# Superhero Saga
# Season 1

Trials, Tribulations, and Trust Issues

Julie C. Gilbert

# Contents

# Chapter 1

---

# Journal Entry 1: I'm a Nobody

If you're hearing or seeing this, my plan worked. Don't worry, it's not a nefarious plan. Promise.

I may need your help soon.

I get that helping a total stranger is bizarre but hear me out.

After I explain my situation, you can decide to shut me out or help.

Name's Jess Turpie. You can imagine what snotty middle schoolers did to that name once upon a time.

Never got a cheesy superpower name because I'm a Nobody. That's not a derogatory term. It's an actual thing.

Superpower names and nicknames stem from the power manifested.

I'm going to use the term gifts, skills, powers, abilities, and probably a few others interchangeably to keep the stupid, overzealous editing program from freaking out.

Her name's Bess. It comes from Bridgeway Editing Software Systems.

Don't worry. She's limited enough that she won't snitch on us.

Unless you do something rash, like post about the experience on your social media pages, our communication should remain private.

If the idea of superpowers is totally new to you, you're a Normal or Normie. Now that I think about it, the terms are probably meant to be demeaning, but since the mind wipers keep you blissfully ignorant of our existence, I guess they don't really strike you that way.

If you're game to help keep me sane, I'll protect your mind from future wipes.

Since powers started popping up in the population a hundred and sixty something years ago, most people get a grand total of one power.

The ability to have a superpower is hereditary, but the nature of the skill itself seems to be completely random.

Mom (Angela) has Superspeed.

Dad (Winston Jamison Turpie III) has Underwater Breath. (Despite his stuffy name, Dad's way more laid back than Mom.)

My older brother, Joe, can change the molecular structure of something so that it's weaker or stronger.

My kid brother, Doug, got Super Strength.

As you can imagine, a lot of stuff got broken around our house.

Nobodies, like me, are rare. We get multiple powers.

They tell me I won the lottery for superpowers.

I have Superpower Mimicry, Gift Transference, Power Suppression, Advanced Self-Healing, Shapeshifting, maybe Immortality (haven't really wanted to fully test that one), and a handful of other gifts that let me try on various super stuffs for a short time.

Not sure who coined the term Nobody. I can't decide if they were jealous or overly practical. Anyway, somewhere before my time, shapeshifters became known as Nobodies because we don't technically have a normal human body.

Over time, the definition expanded to include those with multiple gifts.

I don't exactly advertise my abilities.

First, that would be awkward, rude, and break about three dozen international secrecy laws. The fact that I'm doing exactly that—breaking secrecy laws—now should show you how desperate I am.

Second, at the risk of sounding idiotically obvious, multiple powers make one more powerful and that attracts trouble.

I've only heard of a handful of Nobodies.

People don't like to talk about us since the government works very hard to control us.

Hence, my predicament.

Remember how I said people get one power and it's hereditary?

Bridgeway Labs (a.k.a. The Corporation, The Evil Corporation, and Those Manipulative Jerks) is a government shell company. There are about nine more businesses that link to it in this country and another two dozen internationally.

That doesn't matter.

I try not to think how far their reach extends.

The point is that they've worked hard for more than a decade on several solutions of bottled superpowers.

Their Research and Development department has requested (read: demanded) I test the various superpowers and rate them on categories like usefulness, entertainment, complications, unexpected downsides, and dangers to the public.

Should I be honest with my evaluations?

On the surface, I'm not opposed to the idea of creating substances that will temporarily convey superpowers. It sounds like there's huge entertainment value there.

I'm worried about the fallout and next day scenarios. If you think Bridgeway Labs is working this hard out of the goodness of their little black hearts, you're dumb.

They want money.

That means these pills, drinks, shots, whatever form they package the Gifts in will be purposefully addictive.

Being a part of this endeavor, even in a small way feels skeevy, but they're not exactly asking nicely.

Oh, they pretend.

My cell here at this campus is nice and cushy.

The food rocks.

The entertainment system is topnotch. Their selection of books and movies is second to none.

That's the carrot part.

The stick part isn't as obvious, but it's there in the multiple cameras and the mix of subtle and blatant threats.

Bridgeway people just love showing me candid shots of my parents and brothers going about their daily business.

The folks are semi-retired. Dad teaches swimming and deep-sea diving classes for the local community college. Mom runs a delivery service. It has all the right fronts, but in reality, she delivers stuff for the chance to stretch her legs.

Joe and his fiancée, Leslie, work for her father, helping keep three coffee shops afloat. Doug's still in high school.

The point of this obscene amount of detail is that my family has painfully regular schedules.

Thankfully, I don't have a lot of friends for Bridgeway to threaten. There's just Ellie Chambers. We've been friends since second grade. She's one of the rare Aware, people who know superpowers exist because they have Supers in the family tree but who somehow missed inheriting.

I can sense your doubts. How did a sweet, crazy overpowered thing like me wind up here? Eh, story for another time.

If I haven't yet sent you screaming for the proverbial hills, I guess I'll get on with the business of doing the job I was *hired* to do. When I get another free moment, I'll share more of the how I ended up here thing too.

I try not to admit weakness or vulnerability of any sort, but I just needed somebody to talk to, so thanks for listening.

# Chapter 2

# Superpower Review 1: Flight

**Background and notes:**

Some of the categories in the guiding form I'm supposed to fill out are redundant or silly, but since that wasn't what they hired me to critique, I guess I'll just have to deal with it.

I've been ordered to use a 5-star rating system since we've all been well-trained to understand it. That's fine with me. I like having an odd number to work with. It leads to less ties.

I feel like there should be dramatic drums playing in the background, and my brain adds the effect.

First up, Flight.

**Explanation of the power:**

Flying is one of the first things that pops into people's heads when they think of superpowers. It's not even the most flashy, practical, or fun Gift, but something about it appeals to the human soul.

**Philosophical aside:** Perhaps the obsession has something to do with a lot of people feeling trapped by their circumstances. If only they knew that the pursuit of a goal is often much more fulfilling than obtaining it.

By Flight, I don't mean flying from one place to another by some sort of vehicle. This is the boots-leaving-the-ground, levitating style movement of a person's body from point A to point B.

(Please don't confuse this with Imbue Flight. That ability allows one to create the right conditions to let someone or something else fly. People most often subject their animals to this. Spoiler alert: pigs can fly, but they have a hard time landing. It gets ugly.)

**Experiments:**

- Test 1 (Indoor): Startled the observers by rising off the ground before they were *ready*. Simple elevating and descending exercise ensued.

- Test 2 (Indoor): Demonstrated movement from side-to-side.

- Test 3 (Indoor): Completed an obstacle course consisting of static objects.

- Test 4 (Indoor): Despite my protests, I did an obstacle course with moving objects and randomly fired projectiles, such as arrows and bullets. Got grazed a few times. Was shot twice but my body changed the molecular structure of the skin to prevent damage. (Got scolded for using multiple powers at once, but I won the ensuing debate by pointing out that letting myself get shot would require healing and set back their precious tests.)

- Test 5 (Outdoor): Flight through a rural zone.

- Test 6 (Outdoor): Flight through a forest and up a mountain.

- Test 7 (Outdoor): Flight through a suburban zone.

- Test 8 (Outdoor): Flight through an urban zone.

- Test 9 (Outdoor): Maximum altitude test.

**Expectations and reality:**

People expect Flight to be 100% fun and games. It's not. There's a lot of work involved. Your body goes through Calories at a frightening rate.

**Random warning:** Do not use Flight as a weight-loss program. You're probably going to overdo it and die.

**What happened:**

Most tests went fine. The indoor tests where I wasn't getting shot at were peaceful and fun. The outdoor tests were naturally messier as they were in uncontrolled environments.

I got crapped on by some birds while flying through the empty field. That was unpleasant.

I almost got hit by a plane during one of the maximum altitude tests. Had to do that test several times because my body kept compensating for the various discomforts.

**Complications and downsides:**

It's messy. Even if you avoid bird excrement, you're still traveling through space occupied by bugs. I might have automatically filtered some of that out of my way, but anybody not me is going to get a face-full of bugs.

I've heard people expect Flight to be easier and less congested than other means of travel, but if this goes the way Bridgeway Labs wants it to go, there will be a Wild West free-for-all. Until traffic patterns get established, I can see that getting messy.

It's cold. If you're not wearing a climate control suit, the flight may not be comfortable.

It does a number on your clothes. You ever seen how flags look after being in all sorts of weather for a few months. Yeah, that'll be your clothes.

Going up is easy. Coming down can be easy, but it's often complicated by a fear of heights.

**Danger Level:** High

**Usefulness:** 3 of 5 stars

Flight works for getting one from place to place across short distances. Vehicles were invented for a reason. They're a much cleaner and more efficient means of travel than Flight.

I would not recommend it for long distances. The definition of long distances will vary from person to person.

Picture it like running. For some Normies, the distance to retrieve the mail at the end of their driveway is considered a long run. Other crazy people run five miles as a warmup.

Flight takes energy and agility. People low on either may wish to stick with conventional means of travel.

**Entertainment value:** 5 of 5 stars

Flying is fun. There's no denying that.

**Overall rating and conclusion:** 4 of 5 stars

Despite the many dangers and downsides, if you're looking for unadulterated entertainment value, Flight has it.

# Chapter 3

# Superpower Review 2: Superspeed

**Background and notes:**

I blame pop culture for this one. People think it's going to be so cool to be able to run from point A to point B in an instant.

**Think of the applications! You could ...**

- Run into burning buildings and carry everyone to safety. (Maybe. This also requires a lot of strength and stamina.)

- See the world in a flash. (Call me cynical, but what would be the point? To say you did? Go you. Here's your participation trophy.)

- Run anywhere and never get tired. (False.)

- Visit friends on the opposite coast and be back within the day. (True, but if you're really going to spend time with your friends, why rush back?)

- Make a ton of money delivering packages. (Maybe. Remember, my mom has this power.)

**Location note:** The Bridgeway Labs facility they stationed me at is located near New York City on the East Coast of the United States.

**Explanation of this power:**

As advertised, this superpower involves running at insanely fast speeds.

**Side note:** It comes with a few side powers.

First, you get a corresponding boost to stamina but not strength. That's why I put maybe on the hypothetical burning building scenario. If all you have is Superspeed, you can pass through a burning building safely, but your ability to rescue others is going to be limited to your natural strength and resistance to fire.

Second, you get enhanced spatial awareness and the instinct to pick a clear path. This keeps you from plowing into a telephone pole, tree, truck, or mountainside.

**Experiments:**

- Test 1: I followed Mom around on some of her deliveries. I now understand why she has a ten-pound limit on stuff she'll deliver. Stuff gets heavy.

- Test 2: Ran from Bridgeway's New York City facility to their San Diego offices. The trip took five seconds.

- Test 3: Ran across Lake Erie. I wasn't positive that Superspeed would allow me to cross water. Turns out, it does unless you hesitate. Then, you get wet.

- Test 4: Ran to Mount Everest and started up it. Had to stop halfway up because I got light-headed. I could compensate fine, but the Research and Development people said an Alternate Breath add-on was a no-go for the Superspeed project.

- Test 5: Ran around the world. I've been asked not to reveal my time since that would only tempt users to try and beat it. Having somebody fail to use a Superspeed enhancement on land would be bad enough, let alone letting them get lost in the middle of the Atlantic or Pacific oceans.

**Expectations and reality:**

People expect Superspeed to be pure adrenaline excitement. Like Flight, it's a lot of work.

**What happened:**

- Test 1: I gained a better appreciation for why Mom naps a lot. I nearly took out a bike rider.

- Test 2: Test went smoothly.

- Test 3: I hesitated and had a brief dunking in Lake Erie. Lesson learned: Do NOT hesitate with Superspeed.

- Test 4: Cut it short because it would have been painful and pointless.

- Test 5: Saw a lot of cool stuff, but the rushed nature of the trip stole all the potential enjoyment from it.

**Complications and downsides:**

People don't realize that increased stamina doesn't mean infinite. You're still human and will eventually get tired and need to eat, drink, sleep, and tend to other bodily functions.

Increased spatial awareness does not always compensate for the unexpected. Superspeed involves you moving faster, not the rest of the world slowing down. It may seem they're slowing down, but they still move. Sometimes, they move right in your way. Same for animals. Accidents are going to happen.

It's easy to misjudge and misuse Superspeed.

Misuse leads to massive headaches and feeling like you spent a few rounds with the Mixed Martial Arts world champion kicking you from one end of the ring to the other.

**Danger level:** High

**Usefulness:** 3.5 out of 5 stars

It's not an ideal way to travel, but I would place it above Flight. If this is going to become a regular thing, I would recommend having paths marked for people to follow or limiting the number of active temporary Superspeed runners.

**Note:** There are military and not-so-up-and-up applications for this power. If this one isn't monitored, I can see the bad guys stockpiling and wreaking havoc in a lot of ways.

**Entertainment value:** 2 of 5 stars

From the expression on Jabrie's face, I can tell that comes as a surprise to my handlers.

People aren't going to buy this for funsies. Oh, maybe at first they will, but it'll lose its shine quickly once they learn how much work it is to use responsibly.

**Overall rating and conclusion:** 3.75 out of 5 stars (Yeah, I know the math doesn't work out. It got a random +1 bump because Jabrie and company started drooling over the military applications.)

It pulled a medium-low rating for entertainment, but a medium-edging-to-high mark for usefulness. I suspect most sales will be to serious buyers not entertainment junkies.

I highly suggest at the very least the sales be tracked and capped. If Bridgeway lets out too much of this stuff out at once, there will be consequences.

# Chapter 4

---

# Journal Entry 2: How I Got Myself Kidnapped

Me again. Is this a good time? You're totally not going crazy, but maybe don't go telling everybody you're hearing voices in your head. Normies don't take that well.

I promised to tell you how I wound up with the unenviable job of testing out superpowers.

Why does everybody think it's cool?

Sure, I get to try out superpowers, but I could already do that on my own.

**Job pros:**

- I get paid well to try new stuff and test my limits.

- My family stays off the scary people's list of things-to-kill-today.

**Job cons:**

- I feel like a lab rat.

- They're always watching, but I'm not sure what they're watching for. It's like they're studying my strengths and weaknesses with evil intent.

It started with an innocuous knock on our front door.

Yes, I still live at home. Try not to get too judgey. I've only been out of college a year, and I haven't landed a steady job yet. Turns out undergrad degrees are mostly a money-making scheme for the institutions.

I can't take most public service jobs like becoming a cop or an emergency services tech or even a doctor. It would be far too tempting to bring Healing Gifts to bear in desperate situations. That's not exactly conducive to laying low.

Tried retail and quit after a few hours because people suck at humaning.

For real. It was quit or set the entitled witch's hair on fire.

Anyway, back to the knock. They timed it such that Mom was busy making deliveries, Dad had a class to teach, and Doug was at baseball practice.

I was home working on my resume. That's devilishly hard to do with no experience.

I hate answering the door, so I usually don't. Eventually, people go away.

After purposefully not answering the door, I swept the front porch for signs of life.

Instead of finding it clear, I found two minds blasting the same message.

***ANSWER THE DOOR.***

That got me curious, so I did the stupid thing and opened the door a few inches.

Before me stood two suit-wearing, sunglass-rocking men who smelled governmenty.

"May we come in, Ms. Turpie?" asks the shorter man.

I could read his name, but I refrain from the slight mental invasion that would entail.

Like a true Northeasterner, I make sure my foot is firmly behind the door to prevent unauthorized entry and say, "No. What do you want?"

That's probably a wee bit harsh.

Never claimed people skills were high on my list of attributes.

My suspicious response prompts twin strained smiles from my unwanted guests.

"We have a compelling offer for you." This too comes from the short guy. "We'd like to give you a job."

My lips betray me by blurting the expected auto response.

"What kind of job?"

But my instincts say: *slam the door in their faces.*

"One uniquely suited to you," says the Mysterious Shorty.

"Not interested, but thanks for thinking of me. Take me off whatever mailing list I've had the misfortune of being on."

I start shutting the door.

The taller man steps forward and places his foot in the way.

"No mailing list, but you're going to want to hear us out."

"For Doug's sake," adds the short man.

Mention of my little brother awakens a protective instinct in me. Flinging the door open wide, I seize both men by their shirts, haul them to the family room, and throw them onto the couch.

At the same time, I reach into their minds and pluck all their surface thoughts.

There's surprisingly little to be found, just names and a vague outline of their purpose. Shorty is Malcom North, and tall-and-lanky is Henry Rathbun. They work as Retrieval Specialists for Bridgeway Labs.

I discovered later these guys were Drones, men prepared for their task by a strong Telepathist.

I don't much care for the term, so I'm going to call such people Mind Talkers or Minders.

When the initial shock wears off, North and Rathbun disentangle their limbs and straighten with a surprising amount of dignity.

"Explain. Right now." I inwardly cringe at how much the words and tone channel my mother.

"You have the chance at a solid paycheck, Ms. Turpie," Malcom North says, still playing nice government goon. "The terms are more than fair." He pulls a tri-folded piece of paper from his breast pocket, waves it, and tucks it away again. "I suggest you accept the offer."

"It could open many opportunities for your family as well," says Rathbun. "Better housing in a safer neighborhood for example." He pauses as if a thought just occurred to him. "Good medical insurance. That's always vital because accidents can happen any time."

I read between the lines well enough, but Rathbun's dark eyes also dare me to peek into his mind again.

Unable to resist, I do so.

The mental images make my heart stutter. They feature car wrecks, muggings, random shootings, and targeted assassinations. Before flipping to the next image, each miniature scene tightens on a portrait of Mom, Dad, Joe, Leslie, or Doug.

Clenching my jaw, I shove the images aside and purge my emotional coffers of the resulting anger and fear.

North and Rathbun have long-since overstayed their welcome.

I glare at them.

"Get. Out."

Almost in sync, they stand and straighten their suit jackets.

"Ms. Chambers is looking forward to working with you," says North. "I hope she's not disappointed."

I freeze like a rabbit hoping the predator will find someone else to eat and try to gauge his sincerity.

Rathbun clears his throat. His voice loses the smooth charm veneer.

"You have a choice between good things happening to you and yours or very bad things. Choose wisely."

After the supreme pussy-footing around the truth, Rathbun's bluntness is oddly refreshing.

So, I choose to let myself get kidnapped.

That's going to be a nasty surprise for the folks, I'm sure.

Whether or not it is a wise choice is to be determined.

# Chapter 5

# Superpower Review 3: Teleportation

**Background and notes:**

I'd love to explore some of the more obscure powers, but I'm working from a list I was given. Apparently, it's arranged approximately in order of people's preference when asked which superpower they'd love to have.

I have no idea who they asked, but the reasoning in the survey seems a tad juvenile. If I truly wanted to know, I could run a mental investigation, but I don't care that much.

If we could guarantee things like number of jumps and the location of jumps, that would be fabulous, but that's not how the Gift works.

I'm getting frustrated by the misconceptions about superpowers.

**Explanation of the power:**

Teleportation involves disappearing from one's current location and appearing at another location.

**More details to prove a point:**

Essentially, your body moves to the 4$^\text{th}$ dimension, travels to the new location, exits that dimension, and reforms elsewhere on Earth.

Jabrie's staring at me like: *So what?*

If people don't know exactly where they're going, they're going to appear in the vicinity of where they'd like to go but not the precise location.

That's going to lead to accidents.

**Experiments:**

- Test 1: I teleported from the fourteenth floor down to sublevel seven.

- Test 2: I teleported home then back to my dorm here in this facility.

- Test 3: I teleported to my favorite coffee joint in SoHo. I didn't have time to stop for anything, but it was nice to visit and smell the coffee fumes.

- Test 4: I teleported to one of the Seattle offices.

- Test 5: I teleported to London, Shanghai, and somewhere in Brazil. (It definitely wasn't a city.)

- Test 6: I teleported to one of the US research outposts in Antarctica.

- Test 7: I teleported to the moon.

**What happened:**

Tests 1 through 4 proceeded as expected with zero hitches. I knew each of these locations well enough or had been given enough information to get there.

Since the latitude and longitude system is already in place and well established, I created a mental map of the 4$^{th}$ dimension that mirrors it.

Test 5 started fine until Jabrie insisted I try without my map. The London and Shanghai visits were fine. Brazil wasn't fine. If I didn't have an instinct to do exact reverse teleportation, I'd probably be dead.

Test 6 was pointless and cold since the likelihood of someone seeking it out is low.

Test 7 was also pointless. I read the contract that's in the works. The distance to the moon isn't covered and there will be safeguards that block those nodes in the 4$^{th}$ dimension. Again, cold. If I wasn't me, I would have frozen to death while watching my liquidy insides move outside.

Being me, my body adjusted, so it was more like stepping outside on a cold winter's day without a coat then coming to your senses and putting one on.

It seems cruel, but that actually makes sense. The people coming into this power for the first time probably won't have the luxury of my map.

I considered offering to provide the map to new users, but knowing Jabrie, he'd kick it up to the execs and they'd want to sell it. So, I lied.

(That note won't be in the final draft, but I can't kick the folks' training aside that easily. When I was a kid who quickly mastered the art of lying, we made a deal that I'd at least tell them later if something was a lie.)

**Expectations and reality:**

Expectations – Teleportation is a clean, easy system to move between point A and point B.

Reality – With one person teleporting—or even a handful of the Supers who have that ability teleporting—the odds of having an accident are slim. However, the 4$^{th}$ dimension is still a place with a finite amount of available space.

It's possible two people will try to move through the same portion simultaneously. I don't think an accident would kill them, but it could kick them out of the 4$^{th}$ dimension at an unexpected location.

Expectations continued – Teleportation is instantaneous, and it doesn't require effort.

Reality – Teleportation is almost instantaneous, and it certainly requires effort. The amount is less than sustaining Superspeed.

Picture it like trying on clothes. It might be fun at first, but by the time you wrestle on a ninth shirt, you're kind of tired.

Expectations continued yet again – It's perfectly safe.

Reality – It's one of the harder Gifts to control. The odds of landing where you're not supposed to be are very high.

**Complications and downsides:**

You know how some people travel in a car just fine and others get a massive headache or want to puke their breakfast all over the back seat?

Those side effects and more are possible with teleportation.

I don't know this from experience. I know it from the reports and videos from the human trials.

The most common side effects are slight disorientation or dizziness.

Fracturing and splitting – Jabrie wanted me to lie about these, but I can't.

Fracturing happens when not all of someone's molecules successfully exit the 4th dimension.

Splitting happens when all the molecules exit but they're arranged with a small amount of space between at least part of their body.

The end result in both cases is missing pieces of the traveler. If they've misplaced a few skin cells, they'll have some discomfort until new skin grows. If they've misplaced part of their brain, we're going to have a big fat lawsuit on our hands.

**Danger level:** very high

I can see this going wrong in so many ways.

**Cautions and concerns:**

Whenever your body ceases to be then needs to reform, you open the way for mistakes to happen.

The human body does a lot of amazing things already. Cells are constantly being replaced. DNA and RNA is being copied. Cell proofreaders are busy catching the inevitable mistakes.

I don't care if you don't think you *need the science lesson*. You asked for my analysis of the dangers. You need to hear this.

My point is that when a lot of stuff happens simultaneously, mistakes happen. A few cells in a billion changes isn't much of a problem, but that's because your body can deal with some flaws here and there.

You don't have the same margin for error when it comes to moving through the 4$^{th}$ dimension.

My body protects me naturally, but you're talking about sending a bunch of Normies through the same space at the same time.

You know how back in the day there used to be problems with the internet when it was in its infancy? Certain times of the day, service would slow to a crawl because too much was happening. That could happen if you start handing out 4$^{th}$ dimension passcards like candy.

**Usefulness:** 4 of 5 stars

**Entertainment value:** 4 of 5 stars

I think most of the fun comes from shocking people you appear before.

**Overall rating and conclusion:** 4 of 5 stars

High marks for usefulness, but also, high marks for danger factors.

I do not recommend creating a public version of this.

# Chapter 6

# Superpower Review 4: Telekinesis

**Background and notes:**

Unlike the previous powers discussed, this one focuses on the immediate vicinity of the user and does not involve travel of any sort.

**Note:** This discussion will be confined to Telekinesis, not Remote Telekinesis. That is a separate power entirely.

**Explanation of the power:**

Telekinesis involves moving objects without physically touching them. It's largely assumed to be moving objects with one's mind.

While not entirely accurate, the explanation that refutes that point once again involves talk of other dimensions. I think my last review might have been a little too thorough for Jabrie's tastes.

Let's leave the slightly in accurate definition in place for now.

**Experiments:**

- Test 1: Move a tennis ball from one table to another.

- Test 2: Move a cup of water filled to the brim from one table to another.

- Test 3: Move a kitchen table and a set of chairs from one side of a room to the other.

- Test 4: Move an ever-increasing series of dumbbells.

- Test 5: Move the CFO's car.

- Test 6: Stop a baseball hurled at me from a pitching machine.

- Test 7: Stop a series of baseballs hurled at me from three different pitching machines.

- Test 8: Stop a bullet aimed at me.

- Test 9: Stop a rocket propelled grenade aimed at me.

- Test 10: Stop a missile fired at me.

**Expectations and reality:**

Expectation 1 – The will automatically means the way.

Reality 1 – Physics doesn't go away. Smaller objects have less mass and are therefore easier to move. Larger objects have more mass, so they require more effort to move.

Expectation 2 – As soon as you gain the ability, you can move as many objects as you want.

Reality 2 – The number of objects that can be moved simultaneously depends on the skill of the person wielding the Gift.

Expectation 3 – You can move objects from wherever you want to wherever you want.

Reality 3 – Precision and accuracy depend on the skill of the user. Like anything, it takes practice.

**What happened:**

- Test 1: I successfully moved the tennis ball by swatting it off of the table. Jabrie complained that I didn't move it from the right spot to the right spot. I told him he needed better directions. From my angle, I never would have seen the X on either table.

- Test 2: The cup was moved from the right place to the right place, but I lost points for spilling some of it. That's unfair because the same thing would have happened if I had carried it from one side to the other. That's what happens when you fill a cheap plastic cup to the brim. Squeeze. Squish. Spill.

- Test 3: I moved furniture.

- Test 4: This test wore me out. I got up to eighty-five pounds before quitting. I could have done much more if Jabrie let me tap Super Strength.

- Test 5: Car moved. He might need shocks sooner than expected, but I'm not telling him that, and I'm pretty sure Jabrie and the rest of the techs and handlers won't either.

- Test 6: This one was harder than it looks. I think by the time I stopped it, the thing was an inch from my nose.

- Test 7: I cheated by using Slow Object to get the baseballs to move at a reasonable pace. Then, I created a miniature whirlwind around me by manipulating the air currents to create a cyclone. The first three dozen baseballs formed a shield against the rest. I think Jabrie forgave me for this one because of the cool effect of my mini-cyclone.

- Tests 8 – 10: I cheated again. Jabrie complained, but I told him I draw the line at letting myself get shot or blown up.

Incidentally, my method of cheating differed for each. To stop the bullet, I dodged. To stop the grenade and rocket, I found the inner mechanisms of their respective launchers and mucked with the internals.

Mama didn't raise no fool.

**Complications and downsides:**

Physics gives Telekinesis some serious limitations.

Given Jabrie's stuffy rule about minimizing other powers that kick in allows the tests to be more realistic, but reality is that the normal human version of me doesn't have bulletproof skin or the ability to exert the exact opposite force to counter a bullet.

Can it be done? In theory, yes, but I'd need Slow Object, Counter Force, and a half-dozen other powers to accomplish the feat. Same holds true for a grenade and a rocket.

**Combat potential:** relatively low

I'm not certain why this question is a thing, but given Jabrie's reaction to every combat comment I've ever made, I'm guessing these tests have an additional motive not being advertised to me.

**Danger level:** at the dosages they're talking about releasing, relatively low

The potency described in the paperwork will last a half-hour to an hour, maybe two, depending on how quickly one's metabolism works. Slower metabolisms will give slightly longer-lasting effects.

Given the natural reluctance of the masses to working out, there will be natural limits to what can be lifted and how far it can be carried mentally.

**Usefulness:** 4 of 5 stars; medium to high

If you want to float a light but awkward object up to a high apartment, there might be a market for this thing.

Grabbing stuff in a grocery store could be fun. Short people could even get stuff on top shelves without climbing.

**Entertainment value:** 5 of 5 stars; high, at least in the short term.

People want what they don't have. I once let my younger brother, Doug, have a few minutes of Telekinesis as a birthday gift. (Again, not something I'm letting Bridgeway know.)

After pelting our older brother with acorns and small sticks at the park, he went back to tossing around a football with our dad the natural way.

**Overall rating and conclusion:** 4.5 of 5 stars

I recommend Bridgeway proceed with their development of commercial Telekinesis offerings. It's a fun skill to play with. Most people will naturally use it for trivial purposes. Physics will provide some natural limits.

Abuse is still possible but harder to accomplish.

Accidents should be minimal, especially if the dosage is kept within reason.

# Chapter 7

# Journal Entry 3: Tired of Being a Shadow

At the end of the Telekinesis experiments, I teleport back to the main campus.

Jabrie had wanted me to bring him back, but I pretended not to hear him.

Don't worry. He has other lackeys with that Gift. They're just not as good as me.

That statement isn't just me being arrogant. As previously noted, most people only get one superpower. Safely accomplishing Transportation requires several Gifts.

Transportation is pretty far down the review list because of the risk factors, but I can give you a quick rundown of what's what so you know what's involved.

Transportation functions like Teleportation, but it also involves moving people or objects too. Anything you hold while teleporting should travel with you just fine. The problems that kick in are the same.

One may be willing to risk fracturing a favorite coffee mug, but most sane people hesitate longer when it comes to living, breathing beings.

My destination of choice is the restroom near the main cafeteria since the last Telekinesis test had been on location in some desolate part of the Sahara Desert.

Bridgeway bought an empty patch of sandy paradise for tests where they'd rather not have too many witnesses.

I should aim for my quarters, but I want to get something to eat since messing with missile controls a few hundred miles away drained a good portion of my energy reserves.

I blame video games for the colored bar representations of health, energy, and current ability reserves.

My older brother and I used to spend hours in virtual reality games. *Pitched Battle* was one of our favorites. Joe was surprisingly good with a medieval flail. I never liked those because of the weird way they messed with my balance.

Yeah. I'm rambling because I'm not exactly eager to share the rest of the tale, but I know I must. According to my shrink, it's a defense mechanism.

The facilities use and washing up part of my tasks went fine, but I ran into trouble stepping out of the restroom.

More specifically, I nearly ran over Ellie Chambers.

Eleanor Rose Chambers has been my best friend forever.

I know I said second grade. That's as close to forever as I can imagine right now.

Our fathers were college roommates who stayed in touch despite moving to different sides of the country. When her parents divorced, her mom moved back to New York with Ellie and her twin brother, Tad. Hence, the delay in us meeting.

Tad's got minor self-healing abilities.

Ellie's either got minor telepathic abilities or a killer sense of intuition.

Unfortunately, Tad passed the Superpower Recognition Test (with a 65, which is the lowest passing score), and Ellie did not.

You can imagine the teasing that ensued. Pretty sure Tad got to practice some of that self-healing after the encounter.

He deserved it.

"Ellie!" My exclamation contains my surprise. I wince and wish I could turn invisible or manipulate time to skip that moment, but the social panic made both moves impossible. "Fancy meeting you here."

The forced good cheer makes me sound out of breath.

She rears back instinctively, so I reach out to steady her balance.

The close proximity gives me a great view of the many emotions moving across her face. I think I miss some, but the rapid changes I see included surprise, shock, realization, and devastation.

Watching her blue eyes fill with tears, I panic again and use Transportation to move us to my quarters.

Anger replaces some of the devastation. I count that a slight improvement but have enough sense to keep that sentiment in and off my face.

She wrenches her shoulders free of my grip. The move presses her back to my closed door.

Though nice, my dorm room here doesn't exactly have a huge amount of open space.

I raise my hands in the universal beast-taming gesture and retreat a half-step to give her emotional space.

Ellie blinks rapidly, causing some of the pooled tears to fall.

"I should have known." Her whispered statement comes out on a rush of frustrated air. Her shoulders slump with defeat.

I admittedly don't have the best people skills, but looking back, I was being particularly dense.

"They ... told me you worked here. I just—"

Like pouring gasoline onto fire, my words bring Ellie's anger back in a rush.

"It's always about you!" The words aren't loud, but they pack the sentiments of a ticked off rhino about to skewer somebody on its horn.

"I'm sorry."

(Wrong reflex response, apparently.)

"Just once! I wanted to do something that had nothing to do with you! Or Tad! Or Mom! Me! Just me!"

My unhelpful brain adds cute little flames and smoke coming out of my ranting friend's head.

I start to smile, then wisely turn it into a cough, which turns into an actual coughing fit because I swallow some spit wrong.

By the time I recover, some of Ellie's anger flips to concern.

"What happened?"

The question might seem entirely vague, but best friend status lets Ellie key in on my meaning.

When manners finally kick in late, I wave her over to my bed. She marches over, sits down, and spills the whole saga in one long, frenetic rush.

I mentally reorder some pieces because she fires them out of order, but eventually, the picture solidifies for me.

Like me, Ellie's been job hunting since graduating college, so she's plastered the usual sites with her resume. She's gotten mostly junk in return. On a whim, she answered a vague ad she'd seen posted on the announcement board at our favorite coffee joint.

Long story short, she came to the Bridgeway headquarters, interviewed with a few dozen people, got told she was a top candidate of several thousand applicants, and had a second interview with somebody higher up the hiring food chain.

Fast forward two weeks, she started what amounts to be a glorified gofer position that pays ridiculously well.

Then, I show up and burst her blissful bubble.

Given the whole story, I kinda hate me too.

Relating the story drains most of the fight out of my friend. Groaning, Ellie scoots further onto my bed and leans against the wall.

"I'm tired of being a shadow."

Since that statement doesn't require a response, I wait to see which direction she takes the conversation, yet Ellie's next question still manages to surprise me.

"Was any of it real?"

# Chapter 8

# Journal Entry 4: Not Settling for the Role

Sorry. I know. I broke my own rules.

I was trying to keep contact with you to a minimum for security reasons, and I know you were put out by the abrupt end (okay, non-end) to my last tale. But you also needed your beauty sleep, and if I had shared the rest then, you would have entertained me because you're a kind soul.

To be honest, I don't know what to do with Ellie's question about her situation being real.

*Of course, it's real. You're either here or a very realistic delusion.*

But that isn't what she means by *real*.

She wants to know if Bridgeway Labs ran an honest search for a candidate with her skills, or if the whole thing has been an elaborate setup to lure her into a fancy trap.

The only surefire way to answer her question involves a display of the current elephant in the room: my powers.

"I don't think—"

"Do it." Ellie gives me a fierce look that says: *if you make me ask aloud, I will hurt you.*

"It won't change anything," I protest.

I know that isn't entirely accurate because motives matter.

Still, I don't want to hurt her.

The thoughts I'd just witnessed told me she'd been genuinely happy with the job until she ran into me a few minutes ago.

*Damage is already done.*

Sitting on the bed near my friend, I hold my right hand out toward her, palm up.

She grips it with her left hand and squeezes hard.

For a moment, I just sit there, clasping Ellie's hand and stewing in my indecision.

I can pause time and have us back up to review that day as it happened, or I can search Ellie's memories, find the people involved, and take a quick tour through their thoughts.

They might try to guard their thoughts from being open books, but after a while, everybody gets lazy. The thoughts in question would be about three weeks old.

Since the Telekinesis experiments had worn me out and running into Ellie distracted me, I never got a chance to eat something.

Therefore, I opt for the easier investigation.

Unless the memories have distinct meaning for the person, they will be filed in long-term storage and largely forgotten.

I love those because they tend to be less guarded since most people have a set-it-and-forget-it attitude about long-term memories.

"Quit stalling," Ellie scolds. She releases my hand wipes it on my blanket and establishes a new hold. "And hurry up. You're sweating."

Holding in a retort, I begin the work. I don't need the physical connection, but it serves as a nice anchor, making the work a hair easier.

Previous experience connecting to Ellie's mind also helps because she purposefully opens some mental doors that are usually at least shut, if not locked.

I find the day of her first interview and watch her agonize over outfits. Speeding past the dithering stage, I follow her down to breakfast and along the short walk to the nearest subway. Annoyed at the detail, I skip ahead to when she steps foot onto the Bridgeway campus.

The lobby and waiting room hum with the activity of people bustling back and forth.

It's not possible to jump to a new mind from a normal memory, but I set a passive ability to record faces and match them to current Bridgeway employees. Only one face immediately registers a match, but that isn't conclusive evidence either way.

I revisit a few places on Ellie's approach to the waiting room to study the expressions.

If I were an expert on expressions, that would have helped, but the brief glimpses available in Ellie's memory speak only of boredom and frustration.

The interview walked through the standard litany of inane questions.

After about a minute, I pause it and switch over to the interviewer's mind.

From Ellie's account of the interview process, I know this is only the first of many people she talked to that day, but I figure it's as good a place to start as any.

Despite the risk of a headache for both of us, I connect my mind to Ellie's enough for her to stay with me while I searched for Elric Ortega.

I find him relaxing in a hot tub in one of the execs' private lounges. Luckily, he is alone, so I don't have to weed out new and old conversations.

Since the man spends most of his day interviewing people, it takes me almost a minute to find the right one.

When the interview with Ellie starts, I back it up and play the few minutes before.

I don't need that long though because most of it consists of him muttering questions to himself or staring at a bright pink Post-it note on his desk.

I'd noticed it during Ellie's part of the interview, but she couldn't read it from her vantage point.

He can.

It says: THIS ONE!

It's vague enough to mean anything, but something in his mindset confirms the meaning for me.

Long before the interviews began, Ortega had been told to hire Ellie.

It stood out because part of him didn't like the order.

Breaking the connection, I open my eyes and look to my friend.

"Thanks. I know you wanted to lie about that." She drops my hand and tries to smile.

It's dim and half-hearted, but I cherish the effort anyway.

"Guess I'll go quit now."

*What? No. Ellie!*

Spikes of alarm stab me in the chest.

"That's not a good idea." I manage the calm words only after artificially cutting off communication with my emotions.

"They can't keep me here," Ellie declares. "I'm an American citizen and—"

"They're the American government," I finish, hardening my tone to bust past her pigheadedness. Seizing upon the stunned silence that falls, I continue, "Possibly international ones too. Your rights—and mine—don't count for much if they place the right label on it."

*National security. Public safety.*

My small speech flips a protective switch on my friend and sets Ellie to glaring again.

"What do they want from you?"

I shrug.

"Not completely sure. I'm testing out powers and rating them for danger and such, but I doubt that's what they're really after."

A calculating look enters Ellie's eyes.

"Who else did they threaten?"

Trying to lighten our moods, I counter with a question.

"You don't think I'd stay just for you?"

"Of course not. You'd Transport me to Timbuktu and explain we need to lay low for a while," says Ellie. "The fact that you're not doing that means it's not just me. So, give."

I consider downplaying the danger, but figure I have a better chance of gaining Ellie's help if I play it straight with her.

Leveling with her is surprisingly cathartic.

I'd forgotten what a good listener Ellie can be. Despite best friend (okay, only friend) status, we've both been lousy with keeping in touch since graduation.

"Looks like we've got a lot of work ahead of us," Ellie comments.

"We?" I ask cautiously.

"I am not settling for the role of helpless hostage." She makes the stubborn face she perfected in the second grade to let me know she is serious. "You're the superhero. You find a way to beat these people, and we'll do it. Together."

# Chapter 9

# Superpower Review 5: Telepathy

**Background and notes:**

If I had to pick one power that people most misunderstand, it's Telepathy.

For the purposes of this investigation, I'm going to set some distinct parameters about what qualifies and what is beyond the scope.

**Explanation of the power:**

I'm going to define Telepathy as any deliberate connection between minds. This includes Mind Reading, Mind Speaking, and Search Memories, but it does not cover Mind Control. That skill involves some of the same mechanisms but typically much darker purposes.

At advanced levels, it may include shaping some images in the minds of others, but it is not full-blown Illusion Making either.

**Experiments:**

- Test 1: Reading unguarded thoughts at the main facility.

- Test 2: Reading guarded thoughts at the main facility.

- Test 3: Reading unguarded thoughts at a random location in New York City.

- Test 4: Reading guarded thoughts at a random location in New York City.

- Test 5: Reading unguarded thoughts in an unknown language.

- Test 6: Reading guarded thoughts in an unknown language.

- Test 7: Directing somebody around a maze in the main facility.

- Test 8: Holding a conversation with somebody in the Seattle office.

- Test 9: Conveying basic messages with images only.

**What happened:**

Each test went fine except for Tests 5 and 6. Reading something in a language you don't understand is kind of pointless.

I could have learned the languages, but that's not a skill they're contemplating including in the package anyway, so I didn't bother.

I could also have told them how to make better tests, but I did not. I don't get paid to do their jobs better. Besides, I don't want to give them any ideas.

**Expectations and reality:**

Expectation 1: Unguarded thoughts are easier to read.

Reality 1: Guarded thoughts are often clearer.

My official report is going to stop there, but you showed a mild interest in what I do. That means you've unwittingly bought the uncensored versions.

Not everybody thinks clearly. I think more than half the Telepathic abilities I use are reordering, reworking, extrapolating, and interpreting the mess I encounter in some people's heads.

Expectation 2: Reading thoughts will give great insights into people.

Reality 2: While fascinating to know if there's a difference between what people say and what they mean, they're just as likely to lie to themselves as to you.

Expectation 3: Everybody has deep, meaningful thoughts.

Reality 3: I often feel like I need to scrub out my head when I spend significant time wading through people's thoughts.

Expectation 4: It's easy and doesn't take energy. It's just thinking after all.

Reality 4: If you've spent much time thinking, you know it can be both daunting and draining inside your own head, let alone wandering unexplored territory.

**Complications and downsides:**

Mind Reading is just that, reading. It does not involve communicating with the person. That's Mind Speaking, and unless the target expects it, the contact tends to royally freak people out.

I spend much of my Mind Speaking time calming people down.

Neither main skill of Telepathy is Mind Control. I can do a rundown of that skill later, but it's also way down the list because it's not exactly a toy.

**Side note:** Telepathy can be used with animals, but the contact is no clearer than speaking with them aloud.

Animals often have their own languages. As yet, humans haven't cracked much of any of them.

The impressions they give through attitudes and actions are mostly accurate. (Squirrels think we're a nuisance. Dogs think we're the best thing ever invented, and cats barely tolerate us most of the time.)

**Range notes:**

This factor depends on the user's skill level and experience. The connection is stronger with closer proximity.

As the distance increases, the accuracy declines, which can be problematic if you want to read a particular person in the midst of a crowd.

**Combat potential:** Medium to high

Combat potential revolves around who you're reading and why you're reading them.

If you want to know the strategy someone's employing and they're actively thinking of it, the thought should be ripe for the picking. If they're thinking of a dozen other things simultaneously, you're going to have a hard time pinning down the exact thought you want.

Search Memories may be the most useful piece, but the more important a piece of information is, the more likely it'll be behind some sturdy locks.

**Danger level:** medium

It's not exactly a skill you're going to blow your head off with, but you could easily ruin relationships.

**Usefulness:** 5 of 5 stars

The best applications I can think of have to do with crime solving. The science is unsupported at this point, but I'd venture that there are still uses to diving into the minds of kidnappers and killers or even pettier criminals.

**Entertainment value:** 3 of 5 stars

I think it will start out with strong sales but quickly decline as people realize how true the statement is that ignorance is bliss.

**Overall rating and conclusion:** 4 of 5 stars

Honestly, I can't make a recommendation for create or don't create until I know the end goals.

Want to sell it to the public for kicks? I think your sales will tank.

Want to market it as a way to solve crimes or figure out the true motives of despotic world leaders? That might work.

It's still probably not a great idea to make vast quantities of it, especially since the skill could be used against you.

# Chapter 10

# Superpower Review 6: Invisibility

**Background and notes:**

I'm a little shocked this one wasn't first on the list.

It's highly popular with teenagers. Once again, I think they might be idolizing only one aspect of that Gift.

Having my Telepathic abilities on high alert the last few days, gave me some unexpected insights as at least three of the tests happened near one of the public high schools in New York City.

**Explanation of the power:**

Unlike many powers, invisibility can be accomplished through several mechanisms.

Erase Memory of Self and Extreme Ignore can accomplish the goal for all intents and purposes beyond the physical. These two were not on my list to test because the Bridgeway people want to concentrate on the more achievable physical means of becoming intangible.

Most people are referring to Turn Invisible. Generally, that means to become incorporeal or make one's physical body impossible to see.

Shrink Self would accomplish the same thing, but that is a different power as well.

Sorry, I try to avoid big, stuffy words, but incorporeal is a lot less clunky than *to turn oneself to an insubstantial state*.

Enter the Fourth Dimension also works as long as you have a tiny anchor to be aware of the normal realm.

**Experiments:**

For testing purposes, tests 1-5 were run with the incorporeal version of Turn Invisible. Tests 6-10 were the same thing with a corporeal version of the Gift.

Turn Invisible and ...

- Test 1 and 6: Quietly move to one of four corners of the room. (hardwood floors)

- Test 2 and 7: Move across a busy lobby.

- Test 3 and 8: Get on and off a subway at rush hour.

- Test 4 and 9: Walk three city blocks without being noticed. (I told them that one was dumb. Unless you're dancing down the street stark naked, pretty sure most New Yorkers are studiously ignoring you.)

- Test 5 and 10: Break into a restricted area at a grocery store, a bank, and a tech security company.

**What happened:**

Tests 1-5 (the incorporeal versions of Turn Invisible) essentially also gives one the ability to pass through solid objects. Even if I blundered into someone, they likely only felt a weird sensation for a split-second.

Tests 6-10 were obviously much harder. Without tapping into Flight or some kind of pulse repel power, I had to plot very careful paths through the moving obstacles.

The obvious happened. Without the ability to see me, people often veered into my path.

Tests 6 and 7 were easy. I failed 8. 9 took me four tries. 10 took me ten tries for the last scenario.

**Expectations and reality:**

Expectation 1: The Gift doesn't cover clothes.

Reality 1: Much like Teleportation, as long as something is a part of your person in any given moment when you activate the Gift, it will be affected. Translation: Your clothes go invisible too.

Expectation 2: Being Invisible will get people to reveal their true feelings about you.

Reality 2: Maybe. You're assuming their thoughts will dwell on you at all.

Expectation 3: It will keep people from seeing how awkward you are.

Reality 3: Invisibility is not a therapy for insecurity.

Expectation 4: Going into restricted areas will be fun and entertaining.

Reality 4: It can happen, but I doubt it will happen. For one thing, Bridgeway Labs can probably make both versions of the bottled Gift. However, you'll only be able to use one at a time. In other words, you'll be able to get into a restricted area, but you won't be able to touch anything.

**Complications and downsides:**

Covered previously.

Being invisible loses its charm very quickly (usually about the third time somebody slams into you full force).

It's a physical Gift. If you really want to know what your friends are thinking, you're better off with an Enhance Insight ability. Going to go out on a limb here and say that spying on your friends isn't going to fix your trust issues.

**Combat potential:** medium to low

This skill doesn't usually come with a side serving of strength or stamina. If you want to equip a highly trained assassin with a corporeal version, that's fine, but it won't help them get close to a target unless they've got a few other tricks up their sleeves.

The most tempting people to knock off tend to have layers of sycophants, advisers, and security guards around them.

Why does the question of killing people keep coming up?

**Danger level:** medium to high

I know enough people who have a hard time walking in a straight line as it is. I don't think giving them the ability to access invisibility is going to improve anything in their lives.

**Usefulness:** 2 of 5 stars

The incorporeal version is obviously more useful for sneaking into places, but it doesn't leave much leeway to do anything once inside.

The corporeal version is harder to use well and still susceptible to most forms of detection. For example, if the sensitivity is high enough, a mass detector could still register the user.

**Entertainment value:** 4 of 5 stars

You may get a favorable response from the practical jokes crowd.

**Overall rating and conclusion:** 3.5 of 5 stars

I'm not sure it's a good idea to encourage bad behavior, but it's probably one of the more harmless ones in terms of danger to others. Danger to self is a different matter, but I assumed Bridgeway Labs has strong hold harmless clauses in all product paperwork.

# Chapter 11

# Journal Entry 5: Fried Dumplings

After our heart-to-heart, I didn't see Ellie for almost a week because they had me doing telepathy exercises and stupid invisibility tests. Not totally sure what they had her doing during that time because I'm not a complete jerk.

I don't randomly read my best friend's mind, even if it's super tempting to do so when she's being cryptic.

***You love it when I'm cryptic.***

And suddenly I regret giving her the thought equivalent of a whiteboard in my mind. It's like texting, but faster and more annoying because she can draw pictures.

A picture of a stick figure girl blows kisses at me.

*You have the maturity of a third grader.*

I place the message on the board in a script font that's way neater than my natural handwriting.

The stick figure sticks her tongue out and sends me a raspberry, complete with spittle sensation.

As I shove the mental whiteboard into a dusty corner of my mind, I notice the stick figure pointing and laughing. She knows she's scored a few points in the arbitrary quest to annoy me.

A knock sounds at my door and kicks up a visceral feeling of disgust.

"It's me!" Ellie's voice carries through the door just fine, but she also places about ninety iterations of that on the whiteboard.

*Don't make me revoke your board privileges.*

"Don't be grumpy." Ellie sounds even more chipper, and normal Ellie—who is not depressed by job disappointment—is like happy-drugs cheerful. "It's dinner time, and they have fried dumplings."

Swinging my door open, I eye my friend critically.

"Why is this newsworthy?"

"Because ... dear friend. I have you," Ellie says with a mischievous grin. Somehow, the slow delivery makes her sentiments worrisome.

I am not following her logic. That much is clearly evidenced by my bewildered expression.

Sighing, Ellie seizes my left hand, yanks me into the hallway, and pivots so she can tuck her arm beneath my elbow and clasp the inside of my wrist.

"I found a way for you to pay me back for being perfect and killing my dreams of earning an awesome job with my own awesomeness."

I wince at her awkward wording and internally protest both points.

Neither situation is exactly something I can control.

Patting my arm with her free hand, Ellie continues her explanation, "Fried dumplings!"

After bellowing her triumphant conclusion, Ellie adjusts her grip so that her taloned paws dig nails into my poor hand.

Two firm tugs get me moving in the direction she wants me to go, presumably the cafeteria.

The whiteboard reappears and fills with a stick figure wearing a large napkin, wielding a fork and knife, and attacking a giant plate filled with steaming dumplings.

One by one, the dumplings disappear as the stick figure shovels them into her mouth.

"I'm so confused," I complain. "What about dumplings?"

I enjoy them as much as the next girl, but maybe not quite as much as Ellie.

She heaves another long-suffering sigh and continues to manhandle my hand as she speeds us in the direction of the cafeteria. Her face goes through all the right contortions to mean: *You're dense.*

"Two words for you: Wildtime Bar." Ellie's good cheer bounces back into her expression and voice.

The reminder brings me to the walk-equivalent of a screeching halt.

"You remember that?" I stare hard at my friend even as my head fills with that awful night.

I don't often get scared, but things I can't control are right at the tippy-top of that short list.

Ellie's smile falters, softening into something more serious and concerned.

"One tends to remember almost dying," she answers.

"You were stone-cold drunk," I say.

"And drugged into oblivion," Ellie adds. "Don't forget that part."

"How—"

"You let me look at your memories to get some closure." Ellie's smile dims to almost nothing before slowly brightening. "That's not the point. It's *how* you saved me that's the point. That's the price."

I finally get it.

Ellie has already forgiven me for bursting her job bubble, but she wants me to atone all the same by increasing her metabolism while she eats herself silly with dumplings.

Maybe I'll tell you that full tale someday, but here's the quick version.

Ellie and I went to the Wildtime Bar to celebrate her birthday and the end of finals. We drank too much because we were young and stupid.

Okay, so it was a few months ago.

We're older and wiser now.

While I was dealing with the natural causes of consuming too much liquid, some smooth talker slipped something into Ellie's drink. Turns out the rohypnol was spiked with something much nastier that did not agree to play nicely with alcohol.

Instead of making her loopy, it knocked her out and sent her into a violent seizure.

I arrived back on scene at the thrashing-on-the-floor stage.

You're not supposed to touch people in that state, but I wasn't thinking. I reacted.

I don't know exactly which powers activated in which order, but the basic solution had been to speed her body through the processing phase so that the nasty substances exited her in seconds.

After double and triple checking Ellie's dumpling proposal, I conclude it is a slightly reckless but ultimately harmless abuse of power. By this time, I decide to give in, but figure my friend needs to know I am not a wish machine.

"I'm not a genie," I mutter.

"But you are remarkably good at making Calories not count." Ellie practically chirps the words at me.

"You know you're insane, right?" I ask.

"I love you too." She beams, then gives my arm another sharp yank to kickstart forward progress. "Let's eat!"

# Chapter 12

# Superpower Review 7: Incorporeality

**Background and notes:**

It makes sense to test out Incorporeality next.

For the record, I hate that word. I can't even spell it right. It's ungainly and long, and Bess (Bridgeway Editing Software Systems) keeps yelling at me. She automatically corrects my sad attempts almost before I finish typing them.

Jabrie's surprised that I go old-school with the typing instead of using a Thought Transfer Device.

Not that it's any of his business, but I don't like TTDs. If you forget to turn them off, they keep recording thoughts, and if you don't calibrate them right, they pick up other people's thoughts. It's more trouble than it's worth.

TTD's aren't on my hitlist of stuff to evaluate, so that's all I'll say on them.

Yes, I'm stalling. These aren't going to be fun tests.

**Explanation of the power:**

Incorporeality as a superpower involves becoming incorporeal (or noncorporeal if you prefer), a state of being without a body. It's typically used in conjunction with invisibility to pass through solid objects, such as walls or people.

Jabrie thinks I should add a section about other ways to use the power. I told him that was unnecessary when it comes to most powers because their uses are self-explanatory, but I suppose I can make an exception.

**Other possible uses of Incorporeality:**

- Dodging bullets – Great, I'm going to get shot at again.

- Cutting lines – Ask stupid questions; get stupid answers.

- Sneaking anywhere – If I have to explain that, I swear I'm quitting.

- Avoiding a sunburn – It's a valid concern for the paler half of the species.

**Side note:** Jabrie wants me to retroactively fix previous entries. It's not happening. I'll add thoughts here, and Bess can move them to the right entries if she so desires.

On second thought, no. If you can't think of the applications of flight, superspeed, teleportation, telekinesis, and telepathy, you don't deserve them. I also believe I gave enough law-breaking ideas about how to misuse invisibility.

**Experiments:**

I systematically tried to pass through …

- Test 1: normal walls

- Test 2: a passenger train

- Test 3: a freight train

- Test 4: dried cement

- Test 5: freshly poured cement

- Test 6: chains and other restraining devices

- Tests 7-8 didn't happen. (They were satisfied with the results of Test 6.)

(I'd seriously like to share a few choice words with Jabrie and his creepy think tank buddies who design these experiments.

Joe always said I was slow, and I'm starting to believe him. It's the sort of honesty you're only ever going to get from a sibling.

This isn't about power reviews. It's about me. I'm just not sure why it's about me.)

**What happened:**

- Test 1: I moved through the walls of the thirty-third floor of Building C. Easy peasy as are most first tests. Pretty sure these are the control tests to establish the baseline. Look at me, remembering Miss R's science lessons.

- Test 2: I stood in front of a moving passenger train and turned incorporeal so as not to die.

- Test 3: Repeat of Test 2 with a freight train. It obviously took a lot longer and was far less comfortable. (Do you have any idea how long those things are?)

- Test 4: I passed through dry cement.

- Test 5: I passed through freshly poured cement. It's doable but also disgusting.

- Test 6: I attempted to escape a variety of chains and other restraining devices. Handcuffs were easy. Only part of me had to be incorporeal to beat those. Ropes and metal chains took me longer. Silver-coated metal chains held me fast.

(That's a lie. I sat there like an idiot, pretending I couldn't access the no-body-button on my power. I don't know who slipped silver-messes-with-powers into the literature but bless them.)

**Expectations and reality:**

Expectation 1: Incorporeality works like a light switch. You turn it on. You turn it off.

Reality 1: It's a conscious decision, more like holding your breath. If you lose consciousness, bye bye control, hello body.

Expectation 2: It doesn't take much energy.

Reality 2: Compared to what? Walking down a city block doesn't take much energy. Walking twenty-five miles takes a lot of energy.

I tend not to get into the nitty gritty details of how the power does what it does, but this one seems important. Incorporeality involves physics and chemistry.

**Short version because Jabrie looks impatient:**

Stuff is made of atoms. Atoms are mostly empty space. Ergo, rearranging the atoms that make up you creates more empty space. It means you can personally take up less space in the universe if you have that Gift.

Think of the body like a toy box. If you chuck your junk in at random, it's going to take up more space than if you carefully place things in like you're doing a puzzle.

Expectation 3: You don't feel anything.

Reality 3: You feel what I'm going to call phantom sensations.

The mind is a powerful thing, and sometimes, it's a jerk. (Ask anybody with anxiety what I mean.)

Passing through chilly wet cement is uncomfortable because the mind already knows what touching that feels like and will happily share the memory with you throughout the whole ordeal.

**Complications and downsides:**

It's less fun than you'd think.

It requires constant maintenance.

It's physically draining and easy to hurt yourself. Presumably, everybody checking out Incorporeality wants to return to their bodies at some point.

Have you ever pulled a muscle? Take that sensation and multiply it by a million all over your body. That's what happens if you lack the control over Incorporeality to get every atom of your body back into its expected location after your little dance with not existing.

It's mentally draining. Your mind (or whatever you call the part of you that's controlling the Gift) has to make about ten thousand adjustments every millisecond.

For the record, that's like taking the span of time of a second, lopping it into 1000 sections, and then selecting one of the time fragments.

**Combat potential:** Very high

**Danger level:** Extremely high

**Usefulness:** 2.5 of 5 stars medium to low

**Entertainment value:** 2.5 of 5 stars

I think the shine's going to wear off this one quickly. The power takes a lot of effort to control.

**Overall rating and conclusion:** 2.5 of 5 stars

Unless you're planning on packing an over-the-counter headache pill with every dose, I don't recommend moving forward with this one.

# Chapter 13

# Superpower Review 8: Super Strength

**Background and notes:**

I'm shocked this one got bumped so low on the list. It's right up there with Flight on the most-requested-superpower list.

(My baby brother, Doug, has this power. We found out when Joe stole Doug's stuffed dragon and threw it under Mom's car.

Toddlers are scary creatures. That's doubly so for toddlers with superpowers.

We were all lucky Doug threw Mom's car at me, and I reacted fast enough to catch it and put it back before the folks found out.)

I don't see the appeal. Use, yes. Appeal, no. I'm sure it's helpful for rescuing people in certain situations, but ordinary people tend not to find themselves in the sort of tough spot where Super Strength would make a difference.

**Prediction:** If you start bottling that and handing it out on street corners, you can expect an increase in stupid stunts, but that's about it.

**Explanation of the power:**

A person with Super Strength will be able to move objects many times their mass.

**Please note:** This Gift enhances physical strength, not emotional. There are a few powers that can boost or alter emotions.

I don't think it's known how much someone can bench press because anybody with the Gift can easily lift whatever weight you throw at them.

**Possible uses:** Once again, this section's irrelevant. It would be a royal waste of my time and yours to itemize a list of stuff you can move with Super Strength. Just read the experiments if you want a starter list of random stuff to lift or try to move.

**Experiments:**

I was asked to lift, pull, or push ...

- Test 1: a 7,000-pound weight

- Test 2: a 10,000-pound truck

- Test 3: a 28.6-ton fire truck

- Test 4: a 120,000-ton cruise ship

- Test 5: a small mountain

- Test 6: the moon

**What happened:**

- Test 1: I lifted a weight. It was greater than anybody's ever lifted on record, but so what? The whole Superpower activation thing sort of kills the bragging rights.

- Test 2: I lifted some poor guy's truck and set it down as carefully as possible.

- Test 3: I dragged a fire truck from one end of a parking lot to the other.

- Test 4: I hauled up the anchor and gave the cruise ship people a little ride.

- Test 5-6: Didn't happen.

Jabrie frowned a lot and required yet another physics lesson about action and reaction.

**Can I lift a mountain?**

Not without a heck of a lot of destruction. I'd have to dig up the mountain first so that it's not, ya know, attached to the rest of the earth.

**Could I move the moon?**

Not without consequences. Have you met people who are lunatics when the full moon approaches? That's them feeling the moon's natural rhythms. Now picture moving the moon even slightly off kilter.

Mom always said not to break the world. She had a valid point.

**Expectations and reality:**

Expectation 1: There's no limit to what a person can lift.

Reality 1: There are several natural limits, including the structural integrity of whatever you're trying to lift. For example, you can't lift a few metric tons of sand if you can't get a grip on it. If it's in the right kind of container, that's a whole different story.

Expectation 2: It takes a huge amount of effort.

Reality 2: That's relative. Sure, it takes effort, like eating, breathing, walking, running, or bike riding. Every activity comes with an energy cost. Having Super Strength active is like slashing the energy costs to a mere fraction of their former values.

Expectation 3: There's a huge sense of accomplishment tied to the power.

Reality 3: It's like playing a video game in god-mode. The fun wears off because there's no challenge.

**Philosophical freebie:** Life has many aspects. There's joy and a sense of accomplishment in overcoming something. Obstacles come in many forms. If you approach them with the equivalent of a cheat code, you risk stealing your own joy.

**Complications and downsides:**

Super Strength is one of the most accidentally destructive Gifts.

With the Gift active, I could pull a tree right out of the ground. I could even shove it back into the earth I removed it from. However, unless I want to tap into some other powers, I'm not going to be able to restore the tree's delicate root system.

**Combat potential:** medium

The answer depends on the type of combat you expect to be involved in.

Super Strength can greatly enhance hand-to-hand combat skills.

It's less useful if you're being shot at.

**Danger level:** medium

Are we talking to self or to others?

People with Super Strength often don't realize the power they wield in situations that don't require it. That leads to accidents, misunderstandings, broken bones, hurt feelings, and a whole load of other problems.

(Most of these examples are from Doug's life.)

**Note:** Super Strength is not Invulnerability. Those granted the Gift may occasionally get to sample Invulnerability, but that is also a separate power.

Accident-prone people should be banned from the Gift.

Jabrie's giving me the *why* look.

Have you ever dropped a phone on your foot? Pain, bruises, possible curses ensue, yes? All righty. Now imagine that's a car you just lifted to impress your friends. If you drop that sucker on your foot there will be pain, bruises, probably curses, but also shattered bones.

**Usefulness:** 4 of 5 stars for certain professions; 2 of 5 stars for the public

Firefighters, police, emergency workers, disaster workers, and soldiers would benefit from having temporary Super Strength. (Criminals too, I guess.)

If the heaviest thing you have to lift in a day is a 20-pound baby, you don't need Super Strength. You need Super Stamina and maybe Infinite Patience. (Yeah, I made that up. Bottle that, and we can talk about usefulness.)

**Entertainment value:** 3 of 5 stars

Are we sensing a pattern yet? Superpowers aren't toys. There may be fun aspects to many of the Gifts, but the joy of lifting large objects will wane as soon as the next wow factor arrives.

**Overall rating and conclusion:** 3.5 of 5 stars

I'd consider endorsing temporary or weakened versions of Super Strength for certain professions.

# Chapter 14

---

# Journal Entry 6:
# Full-Name Summons

Fate and mothers have a lousy sense of timing.

As I return to my room after a long day—part of which involved educating a grown man with two doctorates on simple science—I receive a summons.

Remember that mental whiteboard I'd given Ellie access to a few weeks ago?

It's technically linked to my telepathic Gifts, but my mother invented the concept.

She and Dad were the first granted access to the board, as it was a compromise of moving back my middle school curfew a few hours. Then, it became an easy way for Mom to check up on Joe and get messages to Doug before he was allowed to have a cell phone or a Quick Chip Computer Link.

Like most new things, the whiteboard got used and abused, then largely forgotten.

Joe and Dad message me on occasion so I know they're not dead.

Doug doesn't bother contacting me.

Mom prefers actual phone calls, but she'll also use the board when she deems it necessary.

Her message this round consists of my name: **JESSICA LYNETTE TURPIE!**

I analyze the message.

*All caps. Black marker. Bold as heck. Single exclamation point.*

Conclusion: Yeah. That's bad.

I want a shower, a nap, and food in that order. Though tempted to manipulate time to squeeze all of those in, I resist for three reasons.

- One, if I showed up looking too pristine Mom will know I didn't drop everything and answer her.

- Two, looking harried might score some sympathy points.

- Three, it's close to family dinner time, so I might be able to steal some leftovers.

My mother's not a large person, but she has a commanding presence. One thing my brothers and I learned quickly in our youth was you do not ignore full-name summons.

I consider forming a clone to stay in my bed while I'm out in case someone comes looking for me, but besides not wanting to exert the effort, they haven't exactly forbidden me from leaving the campus.

Occasionally, I get that creeped-out feeling like something is monitoring me. Otherwise, good old-fashioned fear has kept me mostly away from my family since walking off with the government goons, Malcom North and Henry Rathbun.

I spend a few seconds in the bathroom splashing water on my face before answering the summons because I need the alertness edge.

Since I don't know where to go, I home in on my mother's presence and appear in the laundry section of the basement.

That should strike me as weird, but I am too busy reading my next clues to Mom's mood: her posture and expression.

*Back stiff. Arms crossed. Frown in place.*

Once Mom realizes I have arrived, she launches her interrogation.

"Why am I being followed?"

The question fires out with characteristic speed.

Most superpowers don't bleed into speech patterns, but Mom's always been a fast talker.

Having an hour to ponder her loaded question would have been great.

Getting only half a second, my reply admittedly isn't stellar.

"I don't know."

Mom shakes her head once in a flat refusal to accept the answer.

"Guess."

Twenty-three years of training kick in, forcing a reflex response out of me.

"My job."

Mom nods a few times like she is silently filing the information away. She uncrosses her arms and braces them on the dryer. Her demeanor morphs from anger to concern.

"Did your new bosses imply we would be easy targets?" The slow delivery lowers the room's temperature a few degrees.

Swallowing hard, I confirm the suspicion and try to think what I'd done or said in our few conversations and whiteboard message exchanges that would have given that away.

"Are you safe, honey?"

Mom's soft question sets off a string of images from the past few weeks.

Slogging through cement.

Waiting for a freight train to pass through my incorporeal body.

Picking up a truck like an awkward Christmas toy.

Staring Jabrie and his cronies down as they clamor for the moon to be moved. (They said I could put it right back. Isn't that generous of them?)

I have enough sense to bottle the scenes, but I think my face or silence spills the beans anyway.

"For now," I answer after a long pause. "It really is a good job."

I shouldn't bother with the lie or the sad attempt at a smile.

Mom doesn't buy either effort. She sweeps across the two paces between us and hugs me tightly. Upon finally releasing me, she picks up both of my hands and clasps hers around them.

"It's just a job. You can quit."

She says the words with such confidence that I almost believe her.

"You never told us what they had you doing." Mom gently increases the pressure of her hands. "Do you want to talk about it?"

Finally, an easy question.

"No."

After one more squeeze, Mom releases my hands and drops a surprise.

"We always knew this day would come. Say the word and we'll go to ground. Together." She emphasizes the last word.

I let my hands drop and concentrate on not stepping back. Her last word reminds me of Ellie's promise to help me escape the precarious situation I've landed in.

"I ... can't ask you to do that." My eyes drift down to stare at my hands.

"You can't stop us either." Mom's tone splits the line between amusement and challenge.

The tone more than the words brings my head up.

A disquiet deep in my soul helps me brush aside her attempt at levity.

"It would mean running. Possibly forever. Is that what you want?"

"Joe's old enough to make his own decisions, and Doug's young enough to get over it eventually," Mom replies. "Your father and I love what we do, but we're capable of doing what we love anywhere. It's you I'm worried about."

A lump forms in my throat.

I desperately want to keep it together and break down crying. Odd combination that.

"I'm the indestructible one, remember?" I mean it in jest, but I think it comes out desperate.

Mom catches me in another tight hug that pins my arms in place.

"Indestructible doesn't mean immune to pain," she says. "I wish you didn't have to carry this burden."

*No arguments here.*

Even as the words form in my head, I sense the lie as crystals of anger ignite inside me.

If I didn't carry this burden, somebody else would.

I'm all for national security, but I also have serious problems with the way the program organizers play the game.

As one of the few people capable of teaching them the error of their ways, I silently vow to do so.

# Chapter 15

---

# Journal Entry 7: Permanent Post

Mom talks me into staying for dinner. (It wasn't a hard sell.) She'd timed her summons perfectly so that the end of our short discussion coincided with Dad getting home from class and the end of Doug's baseball practice.

I endure small talk with my kid brother and answer a ridiculous number of questions from my folks, but the homemade chicken pot pie, warm spiced apples, and triple berry pie offset some of the annoyance.

As I help clear the table, a knock sounds at the door.

Everybody stops moving.

Mom and Dad exchange concerned looks.

Doug knows something is up but nothing of the details. I can tell that from his expression, which consists mostly of confusion. His eyes dart from Mom to Dad to me and around again.

*Do we answer it?*

I can practically hear an echo of the question from each family member.

Doug cocks an eyebrow to ask if we want him to get the door.

Shoulders slumping, I shake my head. I'd already swept the front porch for minds and found two familiar presences.

"I've got it." I make quick rounds of farewell hugs, starting with Doug and ending with Mom. "It's probably just my ride."

Mom's return hug hurts. When she finally lets go, she immediately reaches for Dad's hand.

I teleport onto the front porch, landing directly behind my old buddies Rathbun (tall, skinny government guy) and North (short government guy).

They flinch but recover their cool remarkably quickly.

"Can I help you?" I try for cordial but don't quite succeed.

"Good evening, Ms. Turpie," says Rathbun. "We came to check on your welfare."

"As you can see, I'm fine." Though only about ten seconds into this conversation, my patience levels drops precipitously.

"You shouldn't leave the campus without letting somebody know," scolds North. "We had to ask Ms. Chambers where to find you."

I bristle at the unnecessary reminder that they can reach Ellie any time.

"You have competent Mind Talkers and my cell phone number," I point out. "Next time, try calling."

"That won't be necessary," says Rathbun.

"We'll be your shadows from now on," North explains.

I really want to tell them I don't need shadows, but the agitated emotional states of my family tells me the porch is a lousy place to continue the discussion.

"Let's go back and talk about it," I say, keeping a tight hold on my irritation.

Too late.

The front door swings in.

"What do you want with my sister?" Doug's posture reminds me of a guard dog about to pick a fight with a trespasser. He's built like a baseball player, thin but strong, but his Super Strength Gift gives him an overdeveloped sense of confidence. (Translation: he's reckless and impulsive.)

Mom and Dad flank him.

Light from the porch extends far enough in to show their conflicted expressions.

"None of your business, kid," says North.

Though I agreed, part of me loves seeing this side of Doug. Maybe there is hope he'll be more than a moody teenager someday. My fingers twitch to transport Rathbun and North away from my family, but I also want to see this play out.

"Just something for work," I say, trying my hand at a diplomatic de-escalation. "Nothing to worry about." I even manage a halfway decent smile.

"Jess, you suck at lying."

I don't protest the point because it's mostly true.

Doug keeps his steady gaze on North.

"And it *is* my business if you're forcing her to do something she doesn't want to do."

"She *wants* to help us," says Rathbun. "Isn't that right, Ms. Turpie?"

Honesty kicks in as patience runs out.

"Not in the least," I answer, "but she *will* help you as long as we get some ground rules in place. One: you play less word games. Two: I get increased say over the tests that get run. Three: I get more contact with my family."

My third condition doesn't sound wise, but they're going to be in trouble with or without me present. At least if I can spend more time with them, I can pretend I have more control over the situation.

"Agreed," says Rathbun.

Predictably, North chimes in a second later.

"Angela. Winston. Douglas." He nods to each in turn. "Jessica is performing a great public service for Bridgeway Labs. She's doing quality assurance tests and viability studies on certain superpowers so we know which Gifts can be released to the masses."

"You don't need her," says Dad.

*Gee, thanks, Dad.*

I know what he means, but his statement still irrationally stings.

"What happens after that?"

Doug's surprisingly insightful question makes my ears perk up.

I've been so busy focusing on the immediate problems that I never considered an after scenario.

I really should start.

In the moment, I wait to see what my new shadows will say.

The answer, as voiced by North, is disconcerting but not shocking.

"This is a permanent post as long as she has her powers."

The statement puts a really crazy idea in my head in the form of a question.

*What if I didn't have my powers?*

For the record, I don't know if I can give up my Gifts. I've never tried. I have Gift Transference, which means I can move a power from one person to another, but as soon as I stop exerting that Gift, it reverts to the original person.

In theory, if control of me is the sole reason to threaten my family, they'll be okay if I cease being a factor.

Unless Bridgeway gets vindictive.

They strike me as greedy and power hungry, but not necessarily vengeful.

These thoughts zoom around my head, but I can't entertain them long.

Doug steps forward.

Not sure if he has a plan or not, but I step in his way and catch his shoulders.

*Not yet. Maybe later. Protect the folks.*

I tuck the thoughts directly into my brother's mind.

Fighting now will get us nowhere. Doug and I can definitely defeat Rathbun and North, but Bridgeway will only send more suited shadows.

I need to know more about what Bridgeway plans, how they function, and what they truly want. Otherwise, I can't make intelligent decisions about how to handle them.

*This will NOT be a permanent post.*

# Chapter 16

# Superpower Review 9: Superhero Clothing Lines

**Background and notes:**

It's not a mistake. This will still involve uncomfortable tests and my solicited opinion.

Correction. It's not a mistake on *my* part.

Jabrie and the Evil Think Tank—which sounds like a bad metal band—and whoever's above them on the corporate food chain have decided that my next evaluation will involve superhero clothing.

That's right: tights, flame resistant materials, and capes. I wish I was kidding. I swear these people got their ideas from comic books and junky spinoff movies.

This is the direct result of letting the marketing department run amok, but I suppose there's some sound logic in play here. Bridgeway intends to sell superpowers. At least for a time, that will ignite a longing to look like superheroes.

One improvement over previous experiences is that they asked for input in designing the tests to run. I'm hoping this heralds good things for future superpower reviews too, but my cynical nature says these guys are just out of their league on the clothing issue.

Their desperation should be clear enough with the fact that they turned to me. Ellie fell into fits of laughter. Surprisingly, they let her attend the clothing trials and give her ninety-nine cents on the fashion side.

**Explanation of the clothing contenders:**

We have three top bidders for the massive contract Bridgeway wants to hand out this week.

**Core components** – adult onesie or tight shirt and tights; impressions from initial tryout session

- Faruchi – High-end; best of the best; silky soft to the touch; very comfortable but feels heavy; likes bright colors; many color options, including purple and pink; earned 9.5 style points from Ellie

- Carmichael – Medium cost; light-weight; cooler feel than the others; sticks to bold prime colors (red, yellow, blue); earned 7 style points from Ellie

- Alazoo – Low cost; bunches oddly at joint areas; obsessed with red and yellow themes; 6 style points awarded; (I think Ellie was being generous. Her facial expressions read slightly nauseated.)

**Accessories** – all the add-ons

Faruchi – Offers stylish customizable sets with cape, matching gloves, mask, full armor or just bracers and shin guards, personalized logo, weapons holsters/sheathes, boots or high heels, underclothes, skirt add-ons, and so on.

Carmichael – Offers custom and common capes, basic armor, boots, and gloves. You're on your own for underwear and logo prep.

Alazoo – Offers basic, useless capes, knockoff armor, and gloves. They didn't give a boot option.

**Experiments:**

- Test 1: flame test with flame thrower

- Test 2: flame test with accelerant-fueled fire

- Test 3-4: arrow tests with hunting bow and crossbow respectively

- Test 5-7: bullet tests with handgun, rifle, and shotgun respectively

- Test 8-9: chemical tests with a strong acid and a strong base

- Test 10: bomb test

- Test 11: laser test

- Test 12: Flight and functionality test run

**What happened:**

Fine. I admit I had fun. It is interesting to see the results when not on the receiving end of fire, bullets, and corrosive chemicals.

- Test 1: All three sets of clothes successfully protected the dummy in the covered areas.

- Test 2: Faruchi lasted twenty-five seconds of sustained fire before melting with one important exception. The purple Faruchi outfit flamed out spectacularly. Carmichael and Alazoo weathered fueled fires for about eight to ten seconds each.

- Test 3-4: Results varied by expected ranges. Within fifteen feet, all dummies became pincushions for arrows. Around fifty feet, Faruchi armor successfully deflected angled arrows. Around sixty feet, Carmichael armor successfully halted arrows. The Alazoo dummy had a bad time no matter the range. As long as the arrow reached the dummy, it went through the flimsy armor.

- Test 5-7: Ranges differed, but results matched the arrow tests. Faruchi provided the best defense, Carmichael came in second, and Alazoo swathed dummies repeatedly died horrible deaths.

- Test 8-9: Carmichael and Faruchi tied on this one, though neither did spectacularly well. I'm told Faruchi has a separate clothing line they could offer us with built-in chemical resistance. (It wasn't part of the original lineup because most of their items are Kevlar based. The material rocks but is significantly heavier than the other options.)

- Test 10: All dummies rested in many, many pieces.

- Test 11: Depends on the laser's intensity. Basic eye beams in two-second bursts scored the armor. Intense eye beams busted a fat hole through all of them.

- Test 12: Faruchi armor was the heaviest by far, but each option was reasonably maneuverable. The Alazoo cape tore off before I reached a comfortable cruising flight speed.

**Results summary (and other life lessons):**
- Tights are weird. They're not necessarily bad. Maybe I'm just overly self-conscious.

- Go cheap only if you don't care about going home.

- Capes. Are. Useless. (And uncomfortable and dangerous.) If you're strutting around a parade, add the stupid cape. If you actually want to use the superpower, skip the cloth hazard.

- If you buy the Faruchi purple line, stay away from fire! (Exception: If you have a natural Gift for controlling fire and want to make your fire more impressive, by all means, choose this one. You may wish to bring backup clothes though. Eventually, these burn up.)

- Superhero clothes offer protection within reason. They're not a substitute for Invulnerability.

- Resistant and proof are very different things.

- Stay away from bombs.

- If you get shot at enough times from close enough range, something will eventually bust through your fancy clothes.

- Don't play with harmful chemicals unless you're okay with your face melting.

- Public Service Announcement: These temporary superpowers are mainly for entertainment purposes. They have limited job applications and are NOT adequate for challenging supervillains.

The distinction between superhero and supervillain lies in the application of the Gifts. Good deeds means: yay, you're a hero. Evil deeds means the opposite.

Lest you believe the cow doo sold by the media, there are evil people in the world but very few flamboyant, in-your-face supervillains. I'm guessing people who misuse their Gifts for profit try to keep a low profile so they can keep on doing what they do in peace.

It's common sense that most low-profile people generally get left alone. Those who make a nuisance of themselves eventually tick off the wrong person and get throat punched (or the equivalent).

**Expectations and reality:**

Expectation: The clothes make the man (or woman) into a superhero.

Reality: False. (See above for wordier version of this conclusion.)

**Individual conclusions:**

- Faruchi – nice and useful but pricey

- Carmichael – functional and modestly priced

- Alazoo – "Hokey, garish, and sad." (This is a direct style quote from Ellie.) I wouldn't go quite that far, but this level won't provide much protection. Only suitable for casual hobbyists.

**Overall conclusion:**

I suggest offering selections from all three vendors. Since they each deal with the manufacturing details, there's no real reason to not let the customers determine their level of seriousness when it comes to superhero clothes.

# Chapter 17

# Superpower Review 10: Shapeshifting

**Background and notes:**

I don't see this one going over well for entertainment purposes, so I'm not sure why Jabrie's jazzed for today's festivities.

Shapeshifting is too complicated to attempt bottling and selling. Anything created will likely only capture one part of the Gift.

I hate to be Captain Obvious, but there's a lot more to shapeshifting than changing shape.

Besides, the cool factor doesn't quite balance the risks of something going horribly wrong.

**Explanation of the power:**

The simplest form of the definition states that shapeshifting involves changing one's form to take on the body and essence of an object, animal, or person.

The media portrays shapeshifting with ridiculous stories of people becoming werewolves or changing their features and body type to imitate someone else.

**Oddball question from one of Jabrie's henchmen:** Could I become a werewolf? In body, sure, as long as I had a clear enough picture of what I should look like. But it's like putting on a very detailed Halloween costume. Taking on the form does not mean falling under the rules that bind magical creatures.

**Back to doing my job:** At its heart, the Shapeshifting Gift is a very close cousin of Molecule Manipulation.

Nobodies (Shapeshifters) usually have a specialty, which involves imitating objects, animals, or people.

It's more of an art than other superpowers.

**Experiments:**

I was asked to form ...

- Test 1-3: a diamond, a soccer ball, and a wooden chair

- Test 4-6: a small dog (Pomeranian), a lion, and an elephant

- Test 7-9: Dr. Aleric Jabrie, Titus Malzeron (the boss man in charge of this facility), and Ellie Chambers

- Test 10-12: a werewolf, a vampire, and a zombie (sounds like a bad bar joke)

**What happened:**

(I was sorely tempted to cheat by tapping their minds instead of forming the actual shapes. Instead, I went with the downplay-the-Gift approach.)

- Test 1: I rearranged the molecules making up my body and fashioned them into a diamond shape. Jabrie looked annoyed. Mission accomplished.

- Test 2: I formed about eight soccer balls.

- Test 3: I became a lovely, sturdy wooden chair.

- Test 4: I became three adorable Pomeranians.

- Test 5: I made a pretty scrawny lion.

- Test 6: Well, if this job fails, I can always make a living as a teacup elephant.

- Test 7-9: I did passable impersonations of the assigned people.

- Test 10-12: I spent a bit more time on the details for these, but really, the results were no better than if I'd been a devoted cosplayer prepping for a con.

**Expectations and reality:**

Expectation 1: Shapeshifting happens like magic. Poof. Done.

Reality 1: It may look like that if the Nobody is competent and comfortable with the thing they're forming, but on a molecular level, about three billion changes happen every microsecond to give you that instant impression.

Expectation 2: Shapeshifters can form anything.

Reality 2: The less changes need to be made, the easier it is to assume a certain shape.

Expectation 3: Forming people is easier than animals or objects.

Reality 3: People are probably the hardest because they're the most familiar and the most complex. There's much more to shapeshifting than fashioning a lookalike face. People are more than their looks. They have beliefs, attitudes, mannerisms, and bad habits.

Expectation 4: Mass doesn't matter.

Reality 4: Mass has to be accounted somehow. That's why I sometimes formed multiple objects or small animals.

It's like building a 4000-piece Lego castle, then trying to make a small hut with the same pieces. You're going to have leftovers. In this analogy, I chose to make multiple small huts to use up some of the excess pieces.

The opposite is also true. The mass making up me is significantly less than an elephant. So, I got the elephant shape and coloring right, but my scale was probably 1:40 of the actual animal.

(I am not admitting to being able to compensate for mass differences because they do not need to know that.)

Expectation 5: If you form an animal, you gain those instincts.

Reality 5: True to a point. You'll still have your human mind, but reflexes may be quicker or slower.

**Complications and downsides:**

(People not me are going to have a very hard time with changes that demand much more than simple facial alterations.

I'm really not an arrogant twit. I swear.

I feel like it comes off that way when I say things like this but changing to a new shape and maintaining said new shape take a lot of microadjustments. I highly doubt the pill form of Shapeshifting is going to come with those instructions.)

Forming an object might be easy, but it's also almost deadly boring and kind of demeaning.

Don't believe me? You become a chair and spend the day letting people sit on you. They move. They fart. They smell. Just because you have the shape of an object doesn't mean your other senses fail, they just move to whatever convenient location you've moved them to.

**Combat potential:** medium

It would ease kidnap-and-replace scenarios, but the art of shapeshifting doesn't convey any other special skills. So, much like going invisible, you'd have to equip an assassin who already possesses the right, deadly skills.

**Danger level:** astronomically high

Have you read the side effects on this one?

- Muscle twitches (could be permanent)

- Dizziness

- Vomiting

- Blankouts – you don't remember what happens for a time

- Death – I don't think it's so much the shifting part that's the problem. Once you take on an animal form, you do pick up some of the animal instincts. If you haven't noticed, many small animals are twitchy and nervous because multiple things are trying to eat them. If I'm reading the reports correctly, the deaths are mostly accidental (zigging when you're supposed to zag in animal form).

**Usefulness:** 1 of 5 stars (at the commercial level)

I can think of a dozen more useful Gifts to bestow upon the hypothetical assassin Jabrie and company keep harping on.

**Entertainment value:** 4 of 5 stars

There might be a market if you target the cosplay fanatics.

**Overall rating and conclusion:** 2.5 of 5 stars

Unless you're wanting to express your existential crisis, this probably isn't the best Gift to covet.

# Chapter 18

# Journal Entry 8: Telepathic GPS

You know that saying about wanting to be a fly on the wall? Anybody who's ever tried it likely stopped wishing for it.

The shapeshifting exercises gave me a lot of down time. It took me about twenty seconds to compose my conclusions about the nuances of forming a chair. I spent the other three-plus hours exploring the compound through Telepathy and a form of Incorporeality.

I discover four interesting facts:

- Jabrie's more of a puppet than previously anticipated. During the experiments, he's in contact with several Mind Talkers.

- Ellie really likes Candy Crush. I think she's on level 22,000 something. I didn't even know they'd made that many. (I think I'm on 6,000 something. That's respectable, but less impressive than you'd think given that I learned to play it as a four-year-old.)

- I'm not the only Nobody here. Three whole floors of the main tower are decked out like a luxury resort. There are at least two people staying there. Their essences change enough to declare them Nobodies. I think they're waiting for something, but I can't tell what yet. (Great. One more thing to make me paranoid.)

- I'm definitely being monitored. I only detected four Mind Talkers. Three shrank from my queries, but one—I'll call him Bob—has been rather chatty.

They rotate shifts, but the monitoring is 24/7.

At first, I am downright horrified, but Bob assures me it's a creepy level of monitoring but not super creepy.

He defines it as a telepathic GPS.

The Minder on duty will check where I am against the schedule of where I'm supposed to be. That's what got me busted when I answered my mother's full-name summons and stayed for dinner.

They can tell if I'm in my room or in the shower, but as far as I can tell, they're not paying attention to everything done in the bathroom.

I test this theory by taking a nap in the bathroom after the last shapeshifting event.

At seventeen minutes and thirty-two seconds, Bob politely inquires if everything is all right. (Apparently, my usual showers clock in at an average of six minutes and twelve seconds.)

Guess I should be grateful for small favors.

I suppose they could lie about how intrusive they are with monitoring.

Ellie and I run some experiments.

She agrees to let me monitor her telepathically. I warn her what day I will try to enter her mind unobtrusively.

The first time, I pop in practically waving an announcement banner.

Ellie notices right away.

The message board fills with welcome balloons.

A stick figure representation of her waves enthusiastically.

I stay for a few minutes. That's where I get my fly-on-the-wall impressions.

The second time, I enter cautiously.

Ellie detects me in about a second.

The third through ninth times, I try different levels of monitoring.

Any time I enter Ellie's mind, she notices.

As previously mentioned, I do not make a habit of entering people's minds, so I guess I'm pretty lousy with being subtle.

The only times I sort of get away with watching Ellie is monitoring from afar. It's like holding a video camera on somebody from a bird's eye view.

I'm not sure I learn anything useful about how to enter a mind without announcing it, but a thorough debriefing over dumplings and ice cream gives me some thoughts about how to detect and track if I do pick up a watcher.

I haven't gotten around to reporting on Underwater Breath, but the experiments stretched over a few days and also gave me much thinking time.

My brief experiments with Ellie kick my sense of curiosity into a higher gear.

While I have hours upon hours of time to kill, I start tracking people's minds.

Everybody feels different.

Some minds are tranquil, almost blank.

Others are like trying to walk across a freeway at rush hour.

Most are somewhere on the spectrum that exists between the two extremes.

Some people even think in pictures instead of words.

Ellie, Mom, and Bob can usually detect me if I join their thoughts.

Dad, Joe, and Leslie can feel something has changed, but unless I announce myself, they can't pin down what's different.

Joe's not really talking to me.

I don't blame him much. It's a crappy situation.

He's upset that the government goons include his fiancée in their general threats against me.

I chicken out before peering into Doug's thoughts.

There's a saying that a person's living space reflects their mind. I've seen Doug's room. I do not need to be stepping into his head.

I'm not even sure why I care. Maybe it's just a rebellion against the idea of being monitored.

There's got to be a way to fool Minders. If everybody has a distinct feel to them mentally, there must be a way to spoof or scramble that feeling.

Maybe Mom and Ellie will let me experiment on them. I have a better chance if I frame it as important to freeing us from this odd situation, but that might be a lie.

Plans are forming, but I've got to keep them buried deep until I know how far the conspiracy extends.

Motives matter.

The review list isn't random.

They're preparing me for something.

Until I figure out what, I'll have to keep my mind sharp.

Maybe you can help me. You're a neutral party. It might help me to practice my Mind Talker skills with someone neutral.

I know you're getting these messages because I can feel the shifts in brain activity.

You have the ability to block me if you so desire.

I'll take your inaction on that front as a cautious sign of support, but I won't drag you into anything without your consent.

Got enough boulders of guilt to bear already.

# Chapter 19

## Superpower Review 11: Underwater Breath

**Background and notes:**

(I should probably be worried about the fact that the superpower review hitlist just happens to cover every one of the Gifts manifested by my family members.)

Dad has this power. That's why he loves swimming so much. He's as close to a merman as we're likely to get in this world. No fins, but if he could get away with swimming for days without those pesky necessities like eating, he would.

I don't need to do the tests to tell you my conclusions. They're pretty much common sense. There's great potential for entertainment value, but also a high danger factor as well.

Marine biologists and those fascinated by the pretty things under the sea will find a lot of uses for Underwater Breath. They're going to be bummed that the physics and chemistry of deep-sea diving still applies.

**Explanation of the power:**

I feel like the title ought to suffice for an explanation of the power. It's the ability to breathe underwater.

It's kind of confusing though.

Underwater Breath and Breathe Water are two different Gifts. Breathe Water is more of a skin absorption thing. I can talk about that, but I was not asked about it for this entry.

The confusion kicks in because Underwater Breath is essentially breathing the water. Essentially, water functions as the oxygen-giving agent.

I don't know the full chemistry and biological explanation, but I think that instead of drawing in air, you draw in water. Then, your modified lungs split the hydrogen from the oxygen, combine single Os with each other to form $O_2$ molecules, use $O_2$ normally, and expel $H_2$.

**Experiments:**

I was asked to breathe underwater in various conditions.

- Test 1-3: pool for five minutes, a half-hour, and five hours

- Test 4-6: the Atlantic Ocean for five minutes, a half-hour, and five hours

- Test 7: water boarding (I argued. They argued. Jabrie had somebody fetch Ellie to *talk sense into me*. They won the disagreement. This one was unpleasant.)

- Test 8-9: fighting in a pool and in the ocean; number of opponents varied

- Test 10: deep sea test

**What happened:**

- Test 1 and 2: The five minute and half-hour tests were fine. I spent the time napping.

- Test 3: The five-hour test was physically exhausting and boring, but I made it. (I had to pee the instant I got out of that pool, but I safely teleported to the restroom in time. I'll have to apologize to maintenance for the flood in the restroom. I didn't stop to towel off.)

- Test 4-6: Had essentially the same results as the pool tests, but this time, I made sure not to drink coffee before the experiment. I did eat a large breakfast though because I didn't want my energy coffers hitting zero mid test.

- Test 7: Once I got over the initial panic, this one wasn't too terrible. The trouble came mostly from the frustration of switching between normal breathing and Underwater Breath. Oddly, the most comfortable moments came when a steady stream of water hit. When the waterflow turned intermittent, my body wasn't quite sure which method of breathing to use.

- Test 8 and 9: Fighting underwater isn't as cool as it sounds. It's devilishly difficult whether you can breathe or not. The scientists wanted me to limit my use of other powers. I tried but survival instincts overruled stupid stipulations.

- Test 10: The deep-sea test went about as smoothly as sandpaper, and I got to try out my eighth-grade science teacher mode again.

**Expectations and reality:**

Expectation 1: Underwater Breath turns any swimming experience into a magical good time.

Reality 1: It lets you breathe underwater. Period. End of use. It does not enhance your eyesight, protect you from riptides, give you greater swimming stamina, or make the ocean inhabitants swim by you singing Disney songs.

Expectation 2: Underwater Breath makes one impervious to the natural pressure differences that exist in the ocean.

Reality 2: See Reality 1 for a complete list of what Underwater Breath does for you.

Superpowers tend to be very selfish, self-centered things. As such, most of them do not have much influence on the world around you.

**Mini science lesson:**

Water has weight. If you go deeper into the ocean depths, there's more water above you. The water presses down on you.

You have a lot of liquid in you, but there's also gases too. Ya know, the oxygen you need to live and all its life-giving buddies.

The gases are easier to push around than the liquids, so they get squished under high pressure. I don't care if that's not a very scientific term.

If you return to the surface too quickly, the gases—specifically the nitrogen in your blood—get so darn excited they just want to escape immediately. Good for them. Very bad for you.

This is why even if you have Underwater Breath, it's best to observe all those pieces of sage advice like return to the surface in increments to give your body time to adjust.

**Complications and downsides:**

Complication 1: People who have the Gift have a hard time gauging their energy levels. (Not everybody keeps convenient video-game-like energy bars like I do.)

I imagine this will be doubly so for those new to the Gift.

Complication 2: Metabolism rears its head again. Namely, people have different rates of metabolizing stuff you put in their systems, such as a substance meant to convey the ability to breathe underwater.

Fast metabolism will mean a shorter time experiencing the effects of Underwater Breath. Slower metabolism might stretch the time a little, but it could also mean it's less effective.

I think it will still work, but the user might feel *winded* if their body doesn't quite buy into the whole suck-the-oxygen-out-of-water thing.

**Combat potential:** low

Unless you know your enemy is hanging out in the water, this one has limited combat potential.

**Note:** There is some terrorism potential. If you want to hide the approach to sabotage some underwater pipes, Underwater Breath can save you the trouble of carrying an oxygen tank.

**Danger level:** medium to high

People have difficulty keeping track of the time with a Quick Chip Computer Link embedded in their skull. What makes you think they'll keep good track of the time they've spent underwater, even if you could predict the duration of an Underwater Breath potion?

**Usefulness:** 4 of 5 stars

I suppose you could also use it for repairing pipes or something.

Perfect for rescuing people in over their heads in the ocean.

**Entertainment value:** 4.5 of 5 stars

If you control this one, it does have decent entertainment value.

It's perfect for tourists visiting some of the wonders on the ocean floor.

**Note:** If you make this easier, be prepared for some ecological fallout. It's a well-documented fact that people are destructive little monkeys when you let them be.

**Overall rating and conclusion:** 4.25 of 5 stars

I approve of trying to sell this one. It has good marketing potential.

# Chapter 20

# Superpower Review 12: Metabolism Manipulation

**Background and notes:**

Somebody's been reading my mind or Ellie's mind. So, that whole bit about the monitoring being telepathic GPS is likely complete baloney.

I guess Ellie could have told them outright. She always was a trusting soul. I could offer to help her guard her thoughts, but then, she'd think I didn't trust her. That alone would cause a headache and a half.

Anyway, a brand-new, shiny, line-cutting power showed up on my to-do list this morning. You guessed it: Metabolism Manipulation.

I'll be the first to admit that research isn't my forte. But I get super high marks for dangerous curiosity. Naturally, I did some standard and deep-dive searches into whether Metabolism Manipulation is an officially recognized superpower.

It is, but as you could guess, it's not exactly the poster child for superpowers. I believe there are four documented cases of people with the power. However, the first twenty years or so of Gifts being a thing were basically the Wild West of anything goes.

**Explanation of the power:**

This is a self-power. (I wonder if there's a less clunky way to say that.)

For the record, what I used on Ellie after the Wildtime Bar incident is technically Imbue Metabolism Manipulation (as in I gave it to her instead of using it on myself.) I plead the 5th on whether I used it during the Great Dumpling Deal.

One changes the speed of their metabolism. Usually, people dial it up so they can throw more food down their gluttonous gullets.

(Bess—Bridgeway Editing Software Systems—is yelling at me for being judgey. She can edit it to something kinder later. I don't have time to sugar coat stuff right now.)

**Experiments:**

I was asked to ...

- Test 1-3: speed up metabolism of fats, sugars, and carbs in isolation of the others. I was allowed to pick the food, so I chose penne vodka with chicken. Alice, the head chef, makes a killer vodka sauce.

- Test 4: speed up metabolism of an 8-course meal

- Test 5: speed up metabolism of a 100-course meal (excessive much?)

- Test 6-8: slow down metabolism of fats, sugars, and carbs in isolation of the others

- Test 9: slow down metabolism of an 8-course meal

- Test 10: slow down metabolism of a 100-course meal

**What happened:**

I feel like these should have been obvious. Darn scientists and their quest for thoroughness.

- Test 1-3: These were kind of useless. I didn't gain much benefit from metabolizing only one element of a food because very few edible things are only one thing.

**Side note:** Derin—Jabrie's second in command—suggested I try the tests again with lard, sugar, and quinoa. I could get behind the sugar test, but lard and quinoa are deal breakers.

- Test 4: speed up metabolism of an 8-course meal – I felt lousy. I felt okay. This isn't rocket science, people.

- Test 5: speed up metabolism of a 100-course meal – I turned the Gift on from the get-go so I didn't die. You think I'm kidding. Normal people who indulge in a decadent 100-course meal would sample—as in take a bite or two—of each offering. Jabrie and the Evil Minions wanted those plates cleared.

- Test 6-8: slow down metabolism of fats, sugars, and carbs in isolation of the others – much like speeding up only one at a time, hindering metabolism didn't do much besides make me feel full faster.

- Test 9: slow down metabolism of an 8-course meal – I made it to course four before hitting food-coma state and quitting.

- Test 10: slow down metabolism of a 100-course meal – I don't know why they thought this would be any different. I basically starved myself for the rest of that day in anticipation of the test. (That messes with the data; yeah, I've been told repeatedly.) This time, I made it to course nine before casting the quit card.

**Expectations and reality:**
Expectation 1: It's an easy to control Gift.

Reality 1: From a turn-on, turn-off and monitoring point of view, that's correct. This one doesn't take a whole lot of brain power to sustain. There's a gigantic but coming. From a self-control standpoint, it's very high on the will-be-abused list.

Expectation 2: You'll know exactly when to turn it off.

Reality 2: Okay, so this is really part 2 of the point I was making in 1. The power is amoral. It does come with an insistent, hey-stop-using-this-dummy gut feeling, but a warning is not an auto-off switch. It's left to the user to decide whether enough is enough. You don't have to be a cynic to understand that people and common sense don't always mix.

**Complications and downsides:**

Massive moral complication: Didn't somebody tell you beauty's in the eye of the beholder? Have you observed any fashion trends from the last four centuries?

I don't care much for fashion. Ellie—of the my-only-friend status—is both a lovable chatterbox and a fashion feaster. She even likes the history of fashion. Anyway, once upon a time, somebody got it into her head that having those plastic bubble balls pinned all over one's dress should be a thing.

My point is that many trends for women's fashion already harp on the ridiculously skinny is the golden ticket to fame, fortune, and good looks. Having something that can make that happen will only make that problem worse.

**Combat potential:** almost none

As a self-power, the user basically controls whether or not to accept the Gift they've been given.

The only way this can be used for killing somebody else is if it's paired with a very strong Mind Control suggestion to ignore all the warnings.

**Danger level:** very high

Getting the controls right for any auto-off setting is going to be next to impossible because the entire point of the Gift revolves around messing with metabolism.

The potential for abuse to the point of self-harm is high.

**Usefulness:** 4 of 5 stars (if used responsibly)

There are some medical benefits, such as safely losing weight in a timely fashion and purging drugs and poisons from one's system.

**Entertainment value:** 5 of 5 stars

It's not entertaining in the ha-ha sense, but I can see mild doses of this being served to the rich and famous so they can keep their perfect figures and indulge in a cupcake now and then.

I'm guessing the black market for the stuff will be lucrative.

**Overall rating and conclusion:** 3.5 of 5 stars

I don't care if the math doesn't work. It loses a point for being psychologically dangerous to those who give a fig about their weight.

# Chapter 21

# Journal Entry 9: Nice Escape

Mom's okay with me hating stuff. Dad's always been a fan of articulating and channeling anger into *more productive courses*. (This is why he got to teach me and my brothers how to drive.)

Guess I'll compromise.

I *strongly dislike* Bridgeway Labs and their Oversight Committee.

New not-so-fun fact: there's an entire committee that specializes in manipulating and controlling certain superpowers.

And I've been unwittingly helping them.

That's right. Every single one of my glorious superpower reports have been forwarded to the Oversight Committee.

I should have seen that coming, but Perfect Foresight as a power doesn't exist because too many things are in motion to accurately predict the future.

The realization puts me in the awkward moral position of continuing to toe the line they've drawn in the proverbial sand and quitting.

The rebel in me highly favors the idea of quitting, but that option will be very messy.

It's inevitable.

Everybody has a limit. Either they'll ask something I can't agree to—I mean more than an ill-conceived experiment they haven't thought through—or the holds they have on me will disappear.

I try not to think about that part. (The curse of practical Immortality.)

I'm disturbed by your question, but I'll answer it anyway because it's a natural question that was bound to be asked at some point.

Sure. I could remove myself from all equations (euphemistic wording for committing suicide), but then, Bridgeway would just pick some other poor Nobody and torment them. So, that's really a terrible solution.

Like it or not, these people chose to mess with me. Thus, it becomes my burden and duty to make them regret that decision.

As if misusing my reports wasn't enough reason to dislike them, they've also turned Ellie against me.

Perhaps that's a bit harsh, but I do know that they've asked her to report on me.

Of course, I look at her thoughts on me. I need to know what she has to say about me. I don't think she gives them anything that could be used against me, but I resent what they're doing.

It's classic manipulation.

(So are implicit and explicit threats, but this is a new level of low.)

What ticks me off the most is that the damage is largely done.

I know Ellie's reports on me are supposed to be hush hush because I had to bust through some Grade A mental locks to get at them.

I'm hoping that is something Ellie implemented on purpose to inadvertently draw my attention to them, but that could be wishful thinking. Maybe in a future visit, I'll have you look at one of her reports. She could be more devious than I give her credit for. I'm rooting for that outcome.

Either way, they've effectively driven a large trust wedge between us.

Translation: I can't confide any serious plans for breaking away from Bridgeway unless I want to channel the information directly to the Oversight Committee.

It complicates things because now I'll have to come up with fake plans to discuss with Ellie that I don't mind being leaked to the evildoers and real plans.

Misdirection is a viable option, but Ellie's such a good sounding board.

Taking the genuine version of that away is downright mean.

Guess that means you get to be my sounding board. Please don't take that as an insult. Trying to handle stuff on one's own is a natural human tendency.

Asking for help stinks, especially for a Nobody. Access to multiple Gifts is great for giving one delusions of Invincibility, and I don't just mean the physical kind.

The past is safe in a way my present won't be until I right these wrongs.

I enjoy visiting your time. It's a nice escape.

I know you want to help, and that alone means a lot to me.

Yeah, I know. Cop out answer usually meant to soothe ruffled feathers.

(Your time-period has so many delightful colloquialisms. I think I'm using them correctly. I made a copy of Bess, modified her attitude, and called her Mess—My Editing Software System, for obvious reasons. Would have gone with Jess but that seemed needlessly confusing.)

But I mean it. Sometimes, the most powerful gift you can give somebody is a genuine, heartfelt listening ear.

For eons, people have been obsessed with superpowers, power in general, or money. Not much has changed on that front. People forget the simplest gifts can mean the most.

I promise to let you know if you can help me in a more tangible way than letting your brain be a private dumping ground for plans and pieces of plans.

Honestly, I want you to continue doing what you do without any changes.

I connect with your mind so easily in part because you're my great-great-great-great-something-or-other. (Give or take a few greats. Numbers aren't my strong suit if I don't have Enhanced Intelligence toggled to on.)

Got to sleep now, but your curiosity concerning how Gifts work is quite apparent. I'll go into that next session. I owe you that much for being my safe haven.

# Chapter 22

# Journal Entry 10: How Superpowers Work

Never really thought about how superpowers work, especially multiple Gifts. It's a moot point to 95% of the people who have a superpower since they only get one.

What do you call them? Supers? Heroes? Superheroes? I guess any of those work.

With only one superpower, it's usually a simple matter of turning the Gift on or off. Take Flight, Invisibility, or Superspeed, you have the intention of using the gift—thereby activating it—and voilà, you fly, turn invisible, or run very fast.

If something knocks your concentration or you accidentally hit something, the Gift will likely preserve your life but not necessarily your dignity.

The Ancillary Gifts—such as an enhanced awareness of stuff around you when using Superspeed—don't count as separate powers because they're usually not offered alone. They're part of some package deal.

Somebody with Enhanced Spatial Awareness probably wouldn't even pass the Superpower Recognition Test because they rarely turn it off.

They might gain a reputation for being exceedingly coordinated, but that's about it.

In fact, most self-powers have a tough fight to be recognized as Gifts.

Self-power is sort of a misnomer. From a certain point of view, most Gifts would be seen as self-powers if we went with a generic definition. In this case, we're using it to mean a power whose application only affects the user.

That's why Metabolism Manipulation falls under that category and Flight does not. You misuse the former, you die. You misuse the latter, you—and possibly random others—die.

You may argue that Enhanced Spatial Awareness can lead to quicker reflexes that can affect others. It might lend you the uncanny ability to dodge a single bullet, but if there are no other Gifts in play, it's just going to announce when you fall to multiple bullets.

Same thing for saving somebody else from a bullet. Your intervening options are not much greater than a Normie with good reflexes.

For whatever reason passes for a whim around here, the Superpower Control Council's Public Relations Committee deemed such things as pseudo powers rather than full Gifts.

That can be a bitter pill for some people.

Mostly because people stink.

They'll use any difference or perceived deficiency to point out why they're somehow better than you. It's a drive to dominate that's turned into a fine bullying mentality.

Spoiler alert: if they didn't solve the worst tendencies of humanity in the few thousand years before you, it shouldn't shock you that they didn't do so in the few hundred separating our timelines.

There are more nitpicky details but that's the basics.

On to your questions.

**Could I do something about it?**

I assume you mean the humans being jerks to each other thing. That's an interesting question. Best answer I can give is no. Anything I do to *perfect* humanity would destroy both the good and the bad parts of us.

It's like weeding with napalm. I guess it's a solution, just not a very good one. If I was a futuristic artificial intelligence your sci-fi books and movies are so fond of, I'd go with it, but I'm not.

**Can I use more than one power at a time?**

Yes, within reason. The closest analogy I can think of is you having multiple tabs open on your computer screen.

Some people have multiple monitors running so they can check different tabs at the same time.

Our Quick Chip Computer Links function much the same as your normal computers and wireless internet service.

Your devices are also capable of playing music, showing you something to read, and running a video, though most phone things are smart enough to stop a video if you're on a different tab.

I know that drives you nuts. There is a workaround, but I'm not sure if I'm allowed to share it with you. The Security Panel—essentially Time Travel cops—get all big-eyed, raving lunatic-y when somebody introduces something before its intended time.

Not that I know this from personal experience.

I might know this from personal experience.

It was a peppermint in the 1200s. A girl had just lost her family to a plague. I was nine, and I panicked. Hence, the ill-fated peppermint. The Security Panel agent who arrested me said the candy wasn't the main issue. The plastic wrapper got me busted. Again: I was nine. End of defense.

Got a Time-Travel Restriction Order that expired when I turned twenty-one. Lesson learned.

**Side note:** Google's still a thing, as are Apple and Walmart. Near the end of the twenty-first century, most of the big companies started paying for posterity protections. That boils down to legal protection from their own heirs trying to change the iconic names.

Guess everybody has a fear of disappearing.

**Explain the *within reason* part.**

Not a question, but point taken.

Multitasking is a thing in your era. I can do the same, but much as you have access to thousands of apps for your smart phone, I have access to different Gifts. You don't use all your apps at once. I don't use all my Gifts at once.

Each one takes a little bit of power. Some—depending on how complicated they are—take a bit more power and attention to maintain. Remember the energy bars I mentioned? Like a battery, they drain faster if I'm trying to do multiple things simultaneously.

The analogy isn't perfect, but it's mostly still applicable to phone or tablet apps. If you had three thousand apps and opened them all, your device would probably be sluggish at best, peevish and unresponsive at worst.

Using too many Gifts burns me out. Because things concerning superpowers are rarely easy, burnout to me is akin to a diabetic crash or extreme fatigue. It's the kind of tired where thinking about thinking hurts.

I've only been in that state twice because my folks harped on responsible Gift use a lot.

**Why don't I use my amazing powers more?**

You mean aside from not liking what burnout does to me?

Fine. I can feel you're not quite with me on the apps analogy, but I also see you like video games. Maybe a second analogy will help.

Some roleplaying games get crazy and let you touch everything in the world. That means every object, animal, or person can be talked to, moved, or chucked. You—should—choose not to do these things because doing so would draw a lot of unwanted attention to yourself.

I don't use most of my Gifts because I don't want to stand out. As soon as you stand out, people want stuff from you.

Win the lottery? Boom. Instant ticket to 400 false friends.

**Isn't that a selfish point of view?**

Maybe. Whose side are you on anyway?

Selfishness is an evolutionary—or God-given, depending on your perspective—default state of being. It's part of self-preservation, which is arguably a good thing.

Notice, I did not say be a meanie head to everybody around you.

My personal philosophy is closer to try not to kill anybody.

It's a good rule to live by.

# Chapter 23

# Superpower Review 13: Lightning Manipulation

**Background and notes:**

Jabrie and Company wanted me to do separate reviews for Create Lightning, Control Lightning, and Negate Lightning.

I told them that one that encompassed all aspects simultaneously would be much more comprehensive, allowing me to address the nuances inherent to each.

(Yeah, I finally got smart. It was a *not-happening*, but instead of a straight version of that, this one sounded prettier. Perhaps my next review should be Manipulate Powerful Idiots, but I digress.)

I had to think hard for non-destructive uses of Lightning Manipulation.

Even before analysis, I don't see myself signing off on a public version of this power unless Bridgeway wants the title of Most Irresponsible Company in History.

**Explanation of the power:**

I feel like this section should henceforth be known as State the Obvious.

Lightning Manipulation involves everything about creating, controlling, and stopping lightning. There are probably other companion Gifts I'm not going to dwell on too, such as Lightning Immunity.

Would do you very little good to be able to create lightning if it ripped you apart in the process. On the other hand, companion Gifts usually work flawlessly, but I wouldn't stake my life on it.

**The subpowers spelled out for clarity:**

- Create Lightning – The art of fashioning lightning.

- Control Lightning – The art of making lightning do your bidding.

- Negate Lightning – The art of turning lightning off.

**How I categorize types of lightning bunny trail:**

For the record, this isn't going to be the boring science lesson on natural types of lightning.

- Zeus lightning – the stereotypical jagged bolt of lightning artists depict people wielding like a spear

- Web lightning – looks like a spider's web; has very regular shape to the bolt distribution

- Tree root lightning – starts at one place then sends out main streaks with baby streaks coming off of those

- Pattern or grid lightning – usually involves smaller, temporary bolts or mini-streaks of lightning zipping around on predetermined paths

**Experiments:**

I knew the day's festivities would do very bad things to my hair, so I didn't put much effort into it today.

I was asked to ...

- Test 1 (creation/negation): create a single bolt of Zeus lightning, then make it go away (Jabrie's instructions were terribly vague, but after some discussion, this is what I concluded he meant.)

- Test 2 (creation/negation): create two bolts of Zeus lightning, then make them go away

- Test 3 (creation): create multiple bolts of Zeus lightning and throw them at targets of varying distances

- Test 4 (control): create a small streak of lightning and move it through a maze

- Test 5 (control/negation): create a streak of lightning, turn it off when it comes to a person, then recreate it beyond the person

- Test 6 (negation): stop a lightning storm

**What happened:**

- Test 1: As expected, I made a bolt of lightning, posed with it a few seconds and let it fade.

- Test 2: It went exactly as the first experiment, only this time, I did it twice. (Then, I couldn't help it. I created a clone of myself and staged a sword fight. You can't not hold a sword fight with bolts of lightning.)

- Test 3: Not going to lie. Flinging lightning bolts around like fastballs was therapeutic.

- Test 4: I did it, but it's a heck of a lot harder than it sounds. Lightning by its very nature is an ornery thing. It goes where it wants to go, usually blazing a path through ionized air.

- Test 5: They must have sensed me having too much fun because they pulled another unnecessary power play by hiring my little brother (Doug) to be the lightning dummy*. I only found out about three seconds before releasing the lightning.

*I'm not just insulting my brother, even though I do question his judgement. That's the term Jabrie used when I got the instructions for the experiment.

(I'm annoyed with Doug, but I don't blame him. $10,000 for standing in a spot for a few minutes is a mighty tempting offer. I can't even begrudge Doug the money, but I don't like that Bridgeway is involving my family.)

- Test 6: Hurt. Figuring out the mechanics in my head and making the umpteen billion frantic particles heed my will were two completely different realities. (It might have looked like I figured it out instantly, but that's a Time Manipulation trick I used. It took me four restarts before learning the basics of lightning wrangling.)

**Expectations and reality:**

Expectation 1: Lightning is an awesome, clean, efficient weapon.

Reality 1: It's visually impressive, but also, dangerous, destructive, and unpleasant to wield. The air surrounding a bolt gets heated to over 25,000 degrees Celsius. That doesn't do nice things to flesh.

Expectation 2: It's easy to redirect lightning.

Reality 2: Unlike an arrow or a bullet, lightning is an electrical discharge. It's energy. It behaves erratically by nature. Controlling that involves hundreds of thousands of fine adjustments every microsecond.

Expectation 3: It's easy to turn on and off.

Reality 3: Creating it involves making the right conditions to let it happen. It's that age-old subatomic particle love story: electrons are besotted with protons. Their mad rush to unite creates electricity. Stopping lightning is the opposite (remove the conditions needed).

Expectation 4: It would be an excellent source of energy.

Reality 4: I do not like where this one is going. If controlled, yes, lightning can be a nice source of energy, but to have a constant source, you'd need to have somebody devoted to constantly creating it in a controlled setting.

You'd need people willing to spend large portions of their life doing one dangerous, monotonous task. Even if you paid them well, you likely wouldn't get many takers on a job where a misstep means you cook your insides.

**Complications and downsides:**

**Summary:** Terribly difficult to control. Lightning does what it wants. If you happen to be in the way and not have the superpower to withstand it, you die. Must we belabor other downsides? I feel like there-are-a-hundred-and-four-ways-to-die-every-time-you-try-this should be enough of a downside.

**Random side effects:**

- My hair had extra volume all day.

- My teeth tingle.

- I have a slightly burnt taste in my mouth.

- I had to erase my memories of burnt flesh.

**Combat potential:** astronomically high

It's not exactly a subtle weapon, but it would prevent the need for hauling dangerous chemicals around. Escort the super into place, target the enemy, and fry them. War over. Go home.

It feels wrong though.

**Danger level:** also, astronomically high

Have you ever tried corralling a dozen cats? Electrons and protons bent on meeting are infinitely more stubborn. To control lightning, you have to do exactly that (corral electrons and protons) to the tune of billions at a time.

There's not much room for error. If you're on a training run using Flight, you might get scraped up. There's no such equivalent setting for Lightning Manipulation.

**Usefulness:** 5 of 5 stars

It could be used to power cities.

**Entertainment value:** 2 of 5 stars

There is something satisfying about controlling something as unpredictable as lightning, but the threat of instant death for a mistake is a buzzkill.

**Overall rating and conclusion:** 3.5 of 5 stars

Highly useful. Very deadly.

Do not recommend you give this one to the public.

Lawsuits. So many lawsuits waiting to happen.

# Chapter 24

# Superpower Review 14: Shielding

**Background and notes:**

Shielding isn't exactly a passive Gift, but it's also not one that gets much media attention because it lacks an offensive side unless one gets creative with how they're formed.

It's not an easy Gift to control, and it requires far more thinking and quicker reflexes than most powers.

**Explanation of the power:**

The wielder forms shields.

**Quick definitions:**

- Personal shields – designed to protect the caster

- Protective shields – designed to extend protection to someone else

**Scope of protection:**

These can be personal shields, group shields, or city-wide shields.

**Types of shields:**

Varies widely depending on the nature of the threat.

**Quick list of common types of things shields can answer for:**

- Blades

- Bullets

- Arrows

- Acid

- Water

- Wind

- Fire

- Concussive forces (rockets, explosions)

- Poisonous gases

- Psychological/emotional

**Note:** It's possible to shield against the effects of poison, but only if such a threat is identified swiftly enough. Basically, this involves isolating the harmful chemical and putting a shield around that to protect the rest of the body.

**Second Note:** Shields aren't going to help much with nuclear weapons.

**Experiments:**

Spent the previous night watching meaningless reels of cute, fluffy creatures being their adorable selves. I figured this series of events would be arduous.

I was asked to shield against ...

- Test 1 (personal): Rathbun, North, and a dozen of their security buddy cronies coming at me with daggers, swords, and other pointy blade-like weapons. Only one dude was weird enough to choose a spear.

- Test 2-4 (personal): a small firing squad armed with handguns then rifles then a M134 Minigun.

- Test 5-6 (personal): a rocket propelled grenade and a multiple rocket launcher

- Test 7-12 (protective): a repeat of tests 1-6 while shielding Ellie, Doug, or both

**What happened:**

- Test 1: I owe the guy who brought a spear to the fight a strong drink because he made my job easy. Jabrie's rules concerning the test said I could only use various shields to defend myself. When spear guy tried to skewer me, I opened my personal shield enough to let the spear poke through. Then, I formed a shield around the weapon and hardened my personal shield. I used the resulting trapped spear as a blunt force weapon. Let's just say it wasn't an elegant fight and the recorders had a mysterious crash right about that time. (Ellie described it as a bizarre belly dance gone wrong.)

- Test 2-4: I insisted the remaining tests be moved to the Sahara Desert training ground. Going from handguns to rifles required the shields to be strengthened. As the number of bullets increased, I had to get creative with angles. It's easier to control a shield around a smaller area.

- Test 5-6: I teleported to within a few feet of the rocket launcher and the guys holding RPGs, then I formed shields. They just happened to be in my way. Jabrie wasn't pleased, but even he knew I'd acted within the parameters.

- Test 7: Doug and Ellie fought the security team. I provided shields so they didn't wind up with a dagger to the gut. (I also might have transferred a few decades worth of hand-to-hand combat knowledge from the surrounding soldiers and security people to them.)

- Test 8-10: Ellie got shot at. I did my best to protect her. (I worked through shields and messed with the soldiers' aim.)

- Test 11-12: Didn't happen. I wove a really nice mental picture of the tests happening with only minor hitches. (Besides not being comfortable with somebody lobbing grenades and rockets at my kid brother, I don't want to die. If I'd let it happen, my folks would find a way to negate my powers and murder me.)

**Expectations and reality:**

Expectation 1: Shielding is a boring Gift.

Reality 1: Any Gift can be exciting. Exciting usually translates to terrifying because people challenge themselves to find a way to overcome whatever you're good at. It's that blasted need to conquer.

Expectation 2: Shields are easy to create and maintain.

Reality 2: That ultimately depends on what you're shielding against, how many shields need to be maintained, and how long the shields need to last.

Expectation 3: Shields are visible.

Reality 3: What you see is an added effect people use instinctively. It's like flinching. When something strikes a shield, one instinctively wants to repair any damage. That's going to change the reflective angles, which will likely catch sunlight, making the shield visible.

Expectation 4: Shields all work the same way.

Reality 4: False. It's not one-size-fits-all. You really need to know what you're protecting against.

- A shield against water needs to be tight enough to repel little $H_2O$ molecules yet loose enough to let oxygen through.

- A shield against poisonous gas will have to be even tighter than the one for water, and you better hope you don't need that for long unless you can make it let only oxygen through.

- A shield meant to deflect a blade can be a little less robust than one needing to stop a bullet.

**Complications and downsides:**

If you're completely suspicious, you probably want to keep a permanent personal shield around yourself. Normal people are going to wait until they perceive a threat to form one. That means somehow, the threat needs to be identified to be answered.

**Complication:** Threats don't always come from expected points.

**Addendum to the Lightning Manipulation review as it pertains to shields:**

When I did the lightning tests, I formed the bolts and smaller streaks of lightning with my hands as expected.

I didn't tell Jabrie and the Evil Acolytes that technically lightning can be formed from any focal point. Generally, such points originate somewhere on the Super's person because it's easier to concentrate when one is using the power close to their body.

**Why didn't I tell them?**

Because I know how people's minds work. As soon as I say *anywhere* their little brains revert to third-grade boy logic and conclude that it means butts.

I can make lightning shoot out of my kneecaps, nose, eyes, armpits, butt, or any other part of the human anatomy. That's not the main point. Get your mind out of the gutter and focus.

If conditions are right or I have the energy to create the right conditions, I can make lightning originate somewhere nearby. Therefore, it's possible to perform sneak attacks that bypass Shielders.

**Combat potential:** high

**Danger level:** to self – low; to others – medium

**Usefulness:** 5 of 5 stars

If you're seeking dangerous situations, shields will help.

**Entertainment value:** 4 of 5 stars

The people who will use this power tend to enjoy war games. It'll thrill their little souls to be able to participate in live-fire war games.

**Overall rating and conclusion:** 4.5 of 5 stars

This is as close to glowing and gushing as you're going to get, but I still say no to a public release of Shielding. Private release to law enforcement and the military should be fine.

You really don't want the criminals getting ahold of this. It's not a toy.

# Chapter 25

## Journal Entry 11: Four-Ring, Voicemail Treatment

Today is the sort of day you just want to go back and hit restart on.

I'd finished my next few reviews early because they relied solely on me and only took one day each to complete.

Sacrificing an hour's worth of sleep let me write up both reports and fire them off to the appropriate entities.

The schedule usually includes two to three days to test each superpower. Many times, the full allotment of time plus some is needed since there's a lot more dithering when you have to coordinate with other people or get approvals to fire missiles in foreign countries.

Logically, one would assume finishing early would mean I could take a few days off to relax before the next scheduled session.

I consider visiting the family or catching up with Ellie. She and Doug have been attending the recent review sessions as a cross between a gawking audience and pseudo assistants.

I should have known Bridgeway wouldn't appreciate efficiency like any normal entity.

It also takes me far longer than it should to figure out something's up. My first missed clue is the empty whiteboard.

Ellie's an early riser, so she usually draws a good morning message for me. Some days it's short and simple, and other days, nearly every inch bears some part of an elaborate design.

When this mess is behind us, Ellie should consider a career as an artist. It's a tough life, but I think she could pull it off.

I usually respond with a generic *hi*. Occasionally, I feign exasperation, but secretly, I enjoy the gesture.

The blank board strikes me as odd, but it has happened before. It's rare, but I do sometimes wake up before Ellie.

My second missed clue is the absence of North and Rathbun. True to their earlier word, they have been my shadows since my brief trip off campus.

Not sure what time they get up in the morning, but they're usually leaning against the far wall outside my door when I emerge for the walk to breakfast.

The lack of babysitters means I can teleport down to the cafeteria, but I sort of enjoy the routine of a walk.

I almost miss North's curt nod of acknowledgement and Rathbun's morning scowl. This is probably how Stockholm syndrome starts.

Breakfast is a peaceful if slightly lonely affair. I indulge in a bacon, cheese, and onion omelet since I don't anticipate doing anything that will make me regret that decision. I even have a hot cup of coffee.

Upon returning the tray and sitting down to nurse the coffee, I call my mother. Her phone does the customary four rings before kicking me over to voicemail. I try her Quick Chip Computer Link and also get a big fat nothing.

Mom's the sort who rarely sets her phone down and checks her email, voicemail, and other messenger systems a dozen times a day. It's linked to her delivery business, so unless it's her unplugged time after 9:00 p.m., I can usually catch her. That's why she's my go-to person when I want to contact the family.

Confused but not completely weirded out yet, I call Dad and get the same four-ring and voicemail routine. Quick Chip, same results.

I try Joe. Same deal.

It could go either way with that being odd because he's been screening my calls for weeks.

I am not sure I should bother Leslie, but now batting 0 for 3 on contacting family, I need an easy win.

Leslie's been in the picture long enough to make a call to her socially acceptable.

We had a little tension when she first started dating Joe seriously. I wasn't used to a female close to my age, and she had a reputation as a flirt.

Being the responsible younger sister, I might have run a background check worthy of the FBI on Leslie.

Joe didn't appreciate my efforts and freaked out.

Dad just laughed.

Eventually, things sorted themselves. Mostly because Mom grounded me to appease Joe's wounded sense of pride.

I rehearse a short speech for Leslie. I plan to start with pleasantries before transitioning over to light inquiries and a request to speak with Joe. Since he's practically two inches from her at all times, it's a reasonable assumption on my part.

My speech crafting is for naught.

The call to Leslie also gives me the four-ring, voicemail treatment.

By the time it happens with Ellie, my thick skull starts to suspect something.

I stare down at my phone, knowing that Doug will be the ultimate gauge of whether I am having a standard run of bad luck or one carefully crafted by Jabrie or his crew.

Not quite ready for rejection, I send Doug a text message and a whiteboard message asking him if he wants to join me for breakfast.

When not playing my assistant, he attends high school classes and plays baseball. Bridgeway must have cut a deal with his school to let that happen.

I'm not privy to the details, but he spends nearly every waking moment here for a few weeks at a time. He leaves to attend practices or a few classes that absolutely must be done in person but that's it.

I can't remember if this is a school day for him or not, but anyway, the breakfast invite is just an excuse to contact him. The wait time lets me finish my coffee.

By that time, I gather enough courage to call Doug.

Ring one.

*Pick up.*

Ring two.

*Pick up. Pick up.*

Ring three.

My heart sinks.

Ring four.

I don't bother hoping for an answer.

As soon as his leave-a-message spiel begins, I carefully place my phone on the table to remove the temptation of hurling it across the cafeteria.

*Who do I call?*

Jabrie is the obvious choice, but the less dealings I have with him, the better.

Leaning over my empty coffee cup, I close my eyes. It's not a must for mental communication, but at this point, it's a hard-to-break habit.

*Bob?*

**I'm here.**

The instant response hits me as a very bad thing.

He's been waiting for my inquiry.

Anger and worry have a shoving match in my gut.

*Where are they?*

# Chapter 26

# Journal Entry 12: Mimic

*Finding them is your next task.*

Six words.

That's all it takes to murder my good mood.

Bob tries to explain further, but I throw up a mental block so I can keep my reaction to myself. It's the mental equivalent of muting oneself to scream a few curses and incoherent chords of pure rage.

Since I am still in public, I bottle everything inside.

The only manifestation to my new mood is a thoroughly crushed empty coffee cup, which I throw out with vigor.

Teleporting back to my room, I toss my phone onto my bed.

I never take it with me while working, and like it or not, I will be working today.

The rest of my preparations involve switching to a more functional shirt and shortening my hair. I usually keep it around shoulder length, but I always shift to shorter for active sessions.

I considered wearing one of the Faruchi getups I had received for the clothing tests, but I really don't want to give the Bridgeway goons the satisfaction.

Right now, I want nothing to do with anything they've been a part of.

*If it offers you better protection, take it.*

I grunt as my logic centers argue with my emotional half.

I waffle on the point until my logical side got tricky.

*Wouldn't it be awesome to use their own provisions against them?*

Changing takes a few seconds because I turn incorporeal to let my current clothes drop away, move my essence to the nearest Faruchi color storm that isn't purple, and reform.

The clothes have a few dozen trackers, which I disable with short bursts of electricity.

A mirror check reveals a scowling version of myself. On a whim, I add some black lines under my eyes like the baseball boys often do. The reminder of Doug tugs at a heartstring.

Shoving the sentiment aside, I contact Bob.

*Where am I going?*

**That is part of the exercise.**

Bob's thought carries the essence of embarrassment, but I accept the vagueness as part of their idiotic test.

*Stupid, but okay. Is there anything I should know?*

**Be careful.**

A short, bitter laugh pops out and threatens to turn hysterical.

I zero my emotions in favor of cold focus.

After being tracked telepathically, I'd decided it might be a good idea to be able to find friends and family, so I left markers with each of them.

I didn't tell them because that would have given them the option to alter or destroy the markers, making them useless. The point had bothered my conscience, but now, I am grateful paranoid me stuck it out.

Tapping into some Gifts involving advanced logic and spatial reasoning, I create a city map within my mind.

**That is beautiful.**

Ignoring Bob's compliment, I populate the map with icons for people I'd marked during my stay. I delete most of them a second later, only keeping the ones for Ellie, Joe, Leslie, Dad, Mom, and Doug.

A few adjustments to the codes let me tap into their minds enough to check their health and emotional states. Since they could be vastly different, I make those two separate settings and toggle between them.

Health status for everybody checks out green, which I'd set to indicate good.

When I switch to emotional status, Joe's icon changes to red, telling me he is some flavor of ticked off.

Dad, Doug, and Leslie are white, which means no emotions.

I take that to mean they are unconscious or drugged.

Ellie and Mom kept changing colors. I take that to mean rapid mood shifts or a high emotional state.

The other notable thing about their icons is that they practically read as one.

Zooming in on the map separates them, and by this time, I pay more attention to location.

A strange feeling sweeps over me.

I add an icon for myself, and the odd feeling intensifies.

Mom and Ellie are here, a few floors above me in Dr. Rolik's office.

I'd never met Dr. A. Rolik. He—or she, I guess—was always just one of many who got a copy of my reports.

Knowing I'd get some answers, I teleport to the office.

Not sure what I expect to find, but Ellie and Mom arguing with Jabrie looking on like a lost puppy certainly isn't it.

"—not ready for this!" Mom declares.

"She'll never be ready," Ellie says bitterly. "There's no way to be ready."

My appearance makes Jabrie perk up.

The door opens behind me, letting North and Rathbun enter.

I don't have to turn to see them. Their mental presences are clear enough.

They move to flanking positions but don't touch me.

I've practically turned to stone anyway.

My gaze darts from Mom to Ellie and back several times.

I settle on Mom.

The face belongs to my mother, but the crisp business suit is completely new. She stands in front of an imposing leather chair and behind a massive wooden desk that takes up a large portion of the spacious office.

Her expression mixes guilt, defiance, weariness, and love.

"Do I need to sit down for this?" My voice stays steady only because I am still actively suppressing my emotions.

"Probably." Ellie raises a hand and telekinetically moves one of the guest chairs toward me.

I stare at her.

*Ellie has powers.*

**Not exactly.**

Bob sounds reluctant to be making that point.

*What do you mean?*

**She's using your powers. She's a Mimic.**

# Chapter 27

# Superpower Review 15: Form Clones (Carbon Copy People)

**Background and notes:**

It's probably easiest if I define what Clones are and what they are not before I begin discussing the experiments and such.

They are not Drones.

Rathbun and North—my faithful shadows—are sometimes Drones when they go on certain missions like the one to fetch me. Becoming a Drone involves having a Mind Talker work through you or prepare your mind in some way.

This entry isn't about Drones. It's about Clones. I'm clarifying because everybody—including some of Jabrie's faithful crew—seems confused on that point.

Clones aren't the stuff of scifi stories or the product of biological mad-scientist experiments either. Rumor has it that all superpowers are the product of secret shady government business, but that's a bunny trail I shan't pursue right now for the sake of Jabrie's delicate nerves.

If you want a storybook comparison, Clones are probably closer to a fantasy thrall or a golem.

The word thrall originally meant slave, servant, or captive, but I think there was a video game that made it more like a temporary body that would fight for you.

A golem is an inanimate substance given life by a ritual.

I'm going to define Clones as Carbon Copy People because that's much more accurate.

As with any Gift, as soon as the power is turned off, the Clone ceases to exist. That's why it's different than creating a being using somebody else's DNA blueprint.

**Explanation of the power:**

Form Clones goes far beyond mere creation of a physical form. It involves monitoring and controlling the temporary body.

**Point of clarification:** By this definition, Clones are not people. They don't have a soul, though I suppose you could say they share a soul with their caster. They're more like a very realistic representation and extension of the caster.

If they are around long enough, the Clone can develop a personality, but I think it's probably just revealing what already exists beneath the surface in the person who makes the Clone.

(Please don't confuse them with clones who have been gotten through good old-fashioned mad science. Lab-born people deserve every advantage afforded somebody conceived the natural way.)

Jabrie's looking at me with all wide-eyed innocence like he doesn't know clones exist.

**Experiments:**

I'm not even going to bother listing the experiments.

I was asked to form an ever-increasing number of Clones and have them do things like walk through a maze, dance, play a pickup soccer game, and synchronize swim.

Next, I repeated the same exercises with Clones of Jabrie, Hal, Ellie, and Doug.

**What was likely reported:**

Subject—that's me—successfully formed one and two Clones and maneuvered them through the maze. After that, the Clones started showing more variation, but they responded well to directions concerning dance, sports, and other coordination exercises.

**What really happened:**

(Around Clone three, I started letting subtle mistakes happen. I am not certain how many Clones I can make before losing the ability to catch mistakes, but it is more than three.)

For kicks and because I needed to distract the Dream Team, I had the Jabrie and Hal Clones faceoff against the Ellie and Doug Clones in an intense half-court basketball game. To make the game fair-ish, I turned control of the Jabrie and Hal Clones over to Bob.

I believe that ability causes some of the naming confusion as the move technically turned those Clones into Drones.

(I let Bob's team win, but I made it a close thing. I do not need any Bridgeway people knowing anything about my tactics.)

**Quick definitions:**

- Clone – body created and controlled by another

- Drone – being (usually already alive) controlled by another

**Expectations and reality:**

I don't think the public has any expectations of Form Clones because it's not a very well-advertised Gift.

There are only a handful of registered Supers with the Form Clones ability. The only one I know who uses the Gift with any regularity is Maria Escobar, owner—and sole employee—of Escobar Cleaning Services.

Basically, she hand-cleans massive structures inside and out through a carefully crafted team of Clones. (She can afford to put the Clones in dangerous situations because if one falls and breaks their neck, she can let it fade and form another. Pretty sure she works only at night because fading and forming can freak out the uninitiated.)

**Complications:**

**Complication 1:** The ability to control Clones is limited to how well the caster multitasks. Usually only two or three Clones can be adequately controlled. I believe Maria's the exception to that, not the rule.

**Complication 2:** There's a proximity limitation as well. Imagine the Clone as an extension of the person.

**Complication 3:** The quickest way to make many Clones is to craft Carbon Copy People from previous Clones. This causes problems because it multiplies mistakes.

Jabrie thinks I'm being lazy with my explanation. He holds that if I just duplicate each copy carefully enough, an infinite number ought to be achievable.

The more anything is rushed, there's a greater chance for inserting mistakes. Any time and effort spent catching mistakes will detract from forming new Clones.

**Complication 4:** Shadows (a.k.a. Echoes) are Clones that only partially faded. Normally, when a caster stops controlling a Clone, it fades into nothing. If something goes wrong with that process, there's a remnant of the Clone left. This may linger anywhere from a few minutes to a few months.

They don't do much but scare the heck out of people. (What do you think caused 90% of the ghost sightings and hauntings?)

**Do Clones feel emotions?**

That depends on the caster's skill level. If the CCP (Carbon Copy Person) is good enough, then yes, but it's the echo of an emotion projected into place by the caster, if you want to get stuffy about what's happening.

**Combat potential:** Medium

There's potential for forming small squads of soldiers, but you'd have to have some intense training to get them to fashion bodies that can work within a fireteam. Also, if the caster catches a stray bullet, bye bye fireteam.

**Danger level:** Low to medium

There's always the chance something goes horribly wrong, but generally, if a Clone gets too far away from the caster, they fade. If the caster stops exerting their will, the Clone fades.

**Usefulness:** Very high

I can see people buying this to shorten the time they spend on household chores. Conceivably, you could do laundry, cook a meal, watch a few children, clean a house, deal with weeds, and pick up sticks simultaneously.

**Entertainment value:** Medium

There's a decent wow factor in play around this Gift. I think it'll wear off quickly, but people will be more willing to do stupid stuff that could get them killed if they could try it through a Clone.

**Overall rating and conclusion:** 3.5 of 5 Stars

I know it's tempting, but I don't recommend releasing this one to the general public. It gets high marks for usefulness, but if you let a bunch of amateurs have the ability to Form Clones, you're going to drastically increase the number of Shadows.

Most eventually fade on their own, but you're still talking about loose energy. It could gather or be harnessed by somebody opportunistic and unscrupulous.

I don't think the chance to do the dishes faster warrants creating an untold number of Shadows.

# Chapter 28

# Superpower Review 16: Body Modifications

**Background and notes:**

I'm going to tell you up front people are not going to use this one responsibly.

It's a great one for making addicts, but you're also likely to get a huge outcry against the dosage being too weak.

Have you seen some of the modifications people make without superpowers? Do you really want to give them the ability to change almost anything about their bodies?

I suppose the fact that Body Modifications have a built-in time limit could be a good thing. People can change stuff out without the sense of permanency. Think dyeing one's hair vs. enlarging one's earlobes.

**Philosophical musings:**

People have a love-hate relationship with fitting in and standing out.

It comes down to raw desperation to be accepted. Some minds are dead-set against the idea that one can be good enough straight from the baby-making factory.

We (the royal society as a whole we) should be more focused on getting people to accept who they are rather than enabling them to change things on a whim.

### Explanation of the power:

Why do we even have this section?

Body Modifications covers the ability to physically enhance or change something about one's personal physical form. This can run the gamut from normal to the deepest recesses of horror very quickly.

Besides the obvious enhancements the less well-endowed members of society will feel the need to generate to compensate for where they landed in the gene pool, the list of possible changes is limited only by the imagination (and the body's natural durability factors).

**Please note:** This one only covers personal—as in doing it to yourself—changes. It does not cover the ability to change things about somebody else's body. That exists and is a whole other problem waiting to happen.

### Shapeshifting vs. Camouflage vs. Body Modification:

There is some overlap.

Shapeshifting could cover some body mods, but it goes much wider to include other types of living creatures and inanimate objects.

Camouflage is also something that may be included in body mods, but it's much more limited to surface changes, whereas Body Modification can cover more than blending in. I'd categorize Camouflage as only one aspect of Body Modification.

### Experiments:

(I may have downplayed the modifications that would be possible.

Though I knew it would largely be an unpleasant series of events, part of me relished the fact that the inherent nature of the power meant the experiments would involve only me.)

I was asked to form ...

- Test 1: a third arm

- Test 2: a 6<sup>th</sup> finger

- Test 3: a 6<sup>th</sup> toe

- Test 4: a longer neck

- Test 5: stripes along my appendages

- Test 6: a different shaped nose

- Test 7: spikes along my back

- Test 8: a tail

- Test 9: horns

- Test 10: permanent tattoos across my skin

I was then asked to lengthen/ grow ...
- Test 11: the long bones in my legs

- Test 12: the long bones in my arms

- Test 13: my torso

- Test 14: my brain

**What happened:**

They had some other asks that I quashed before the list was finalized. Tests 1-10 proceeded as expected.

The scientists' expressions almost convinced me to keep the tattoos, horns, and tail. Those people deserve a little more fear in their lives.

Doug's face made me return to normal. I would never intentionally scare him, not like this. Under different circumstances and during one of his moody-teenager moments, sure, but not simply to torment him.

Tests 11 and 12 were unpleasant. Once I returned to normal, I used Healing Gifts to deal with the pain.

Test 13 hit both unpleasant and weird notes. Newsflash, if you expand the outer package, the stuff inside is going to move. When packing books, that means you're going to ding the corners. When packing organs, it means the slippery suckers move where they want to, which wreaks havoc on everything.

Test 14 didn't happen. The idea of it earned Jabrie yet another science lesson. Letting my core organs get out of place is one thing, but messing with my brain—you know, the thing controlling how I use the Gifts—could easily mean the end of my abilities.

**Expectations and reality:**

**Expectation 1:** It'll be painless.

**Reality 1:** Normal growth is painful sometimes. Why would this be different? You might be able to include some painkillers in the mix, but I suspect some people will be oddly disappointed if it doesn't cost them anything.

**Expectation 2:** It will improve mankind.

**Reality 2:** I'm not opposed to progress on principle, but I'm also doubtful that horns and scales are our next big steps as a species.

**Expectation 3:** The changes are permanent.

**Reality 3:** They are not.

**Complications and limitations (and distinctions):**

**Complications:**

- Some bodies are going to reject new additions.

- People aren't used to extra limbs. The human body wasn't meant to have a third arm.

- If everybody has something, nobody has anything special as long as people can pay the asking price. Imagine growing a sixth finger becomes a trend, those with will look at those without with disdain. Then, some twit will get it into their brilliant head to grow a seventh finger and that will be a thing.

**Limitations:**

Did I mention Body Modification would be temporary? How fleeting depends on all those usual factors about metabolism.

**Combat potential:** 3.5 of 5 Stars

I suppose the camouflage portion could be useful.

While I guess a third arm and hand could help in a hand-to-hand contest, I don't see it being a make-or-break point when guns can easily be involved.

More hands to hold guns could get interesting, but despite movie depictions, accuracy goes to heck in a heartbeat if you try to aim two guns at once. It's also murder on the wrists.

**Danger level:** Medium

Extra height is going to be a common shift. People not used to an extra few inches of height will be a lot clumsier than normal. I guess that could lead to being accident-prone.

**Usefulness:** 4 of 5 Stars

People who lose limbs can have them back as long as you give them a great enough supply of this Gift.

You're better off getting somebody with a strong enough Healing Gift to restore the missing piece.

**Superficial changes made easy:**

If you get good enough with the Gift, you won't need makeup, you can simply change the skin cells on your face to reflect what you want.

**Entertainment value:** High

It's not my idea of fun, but those who get jazzed about normal level of body mods will enjoy exploring a wider range of options.

**Overall rating and conclusion:** 3.75 of 5 Stars

There's crazy-high potential for good, but I can easily see it spinning out of control.

# Chapter 29

# Journal Entry 13: Not-the-Ellie

Bob's announcement gives me a gameplan. It isn't a good gameplan, so I hesitate to enact it.

Mom's sad smile stirs up some conflicting emotions. I feel anger, horror, shock, blind denial, and love crawling about my body as my distraction pokes holes in the active emotional suppression.

Ellie's mocking expression gives the anger and denial an edge.

"Need some tissues, Jess? You look like you might cry."

The cold tone is so anti-Ellie something clicks in my head about Bob's earlier statement.

*She's a Mimic.*

Mimics get to try out other people's looks and unguarded powers.

Thus, my not-so-good gameplan involves shutting down each of my abilities.

I immediately lock down the most dangerous ones like the various pyrotechnic stuff, but I have to leave most of the Gifts alone to mask my actions. Plus, if I shut everything down, I'll be practically defenseless.

Bob didn't say the woman before me is Ellie, only that she is a Mimic. Whether she's Ellie and a Mimic has yet to be determined.

I have a hard time picturing my annoyingly upbeat best friend as a fraud, but most Mimics are masters of disguise, that's kind of the main selling point of the power.

Dividing my thoughts, I set part of my brain to working through that puzzle.

The rest of me tackles the tricky business of determining the nature of the proposal to come and the various ways I can handle the situation.

Self-preservation makes me do a people check too.

Mom and the Mimic haven't moved.

Jabrie drifts closer to Mom.

North and Rathbun stand dutifully out of the way.

The expanded awareness lets me sense the five-man security team waiting in the conference room off this office.

Marching over to the chair Possible-Not-the-Ellie has placed at the room's center, I sit down, absorb some cool calm from the Mimic, and squarely face my mother.

"Explain." I mean to go for something less direct and hostile, but the command will have to do.

My mother is no stranger to my attitudes, but our previous conflicts usually involved how late I could stay out, what I could wear, and where I could go.

A horrible thought hits me.

*Is she even my mother?*

All my sense of belonging and identity brace for devastating impact.

"Not even sure where to begin," Possibly-Not-My-Mother admits.

"Are you my mother?"

My impulsive question brings forth thoughts of an old children's story with that title. This woman—I can tell because of the mental marker—has read me that story countless times.

The wounded look convinces me before she utters a word.

"Of course! That will never change!"

My mind unhelpfully provides all the ways that could change.

*It will if they kill you.*

The Mimic waves to snag my attention.

"Touching as this reunion is, dear Jess has a scavenger hunt to embark upon." Bestowing her sickeningly sweet smile upon Mom, the Mimic continues, "You should tell her about that, doctor."

The reminder hits me like a light slap, as intended.

If my mother has a reaction to the jibe, I miss it.

Staring down my mother, I ignore the Mimic.

"But you're also Dr. Rolik, aren't you?"

"It's been a while, but yes." The confirmation comes out slowly, but the rest of the words recover some of Mom's characteristic speed. "I worked here long before I met Winston. We met here. He was among the first batch of volunteers for the Underwater Breath study."

That was not the story I'd been told before, but I gather a lie was easier to get behind than explaining ties to shady government entities to your elementary-aged kids.

"So, you met a handsome study subject, married him against company policy, and had a beautiful baby boy and then the girl wonder and then another bouncing baby boy. How sweet."

The Mimic's attitude starts to grate on me, but I want to hear what my mother will say to the mocking summary.

"Not exactly the whole story, and some things are out of order." Mom shifts her sad eyes to the Mimic.

"They tried to hide their relationship," says Jabrie, sounding bored. "It's in her file. You can read that later."

The analysis of the Mimic's brain scan comes through, confirming her as Not-the-Ellie.

I look from Jabrie to Not-the-Ellie to Mom, trying to figure out who will get to the point the quickest.

"I'll explain someday," Mom promises.

The award for most impatient is a tossup between Jabrie and Not-the-Ellie. Since that mental moniker bothers me, I decide to get that cleared up next.

"Do you have a name, or should I continue to think of you as Evil Not-My-Ellie?" I make direct eye contact with the Mimic. "And where is my Ellie anyway? Is she okay?"

She has to be close.

The Mimic would need frequent inspirational updates. I don't know exactly how that works. It has been some time since I devoted myself to Mimic studies. Like the Shapeshifting Gift, Mimicry is an art that takes a lot of practice to get right.

I think back to the last few interactions with Ellie and try to figure out when she got switched out for the Mimic.

The Mimic glares at me.

"Which question do you want answered?" she demands.

"All of them," I say, inserting as much bite as she had put in. "Let's start with Ellie's status."

"Safe," answers the Mimic with a smirk.

We trade short, quick answers.

"Location?"

"Here."

"When can I see her?"

"Soon, but after the morning exercises."

"What's your name?"

Out of the corner of my eye, I see very different reactions from Mom and Jabrie.

Mom looks strained. She lowers her gaze.

Jabrie is positively gleeful. He watches me intently, then he glances at Mom to see if she will make the introduction. When nothing happens, he slides his attention my way.

"Don't." The hoarse word slips out of Mom. "This isn't the time or place."

"I disagree. This is the perfect time and place." Jabrie clears his throat and straightens his shoulders. "Jess, meet Jasmine. She's your twin."

# Chapter 30

# Journal Entry 14: Timer

My head does that swivel thing from Mom to Jasmine to Jabrie and back to Mom.

A brief nod from Mom confirms Jabrie's announcement.

Once again, thanks to emotional suppression, I don't react much even though I have a few months' worth of stuff to process.

I suppose Jasmine could be tapping my Suppression power too in order to bury a reaction, but it's more likely the lack of reaction means she already knew.

The glittering resentment in her eyes adds weight to the already-knew theory.

"Is that supposed to mean something to me?" I ask.

"It means I'm going to kill you someday." The Mimic speaks with quiet, terrifying confidence.

*Eh, nice to meet you too. Who peed in your tea this morning?*

**She was raised here.**

I mentally growl at Bob. The revelation muddies the emotional waters even more. If my emotions got to play out normally, I'd be reeling.

Even with my exciting life, it's not every day you find a Mimic impersonating your best friend, meet a long-lost twin, and get a death threat in the span of three minutes.

"Jazz, please! There's no proof Mimic Absorption even works like that."

*Gee, thanks for the ardent defense, Mom.*

**Go easy on her. She didn't have much of a choice about anything.**

*I'm going to need a better explanation than that, but later.*

Needing something safe to think about, I focus on the Theory of Mimic Absorption. It holds that certain powers can be permanently transferred to a skilled Absorber as long as the original Super doesn't need that Gift anymore.

*That last bit's probably a lie to soothe people's fears about the Gift.*

According to the theory, Mimic Absorption isn't a full Gift.

A textbook I read once upon a time claimed that it's merely a flashy display of Mimic power.

Mimic Absorption is often confused with Gift Absorption or Gift Transference. Those are always temporary. As soon as you turn them off, the power returns to the owner.

"No killing yet," says Jabrie. "Maybe after the studies complete."

He sounds like he's telling the Mimic she can't eat a cookie because it'll ruin her dinner.

*Are they all psychopaths?*

**Geniuses, maybe, but—**

*It's an expression, Bob. Shut up. I'm trying to think.*

**You'll need to hurry to get to Joseph and Leslie. Winston and Douglas can hold out slightly longer.**

*What is happening to them?*

Predictably, Bob doesn't answer.

I make a hybrid noise that's part sigh and part growl.

"I don't have time to deal with you people. I need to know what you did with the rest of my family, and which stupid hoops you need me to jump through to get them back."

"First the ground rules," says Jabrie.

"No running," says Rathbun from behind and to my left.

"No hiding," North adds from behind and to my right.

"And don't be late," Jabrie finishes.

The surround-sound admonishments are disorienting, but I resist the urge to turn to either shadow.

"You're terrible at instructions." I direct the statement to Jabrie.

"Find them and save them. That's all we're *allowed* to say." My mother's expression says she wants to say more.

"Says who?" I demand.

"The man controlling their fates, of course." The voice descends from speakers hidden in the ceiling between light panels.

Jasmine stiffens.

Jabrie stands a little taller.

Mom looks like she chomped down on a raw lemon.

"You've done good work so far, Jessica, but you're not tapping into your full potential. We need to see you in action with stakes you genuinely care about. You too, Jasmine."

"Good luck with that," says Jasmine. "I don't care about anybody, so there's nobody for you to threaten."

The Ceiling Voice releases an amused noise.

"Not completely true, but I do believe compensation is a better motivator for you. I need your sister alive for now, but I'll let you know when that changes. Meanwhile, I'll have your allotment of subjects doubled for a month."

"Two months," Jasmine counters.

"Deal," says the voice.

*What just happened?*

**Your grandfather has been giving your sister Supers to practice her Absorber abilities.**

*How big is my dysfunctional family?*

I hold my breath and wait for the answer that will never come.

"Angela, please be seated." The voice speaks reasonably, but there is no mistaking the instruction for a request. It's 100% command. "I believe Jessica requires some convincing."

"I really don't," I argue. "Clarity, yes. Convincing, no. I believe you're serious."

*And unstable and dangerous.*

Mom's only sign of protest is a tightening in her jaw from her teeth clenching. She sits on the large leather chair without a word.

Rathbun and North leave their flanking positions behind me and move to the leather chair holding my mother.

Mom places her arms on the armrests and waits for the grunts to secure her wrists with straps sprouting from the armrests.

Rathbun gently holds Mom's shoulders in place while a silver, two-inch band emerges from the chair, snakes across Mom's stomach, and hooks into place on her other side, pinning her in place.

North guides another silver band into place across her forehead.

Before any of the many questions crowding my head make it out of my mouth, my mother closes her eyes.

She shudders, but the bands hold her in place.

I check the health bar I'd assigned her in my head. It flashes then changes to yellow and dips to about three-quarters full.

I teleport to Mom's side intending to deal with whatever she'd been injected with.

Before I can touch her, Jasmine catches my shoulders from behind and holds me back.

"She's all right. The poison won't work that fast," says Jabrie.

"Why would you poison her?" Before Jabrie or the voice from on high can answer, I blink back tears and fire a similar question at my mother. "Why would you let them poison you?"

Mom's eyes open and fix on me.

"Because I'm tired of living like this, and you're the only one who can beat him." She moves her gaze to over my shoulder. "Both of you." Then, she closes her eyes again.

I don't see Jasmine's face, but she goes very still for a moment.

"Your mother is now a living timer," explains the Ceiling Voice. "She has roughly an hour to live. You have that long to save the others and return to remove the poison."

# Chapter 31

# Mission Report 1: Rescue Joe and Leslie

**Objective:**

Rescue Joe and Leslie.

**Location/Setting:**

Rickety cabin. Creepy woods. Upstate New York.

(I put in the name of the forest, but my buddy Bess—Bridgeway Editing Software Systems—redacted it.)

**Background and notes:**

I don't see why this report can't wait until after the search and rescue mission.

Just because I can multitask well enough to divide my attention between actions and report writing does not mean I should be doing such.

The closest analogy I can think of is Capture the Flag.

A few squads of soldiers are guarding my brother and his fiancée.

I'm guessing the pair is unconscious.

Joe's ability to change the molecular structure of things makes it very difficult for him to be held captive. Leslie's got stellar intuition, but I don't think she passed the Superpower Recognition Test.

When I check their emotional states, they're both reading white blankness.

**Situation/Problem:**

Joe and Leslie have been stashed in a nearby cabin.

I'm about a half-mile away since that's the closest I was allowed to teleport to them.

I'm not sure why the sadistic powers that be ruled out precise Teleportation.

It's not exactly a true test of my powers if they keep ruling out the most basic responses.

**Possible powers required (and why I think I'll need them):**

For the record, it's dumb to put this section before the mission report. I get planning ahead, but it's not going to be a complete list because I haven't done anything yet.

- Locate Target – Already done, unless they're giving off false mental readings.

- Locate Hostiles – It's nice to know which direction somebody's going to shoot you from.

- Superspeed – It's a long hike, and my mother doesn't have time for me to take a leisurely stroll here.

- Personal Shielding – The soldiers are armed.

- Shield Others – Did I mention the soldiers are armed?

- Camouflage – My Faruchi outfit would make me a fine target.

- Induce Sleep – (I'm still not going to admit the ability to kill from afar. There's no Press-Here-to-Kill-this-Person button, but there are ways of inducing allergic responses, causing heart attacks, affecting a person's ability to breathe, and such that would get the job done.)

- Super Strength – If I read the situation correctly and Joe and Leslie are indeed unconscious, I'm going to need more than normal muscles to haul their butts out of that cabin back to the point the arbitrary idiots are *allowing* me to teleport from.

- Transportation – The current location is almost a hundred miles from the main campus. The risks are higher, but the total energy cost is lower than the other method of getting us from the woods back to Bridgeway's New York headquarters.

- Record Event – Conventional recording devices aren't capable of tracking stuff in superspeed. I essentially have to make a memory reel of the festivities and let someone copy it from my head later.

**Note:** Many of the things listed above are not powers in their own right. They're manifestations of Minder (Mind Talker) Gifts.

**Second note:** Jasmine is here as my babysitter since she can pull from my Gifts to keep up.

**Live mission report:**

I used Locate Hostiles to identify each place that held a soldier.

Five surrounded my older brother and Leslie. Their guns are trained on the unconscious forms.

Two more hover near the door. They're probably waiting for me to stroll through.

About twenty feet of open space is between the cabin and the woods. Four soldiers roam the open space, but the rest—another thirty-two, judging by the number of distinct brainwave patterns—are hidden in groups of two and three throughout the woods.

It takes me almost a minute to check and double check that I've located each mind. Once I'm sure, I amplify my ability to Induce Sleep and hit every soldier at once.

Simultaneously, I use Superspeed to dash up to and then into the cabin, gather up the five grenades that got dropped, dump them into a shield just outside the cabin, and wait for the explosion. It rattles the windows but does little more.

Next, I battle the two soldiers I missed due to a mental shield. They didn't get a chance to kill the hostages because the shield worked both ways. I couldn't sense them, but they were also blinded to my approach.

Finally, I got to check on Joe and Leslie. After confirming they were fine, I gave them both thin personal shields, tossed them into a dusty blanket stolen from the bed, and lifted them onto my back like a bizarre Santa Claus.

The trip back to the teleportation spot was awkward, but I made it by combining Super Strength, Superspeed, and a wee bit of Enhanced Coordination.

The Transportation trip back was simplified by the large blanket since I concentrated on moving that instead of two separate people.

When I got back to Mom's office, Rathbun directed me to drop my charges off in holding cells.

(I did as asked, but I also left them with the personal shields.)

**Mission outcome (results):**

- Hostage rescue was successful.

- One soldier broke his arm when he fell.

**Mission grade:** 89 of 100

Wait. I'm getting scored on my performance?

**Penalties:**

- Overuse of Induce Sleep. – Not a fair fight. No parlay.

- Overuse of Shielding.

- Overuse of Superspeed.

- Use of two undocumented powers.

- Removing a blanket from the site.

- Injury to soldier.

Who exactly is qualified to say whether my use of Shielding and Superspeed was justified? Was the point not to get shot?

**Private reflections:**

Joe and Leslie are alive.

They're ticked at being in this situation, though I can't exactly blame them for that without being a complete hypocrite.

I'm a little worried at the arbitrary score. I don't know what it means. I know that an 89 in most scoring systems translates to a B$^+$, but since Bridgeway's terrible at communication, I don't know what that means in the practical sense.

I think I'm due for some time searching the past. I need to know what went down between Mom, Dad, and Grandfather. That information could give me the insight I need to fulfill Mom's vague hope of beating Grandfather.

I'd also like to see what I'm up against here.

# Chapter 32

# Superpower Review 17: Time Manipulation

**Background and notes:**

What is Time Manipulation?

The thing I am currently doing because I have less than an hour to rescue my dad and brother when this extremely important review task landed on my mental to-do list.

Jabrie's glaring at me. He says, "Sarcasm is not a superpower."

I beg to differ. I might just make that my motto.

**Explanation of the power:**

Time Manipulation has tickled the fancy of human minds for millennia.

**What does Time Manipulation cover?**

Any start, stop, or pause in time.

**This includes:**

- Visiting the future – It's less exciting than you think. It's more like a vision.

- Visiting the past – It's less exciting than you think.

- Stopping time – Not recommended for long.

-

Speeding up time – Also, not recommended for long.

- Slowing time – Okay in moderation.

**This does not include:**
- Time travel – That's a different power.

- Changing the past – See <u>Time Travel</u>. (I'm aware the document doesn't exist yet, but if you have Manipulate Time set right, you could visit the future wherein it's written.)

- Change the future – See Time Travel. (Spoiler alert – the best you can do is mildly influence circumstances that might alter the future.)

**What's it good for?**
- Stretching out time or pausing it so you can delay danger.

- Stretching out time or pausing it so you can attend to stupid tasks.

- Speeding up time so you can skip over boring stuff.

- Speeding up time so you can see outcomes you've been awaiting impatiently.

- Slowing time so you can dodge bullets.

- Speeding up time so you can stab the person making you dodge bullets. (Hypothetically, of course.)

- Reset small sections of time to get a do-over.

**Me stating the obvious:** Resets aren't foolproof. If you get shot in the head, no more Time Manipulation. No more reset.

**How does it work?**

A thorough explanation would involve some 400-level physics jujitsu, so you're going to have to deal with my layman's terms, kiddie version.

Consider the concept of equilibrium. The gist is that nature exists with a delicate balance. It's also kind of a momma bear with threatened cubs if you knock that balance out of whack.

The clearest examples are reversible (means it goes both ways) chemical reactions. If you add more of the reactant stuff on the left, the reaction will go on a reactant stuff spending spree and consume it to make more products.

If you start hoarding products, there will eventually be too much, so the tables will turn, and products will start breaking down to form reactant stuffs.

I know. I know. Yucky chemistry. It's over. Back to my Time Manipulation point.

If you slow time down, it will fractionally speed up until the lost time is recovered.

If you speed up time, it will do exactly the opposite.

If you stop it completely for too long, the universe may decide you are a nuisance that needs dealing with and break something in your head. Once you stop exerting the Gift, time returns to some version of normal.

**Range:**

Most Time Manipulation events take place locally.

When you engage the Gift, you'll get something called a Sphere of Influence.

In theory, you can expand this to affect time across the entire globe simultaneously, but that would be a lot of effort for no good reason.

**Experiments:**

- Test 1: Move time forward to finish a 50-minute cooking time.

- Test 2: Slow time to plot a safe course through a hail of bullets.

- Test 3: Stop time to freeze a bullet in place.

- Test 4: Stop time to freeze many bullets in place. (Gracious, these people are uninventive.)

- Test 5: Time skip to listen to a 35-hour audiobook in four minutes of real time.

**What happened:**

I told the scientists that these experiments would be largely useless. I can tell you exactly how each test should or would turn out.

But Jabrie insisted.

**(Three points:**

- I think the man just looks for excuses to have me shot at.

- I'm aware I am the experiment.

- I definitely cheated on these tests.

Skipped to the end of tedious exercises. Oh look, I'm done.)

**Expectations and reality:**

Expectation 1 – Time Manipulation will right all the world's wrongs.

Reality 1 – Time Manipulation is about messing with time on a small scale in the moment.

**Note:** You need Time Travel to alter the past, and then, you need Perfect Luck to avoid the Security Panel agents who will pounce all over your hide if you mess with the time laws.

Remember my adventure with the ill-fated peppermint in the 1200s? Security Panel agents are a grouchy lot.

Expectation 2 – Time Manipulation is the perfect response to a hail of bullets.

Reality 2 – It is until it isn't. It's not always all about you.

There's no such thing as an exclusive power. That means, if you have a Gift, likely somebody else has it to. Ergo, if you can slow time to give yourself extra thinking time about graceful ways to dodge bullets, somebody else can do the opposite.

If equal and opposite stuffs collide, nothing happens.

In the hypothetical case of you playing with murderous, trigger-happy people—you slow, they speed up—the bullets will continue on their merry way at normal speeds.

**Complications and downsides:**

Complication 1 – Time Manipulation gets more difficult if you try to maintain multiple Spheres of Influence or need to work at a distance.

Downside – Statistically, the number of people who develop this Gift is on the high side, so the likelihood of running into somebody with it is also suitably high.

Complication 2 – Time Blips. It's what I'm calling universal whoopsie righters. If you slow things down too much, it's eventually going to right itself rather violently.

Picture it like yanking back on a very strong rubber band. Even if you're prepared, you're going to feel the sting.

Complication 3 – Interference. If two people use Time Manipulation simultaneously and their Spheres of Influence overlap, one of three things happen.

- Negation – It's like a light switch. You can turn it on, letting light flow, but if someone flips the switch the other way, poof, no more light.

- Amplification – The effects get greater.

- Mix – Some things get sped up, and others will slow down.

Complication 4 – Time outside your Sphere of Influence continues as normal. So, in the case of cooking times, you need a strong enough dose to affect the whole house, or you'll be tied to the kitchen for whatever time you are attending to the cooking.

**Combat potential:** moderately high

If nobody around your hypothetical assassination target can manipulate time, you should be able to get somebody close enough to strike with a close-range weapon.

**Danger level:** moderately high

Stuff like this goes straight to people's heads. If they get the illusion of being invincible, they're going to wind up dead.

**Usefulness:** 3 of 5 stars

That depends on what exactly you plan on doing. If you anticipate a high probability of needing to dodge something, then you may want this Gift on your side, but there are other powers that can accomplish the same thing without risking Time Blips.

The Gift may also have some applications for lazy cooks.

**Entertainment value:** 3 of 5 stars

Unless you dodge dangerous stuff for funsies, I can't see this one flying off the proverbial market shelves.

**Overall rating and conclusion:** 3 of 5 stars

In moderation, this one is safe enough to release, but you don't want too many people in close proximity using it or their efforts will negate or unexpectedly amplify.

# Chapter 33

# Journal Entry 15: Counterproposal

Between rescue missions for Joe and Leslie and Doug and Dad, I stop back at the Bridgeway headquarters to check on Mom and Ellie.

Predictably, they don't let me see Ellie, for fear I'll whisk her away. I'm not sure why that would be a bad thing.

They still control my mother, and besides, Jasmine doesn't need to sneak around pretending to be Ellie anymore.

I know they'll deny the request to see Ellie.

I also guess they want to seem reasonable and benevolent as all evil entities do, so they will let me gaze upon my mother's still form from afar.

Guess they also expect me to mount a daring rescue there too.

The visit lasts twenty real-world seconds, but it's enough.

I throw up the strongest mental shields I can muster, set some timers for the various Time Manipulations Spheres of Influence I currently maintain, freeze time down to a microcrawl, and dive into my mother's mind.

In some ways, navigating the thoughts of a sleeping person is harder than dealing with alert people.

People assume that infiltrating a slumbering person's thoughts will involve Dream Manipulation.

All I want to accomplish here is some simple memory swipes. I don't have time to process them completely, but I can scan and snatch the most likely candidates to give me answers and go from there.

One never truly knows what they'll encounter in another's mind.

For some, sleep means a lowering of mental guards, and for others, it means the mind is locked down tight.

Unfortunately, my mother falls into the locked-down variety.

Guess that comes from a lifetime of secrets, half-truths, and lies.

That's not entirely fair to her, but it's my tale. I'll whine if I want to.

This investigation is precisely because I need the answers to some huge questions like what went on before I was born, how I've gone a few decades without an inkling of having a twin, and why said twin was raised by psycho-grandpa and the evil corporation.

You know that old nature vs. nurture debate? Yeah, both matter, but nurture's got a heck of an edge from where I'm standing.

The scan-and-snatch mission goes well since my mother's long-term memories are catalogued in a very organized manner by multiple means.

Score one for scientific minds.

Given the choice to sort by date or topic, I choose date first.

After sorting the memories by year, I pull up the ones from three years before Joe's birth to three years after Doug's birth. Figure Jasmine and I will be in there somewhere.

Each distinct memory has a preview that plays a few seconds of the thoughts contained within when I focus on them.

Can't say I've given too much thought to the best ways to sort other people's thoughts. This blatant invasion of privacy for a good cause is new to me.

When I sort by Bridgeway, family, fears, guilt, happy, notable, and painful, each preview gets a colored border that matches the labels.

My brain instinctively applies titles to each memory.

Letting them sort themselves by date again, I scan a few titles:

- Father

- Meeting Winston

- First Date

- First Fight

- Wedding/Elopement

- Honeymoon in Barbados

- Joseph's Birth

- Running

- Captured

- Joseph's Gift

- Father's *Reasonable* Proposal

- Happy Years

- Jessica and Jasmine

- Price of Peace

- Douglas

- New Normal

Instinct tells me which entries to avoid.

I use Advanced Logic to organize the thoughts and summarize them so I can make a better decision about which to check.

I have enough time to experience maybe one or two memories in full.

Plucking the first from the lineup, I get my first glimpse of Ceiling Voice.

All in all, for someone who causes some serious anxiety spikes in my mother according to the color code, dear old granddad looked surprisingly normal. Graying dark brown hair. Nice but ordinary face. Cruel, calculating dark eyes.

(Okay, I might be biased.)

Father's *Reasonable* Proposal promised to leave Angela and Winston (my folks) alone as long as they stopped by once a year to have their child—and any future children—tested for new Gifts.

As my time ticks down the last few seconds, I stretch them and check Price of Peace.

When the flat 2D version fails to satisfy me, I glance at the timers, activate another mental Gift called Extrapolation and Interpretation, and jump into the memory properly.

(This is so I can view the scene from the fly-on-a-wall perspective instead of being confined to my mother's first-person viewpoint.)

The scene opens eerily in the same office, or one with an identical design.

Only, this time, my father occupies the grabby chair. His wrists and forehead bear red marks from his futile struggles.

Two large goons—North and Rathbun prototypes—hold my mother's arms.

She looks like her entire world is ending.

Evil Grandpa stands near the chair holding my father.

A third suited, silent muscle-type holds a limp five-year-old Joe a few feet from Mom.

A pair of baby carriers sits on the large wooden desk.

Baby Jasmine and Baby Me sleep soundly.

"Don't do this!" The plea holds enough frustration to tell me Mom knows it will do little to no good. "I'll stay. Let Winston take the children away. Please."

"Get your hands—"

Dad's protest ends abruptly as the chair does its knockout thing.

"Don't hurt him!" Tears underscore the frustration streaming off my mother. "Tell me what you want." The fear in her expression shouts doubts that she can fulfill any requests.

Evil Grandpa looks at my mother coolly.

"I have everything I want right here. Jabrie was saying Joseph's showing signs of Molecule Manipulation. That's a rare and exciting Gift to explore, and initial tests on the twins are even more promising."

"You can't keep them in a lab!" Mom argues. "We don't even know what Gifts they'll get, if any. They need a normal life. That's how Gifts grow. The lab studies have failed."

"Been set back." Evil Grandpa's expression changes from cool to thoughtful. "But you may have a point. I had planned on keeping all three children and letting you go on your merry way with dear Winston. Do you have a counterproposal?"

Mom's jaw trembles. Her gaze flits from Baby Me to Baby Jasmine to Joe.

For a second, it looks like she'll break down into uncontrollable sobs, but then, something hardens in her expression. Her hands clench so hard her arms vibrate.

When she speaks, only two words come out.

"Take Jasmine."

Guess that explains the strained relationship between Mom and Jazz.

*How did Mom even make that decision?*

# Chapter 34

---

# Journal Entry 16:
# Nullifier

When this is over, I'm going to need some serious processing time or therapy or time without people. Preferably all three.

Having just learned I was a hairsbreadth from being raised here at Bridgeway by Psycho-Grandpa and the mad scientists, my emotions spiral.

I had to dial them back to near zero to keep functioning with so many Gifts running.

I am using Time Manipulation at the Bridgeway headquarters and down by the docks around Dad and Doug.

Simultaneously, I raid my mother's mind for memories that would explain the hot mess of my family situation.

Wee bits of attention also go into tracking Mom's progress with the sleeping drugs, monitoring Jasmine's hovering presence next to me, searching the campus for my Ellie, and sending mental feelers toward dear Granddad.

If I can figure out his end game, I stand a better chance of keeping the family safe.

Like it or not, Jasmine now ranks among my concerns. Now knowing her backstory, I can't even hate her for being a few eggs shy of a dozen up top.

*That could have been me.*

Jasmine's voice blasts through my mind.

**If you pity me, I will punch you. Go save your family.**

*They're your family too.*

**I have no family.**

This isn't a great time to have a heart-to-heart discussion, but Jasmine's statement makes me sad.

Since she's using my Gift to establish the telepathic communication, I also gain some other fun—and disturbing—facts.

Fact 1: She's eight minutes younger than me.

Fact 2: Her natural facial features are close to mine, confirming us to be identical twins.

Fact 3: She prefers keeping her hair longer when given a choice.

Fact 4: She's done an obscene amount of martial arts training.

Fact 5: She prefers knives as a hand-to-hand combat weapon.

Fact 6: She's known about me for almost fifteen years.

Fact 7: She's never learned how to drive. (Bridgeway has enough people with the Teleportation Gift that finding someone to Mimic usually isn't an issue.)

Fact 8: She has a black cat named Albion.

Fact 9: She doesn't like the nickname Jazz.

**Are you done being nosy?**

*Jazz, you busted into my head, and you haven't exactly hidden these surface factoids.*

She bristles at the nickname.

I bask in the moment and kick her out of my head.

We've been separated for over twenty years. I have a lot of annoying to catch up on.

Letting time resume normal speed, I hold my right hand out to my sister in a visible gesture of peace.

We need to teleport shortly.

At this distance, she can tap into my power, but going with me will save her the effort. I don't know how much energy use of her Mimic Gifts takes, but we are headed in the same direction anyway.

She stares at my hand like it's a rat and leaves me hanging.

**I don't need your help!**

Even though we could have held the conversation like normal human beings, she chooses to go all shouty telepath on me.

We have a staring contest while the chat continues within my head.

*I could say the same, but I was ordered to take you along as a babysitter. If you'd quit being childish, we can proceed to the next phase of saving our family.*

I'm a little disturbed by how easily that lecture pops into mind. No wonder Joe launches into them so frequently.

**Fine. But don't touch me.**

*Sheesh. Someone didn't get enough hugs as a kid.*

The absolute truth of the statement hits me with gut-wrenching force, bringing tears to my eyes.

Pain flashes in Jasmine's eyes before emotional walls slam into place.

Instinctively, I slip behind her and wrap her in a tight embrace.

She elbows me in the ribs, but the blow doesn't have much force because my arms are in the way.

Besides, I do deserve that.

*Sorry.*

The thought is barely a whisper.

*I'm new at this, and so are you. Let's just get through today so we can have it out and catch up on twenty stolen years.*

**Let go.**

Her thought splits the line between dead/lifeless and deadly/edgy.

*Promise to be civil about this?*

She tries to break free, but I increase my strength to tighten my grip.

I could have teleported us then, but I want Jasmine's cooperation. It will lessen the chances of having her blatantly working against me.

**Fine. For now.**

Knowing I won't get a much better response, I release my baby sister, wait for her to face me, and hold my hand out to her once more.

The disgusted expression remains, but she tentatively takes my hand.

I teleport us to the docks.

And nearly slam into some guy.

A microjump moves us back ten feet where we nearly crash into another guy.

The near misses confuse me. Generally, the teleporting Gift comes with stellar avoid-plowing-people-over side powers.

Both men, plus the other eight arranged around us in a loose circle, wear black body armor from head to foot. They also wear gray helmets that look like they would be better on the set of a terrible science fiction movie. Their weapons of choice alternate between traditional police truncheons and stun guns.

One holds an awkward black box that reminds me of an ancient camera.

Still confused, I revisit the last few seconds. This isn't where we'd been set to land.

*Jazz must have moved us.*

"Sorry," says Jasmine.

I really want to hear true regret in the word, but instead, I detect mocking overtones.

Shaking my hand free, Jazz steps back twice, effectively joining the circle of well-armed thugs.

A second later, the transformation completes as Jasmine mimics the aspiring attackers' fashion choices.

Expecting a betrayal doesn't keep it from stinging.

"It's just a test, Jess. Nothing personal."

The man holding the odd black box points it at me.

The sides retract, revealing a silver cube.

*Nullifier.*

Accessing Superspeed and Time Manipulation, I boost both to dangerous levels then set them in stasis.

Time Manipulation requires a brand-new Sphere of Influence. This is some of the most complicated and delicate work I've ever done.

At the same time, I reverse the retraction process on the box, making the lead-lined walls come back up and around the nullifier.

For good measure, I drill an atom-sized hole through the opposite side and use Molecule Manipulation to swap out enough protons to change the alloy making up the nullifier into a harmless lump of coal.

Before I can relax, a wave of weariness and an intense headache hit me at once.

I stagger.

The timers I'd set in my head flash and crash from thirty-four minutes down to zero.

I drop to one knee and brace my arms on the ground to avoid keeling over.

"I told you we'd need two of them." Jasmine sounds highly self-satisfied.

"It worked perfectly, ma'am. Should I release her now to finish the first task."

*Say yes. Say yes.*

With the active nullifier in place the thought is only shared with me, myself, and I.

A long pause ensues before Jasmine finally answers.

"No. We need to know how long the effects will last."

*Not long. I hope.*

# Chapter 35

# Superpower Review 18: Mimicry

**Background and notes:**

The Mimicry Gift can refer to one of two distinct skillsets: matching features and duplicating Gifts.

Most Mimics can do both, though usually one type is dominant.

Jasmine can do both. Her ability to Shapeshift is limited to people (no animals and no objects). Mimicking Gifts has been her strong suit. I think that's how we wound up in this mess.

I'm doing this review now and storing it for later because I don't need to do experiments. I accidentally left the scan and snatch protocols on while Jazz was an uninvited guest in my head.

She left behind a working knowledge of how she does what she does.

Jabrie will insist there be demonstrations, so I'll give him relevant clips harvested from Jazz's memories.

(Yes, it's intrusive. I am so far beyond quaint moral lines at this point. I'll move to a different time and repeat anything as needed, so the nuances of the power can fairly be evaluated. Still, I see no reason to not use thousands of hours of questionable experimentation that's already been done.)

**Explanation of the power:**

Mimics duplicate the features and Gifts of their current target.

If the target doesn't have discernable powers, the Mimic can get into more detail, right down to matching brainwaves.

Depending on their skill level and the demands of the job, the Mimic may require frequent inspiration updates.

Inspiration updates involve studying the subject.

That's how I know Ellie's got to be alive somewhere Jasmine could access easily.

Mimicry is often confused with Gift Transference, Gift Absorption, and Gift Suppression. While those are very similar, Mimicry is a bit more hands-on.

## Quick list of definitions:

- Mimicry – Involves becoming the target, including quirks, Gifts, and talents.

- Gift Transference – Moves a gift from one person to another person. It can be done between the target and the person with Gift Transference, but it's more common between two external targets.

- Gift Absorption – Takes a person's Gift and gives it to the caster. It's like Power Mimicry without the frills of looking like the target.

- Gift Suppression – Denys the target use of their Gift for a time. This does not include the caster enacting the suppressed Gift in any way.

## Demonstration highlights (experiments in previous entries):

Jasmine has performed dozens of experiments over the years. It's hard to tell if she legitimately has several Gifts or if she's simply an exceptional Mimic.

- Demo 1 (Telekinesis): Jazz's first attempt at mimicry happened when she was a toddler. She wanted a ball located outside her playpen. The person watching her must have had some telekinetic abilities. Jasmine's tiny face took on the features of this woman and harnessed her Gift to summon the red ball.

**Commentary:** The incident likely would have gone unnoticed except that the woman's natural skin tone was many times darker than my sister. Jazz also didn't have enough control over the Gift to turn it on and off at will, so the skin tone change lasted a few hours.

- Demo 2 (Underwater Breath): Jasmine and a brave Bridgeway soul sat chained underwater in the deep end of an Olympic size pool.

**Commentary:** The dude had the Underwater Breath Gift, but it still took some serious trust to let a five-year-old Mimic practice on him.

- Demo 3 (Superspeed): Seven-year-old Jasmine and Mom toured the campus several times before venturing to other things like a large, empty patch of Pennsylvania to practice.

**Commentary:** Am I that oblivious? Everybody's folks keep secrets and general mundane boring information from them, but one would think, *hey, I'm off to spend a week teaching your kid twin sister how to use my Gift* would warrant at least a passing comment.

- Demo 4 (Teleportation): Pre-teen Jasmine and another Bridgeway grunt popped in and out of safe rooms.

**Commentary:** Safe rooms are padded so people training in teleportation risk only bruises instead of death during the training process. I suppose if someone's exceptionally incompetent they might manage to teleport out of the safe rooms, but most first jumps are closely monitored by a Guide.

- Demo 5 (Project Ellie Doppelgänger): Jasmine replaced Ellie.

**Commentary:** While I'm disturbed by that whole affair and still want my Ellie back, I have to admire Jazz's skill. She legitimately had me fooled on several occasions.

**What happened:**

The Superspeed demo was initially going to be Flight, but Mom convinced Jasmine to try Superspeed before the one that would kill her if she flubbed the training.

Evil Grandpa signed off on it.

If you have the time, you can continue the list of demos, but I'm only going to include five in the official report.

Suffice to say, Jasmine's early attempts at most mimic events were rough, but she improved rapidly.

**Expectations and reality:**

Expectation 1: Mimics can do anything Nobodies (Shapeshifters) can.

Reality 1: Mimics do people impressions way better than Nobodies. A Shapeshifter can match any surface thing, but a Mimic can recreate the way someone breathes.

Expectation 2: Mimics can duplicate any Gift.

Reality 2: They're better at visible powers.

Expectation 3: Mimics can enact changes instantly.

Reality 3: All they'll show you is the instant part. There's quite a bit of close study first for most mimics.

**Complications, downsides, limitations:**

Limitation 1: Mimics can use both halves of their Gifts simultaneously, but they can only have one target. Since most people get one Gift, most Mimics are used to dealing with one Gift.

Jasmine has used her abilities on me several times, but the Gifts she's pulled have been ones she's had extensive practice with. (Perk of being raised in a scientific compound by psychopaths.)

Limitation 2: A perfect copy is still a copy.

Mimics are particularly good at getting physical details right, but some things have to be born of instinct and practice.

Think of it like playing a sport. Learning the rules to any sport can be relatively easy, but knowing what moves to make in specific situations takes time, patience, and practice.

Limitation 3: Inspiration updates required. One doesn't get consistent realistic detail without being near the target.

**Combat potential:** medium to low

A Mimic could essentially become the strongest fighter, but they would revert to their natural state if the target gets killed.

**Assassination potential:** terrifyingly high

(Included because Jabrie and Co. keep asking about this.)

You don't even need other superpowers. Kidnap someone close to the one you want to off, study them, replace them, and you have instant intimate access to that person.

**Danger level:** moderately high

There's always the chance something goes wrong.

Mimics have a higher accident rate than most supers because they regularly play with unfamiliar Gifts.

**Usefulness:** 4 of 5 Stars

I don't even have to check to know this one isn't slated for wide release. It's useful, but the liability factors are insanely high.

**Entertainment value:** 3 of 5 Stars

You may think trying out new powers is fun, but it's also a lot of work. You can skip the work part, but that's asking for trouble.

**Overall rating and conclusion:** 3.5 of 5 Stars

Use with caution.

I'll have an annotated version of the report that references several demos that illustrate the point that trying on unfamiliar powers can be unpleasant.

# Chapter 36

# Superpower Review 19: Nullification (Suppress Gift)

**Background and notes:**

As with Mimicry, the Bridgeway people are not even pretending Nullification will be marketed to the public.

That said, I was asked to move it up from the bottom of the list where somebody sensible had originally put it.

(Probably going to hold some serious things back on this one. Sorry, Mom, but getting us out of this jam is going to require some surprises. I can't do surprises if I do completely honest tell-alls about each power.)

Jasmine could give you a far better review of this Gift than I can. She has Mimicry and Nullification, which likely means she has others too, but those are the only two she's centered her research around.

(Multiple Gifts are still a rarity in the general population of Supers. I suspect Bridgeway's responsible for that. So, I'm not just normal special. I'm lab-soup-special. That's disappointing.)

I didn't know I had the Gift of Nullification because I've previously had no reason to try it out. Contrary to popular belief, not every Super wants to make a name for themselves.

(Just because we largely keep out of the affairs of Normies does not mean isolated towns and cities with Supers don't have showoffs.)

**Explanation of the power:**

Nullification involves turning the target's Gift off.

That's where psychos got the inspiration for inventing nullifiers. I'll get to that shortly, as it was *suggested* I cover that item.

Let's get the obvious part out of the way. Nullification can be exceedingly dangerous if it falls into the wrong hands.

**Demonstration highlights (experiments in previous entries):**

Once again, I'm not going to conduct my own experiments. Jasmine's already done many hours of research into the topic.

(The research was probably done with the idea of controlling me, but I'm going to ignore that fact for now. Baby sister and I are long overdue for a sit-down conversation.)

Where possible, I will pull demos that deal with the same ones I drew before to study Jasmine's approach.

- Demo 1 (Telekinesis): A Minder Gifted with telekinetic abilities tossed tennis balls at Jasmine. She dodged, then attempted to mess with the Minder's abilities.

- Demo 2 (Underwater Breath): Jasmine hung out by the pool while Bridgeway employees spent some down time. Those with Underwater Breath like to hang out and hold conversations with hand signals from the bottom of the pool. She interrupted one such mini-club meeting by shutting off their Gifts.

**Commentary:** Jasmine's experiment here was unauthorized.
- Demo 3 (Superspeed): Jasmine practiced suppressing the Gift of

a Bridgeway volunteer speedster.

**Commentary:** I'm selfishly relieved to know these experiments weren't done on our mother.

- Demo 4 (Teleportation): Jasmine tried to prevent a Bridgeway teleporter from moving around one of the large training rooms.

**(Note to self:** She might have improved, but her success rate here was abysmal. Keep in mind for possible future conflicts of the knock-down variety.)

- Demo 5 (Invisibility): Jasmine walked through a room with three invisible Bridgeway people hiding.

**Commentary:** That was the single most bizarre session of hide-and-seek I've ever witnessed.

**What happened:**

- Demo 1 (Telekinesis): Jasmine needed to get within twenty-five feet of the Minder before she could adequately suppress the telekinetic abilities.

- Demo 2 (Underwater Breath): The Underwater Breath crew nearly drowned. They were in about eight feet of water at the time, so it wasn't hard for them to get out. But three of the four panicked. (Pretty sure Evil Grandpa paid some timely bonuses to soothe ruffled feathers here.)

- Demo 3 (Superspeed): Jasmine succeeded whenever she caught the volunteer before he engaged his Gift. They tried multiple instances of her trying to suppress the Gift while he ran past her. Of the ninety-two trials, I believe she succeeded eight times.

- Demo 4 (Teleportation): Once again, if she caught them before they engaged the Gift, Jasmine could effectively stop a teleportation event from happening. However, most of the time, she had to be very close to the target, like all up in their personal space kind of close.

- Demo 5 (Invisibility): Jasmine found the targets easily when they didn't move. She chose a regular grid pattern to walk the first time, so when she came within twenty feet of them, they appeared. The four trials they moved were harder, so it took her much longer to find them.

**Do I think I could have done better?**

Likely, but I have other Gifts to play with. If I limited myself to Nullification only, no, I would not have fared better.

**Expectations and reality:**

Expectation 1: It's an on-off Gift.

Reality 1: That depends on the nature of the Gift being suppressed. In the case of Invisibility, yes, this is an on-off Gift. Now you don't see me, now you do.

For most powers (Lightning Manipulation, Superspeed, and such), it becomes a supernatural game of whack-a-mole to keep the Gift down.

Expectation 2: Whatever is in visual range is fair game.

Reality 2: The range depends on the Gift being controlled. There's probably a motivation factor too. If someone is lobbing tennis balls at you in an exercise, you strive to win. If someone's trying to cook you with a freshly conjured lightning bolt, you strive to survive.

Expectation 3: Applying the Gift is easy in every situation.

Reality 3: Things involving high levels of movement are difficult to target.

**Complications, downsides, limitations:**

Complication 1: Movement messes with accuracy.

Complication 2: Unless you're like Jasmine and Evil Grandpa, you're not going to find many playmates to help you test your abilities. (Let us experiment on you. Plus, please sign this waiver in case of your death, usually doesn't go over well.)

Complication 3: It's got a heck of a learning curve.

Downside 1: Once someone realizes you're trying to shut their Gift down, they tend to attack.

Downside 2: Once you actively stop suppressing the Gift, the person should regain that ability.

Limitation 1: Range is going to be a limiting factor in most situations.

Limitation 2: Targeting varies with the caster's skill level, but you essentially need to develop a knack for prediction of where your target will be rather than rely on normal targeting cues.

**Combat potential:** fair to moderate

In the hands of a well-trained person, the combat potential could be bumped higher, but range and targeting limitations dictate how useful it can be right now.

I guess it depends on the situation. In a straightforward fight, it would be handy to have.

(If you can overcome the issues with range and targeting, this changes significantly.)

**Danger level:** to user – low, to target – high

The caster controlling the Nullification Gift should be fine.

The target should be fine in most cases, unless the nullifier is actively trying to sabotage someone in the middle of Flight or Underwater Breath or something similar.

**Usefulness:** 3 of 5 Stars

It might be good for society to have law enforcement trained to use this.

The population of Supers is reaching the point where revelation and integration with the Normie society is just around the corner. That's why Bridgeway's so jazzed about the marketing potential of each superpower.

**Entertainment value:** normal people – 2 of 5 Stars, crazy people – 5 of 5 Stars

People bent on mischief would have a blast with this one.

**Overall rating and conclusion:** 2.5 of 5 Stars

I know what I was told about this one not being earmarked for release, but given the ever-shifting nature of my to-do list, forgive me if I don't fully trust the statement.

Not recommended for wide release.

Limited release to responsible, highly trained individuals, sure, but you do not want this in the hands of the hold-my-beer crowd.

# Chapter 37

# Journal Entry 17: Snapback

Remember what I said about bringing time to a dead stop? (The universe eventually decides you are a nuisance that needs to be dealt with.) I don't usually tempt the universe to smack me around, but I don't have much of a choice in this case.

Jasmine and the Bridgeway goon squad just hit me with a second nullifier, putting me in superpower timeout. I'll give you my thoughts on those evil things later.

Not having superpowers doesn't make one completely helpless, but the circle of Bridgeway lackeys, which now includes my sister, prevents me from running far enough to escape the nullifier's effects.

I'd put Superspeed and Time Manipulation into stasis shortly before losing access to my Gifts. In theory, that will let them return to me when the universe rights the part I'd slammed to a halt.

That is the backup plan.

Turns out, I don't need the backup plan because Snapback's got a killer full-body slam.

Slowing stuff down for a while requires speeding things up for a while.

Stopping stuff completely apparently means violently restarting when the universe has had enough of Time Manipulation's shenanigans.

Hence, Snapback.

I didn't talk about it before because it's previously been an obscure, hotly-debated theory I wasn't eager to test out.

If you'll recall, I cheated on the Time Manipulation tests.

In hindsight, that's a major blessing because it keeps the Bridgeway people from anticipating the move that ultimately saves me.

Picture slowing time like gradually compressing a spring that's the size of your entire body.

Halting time is like mashing that large spring to the ground.

Snapback is revenge of the spring.

The resulting blast turns me into an honorary human missile.

Have I mentioned I don't like physics much?

Don't care if it saved my life.

Still not a fan.

My body busts through the Bridgeway picket line like I've been shot from a cannon.

My back and shoulders strike two different guys simultaneously.

They're lucky.

A direct hit might have killed somebody instead of breaking a few arms and dislocating a shoulder.

After being used as a battering ram, my body continues sailing along a few feet off the ground.

I regain Flight a hairsbreadth from scraping the asphalt with my skull.

Without bothering to bring myself to a natural stop, I tap Teleportation to microjump over to the guy holding the second nullifier.

After plucking it from his hands, I spin a few times and use Super Strength to hurl that thing like a discus a few miles out into the ocean.

Littering in the ocean isn't recommended, but I don't want to take a chance they'll be able to fix the nullifier if I smash it to the ground like a toddler so done with a toy.

Next, I cure myself of a ringing skull and drive off severe back pain. Given the metallic taste of blood in my mouth, I probably also fix some internal bleeding brought on by my bowling ball impression.

Once free and feeling good, I reset my time holds around Dad and Doug.

I am careful to keep them at some level of slow instead of stop. I don't think Snapback will affect my father or brother, but since neither of them can self-heal, I figure it's best to avoid the possibility.

I cast out mental feelers to analyze the separate situations with Dad and Doug, but I don't move immediately because I still have eight Bridgeway problems and a wayward sister to deal with.

The two guys I'd hammered through are conscious, but they aren't in any condition to get up, let alone threaten me.

A streak of lightning barrels past me.

I slam the internal off button on that power and spin to face Jasmine.

The remaining security force spreads out to either side of my sister.

Sensing Jasmine's Mimic touch upon my mind, I duplicate then triple the most harmless powers I can think of and bury the more useful ones. I even make some up as a decoy. The smoke and mirrors routine won't fool her for long, but I don't need long.

I need half a second to stick her in my personal version of timeout.

Technically, I provide her with an impenetrable protective shield. I just go a step further and superglue the edges of said shield to the ground by borrowing Joe's Gift of Molecule Manipulation.

As an afterthought, I leave a few holes in the shield for her to breathe.

If looks could kill, we wouldn't be having this conversation.

Seeing how well Jasmine's mini-prison turns out, I do the same for the Bridgeway guys.

They aren't as lucky as my sister.

I don't have time to create personalized prisons, so I opt for the mass model.

First, I create a new shield from the ground up until it is a large, man-sized, invisible playpen.

Second, I run around collecting the Bridgeway guys like Easter eggs and tossing them into the holding pen. They try to run, but Superspeed and a few miscellaneous other Gifts make chasing them down child's play.

Hurling them into the forming shield prison requires more blasted physics calculations, but Enhanced Intelligence takes care of that.

To prevent escapes, I stretch the walls up and curve them in.

Okay, so it isn't so much a playpen as a fishbowl.

Screams and curses emanate from the fishbowl.

I stop curving the walls in with a few feet to spare so they'll have some air to breathe.

A little reshaping brings all sides inward, forcing the boys to get cozier. Once certain the size will cause discomfort and not death, I stop and fuse the molecules along the shield's bottom with the ground.

As a final touch, I add some bars to the top in case they get creative and teamwork a human tower when I'm not looking.

I can't exactly turn off Molecule Manipulation while using it, so Jasmine gets smart and taps into it to free herself as I finish perfecting my Bridgeway grunt holding tank.

I shut down the Molecule Manipulation Gift before Jasmine can access it in time to free the guys.

Do the same for Shielding too.

Of course, that means I can't touch them either, but at least the nine-to-one odds are down to one-to-one odds.

# Chapter 38

# Journal Entry 18: Throwdown

Unfortunately for me, the one-to-one opponent I face is my baby sister: the Mimic. I finally understand why people get all hot and bothered when a sibling touches their stuff. It's even more personal and annoying when that *stuff* is superpowers the sibling is trying to turn against you.

As per the unwritten rules of engagement, I try reasoning with her first.

"Can I have a raincheck on the throwdown? I need to launch a few rescues first."

Jasmine is not in a talking mood.

She borrows one of the powers I'd labeled Blast and uses it against me.

I get smacked with about thirty water balloons at once.

Aside from being soaked, I am more amused than hurt. The effort not to laugh hurts, so I indulge a little.

The Faruchi getup I'd donned ages ago earns its keep by being almost completely waterproof.

Jasmine tries Bombard next.

About the same number of small rubber duckies pelts me.

Those hurt more, but they also make me laugh harder.

I probably sound like a raving lunatic villain.

Who am I kidding? I definitely sound like a raving lunatic villain.

But it's so worth it.

Apparently, I can create new superpowers. (Albeit, mostly useless ones, but whatever, I'll take the win.)

Jasmine makes a noise like a ticked off bird of prey crossed with a blood-curdling battle cry and sprints at me. She uses Superspeed, and the distance between us disappears immediately.

I phase in time to avoid an unpleasant, back-jarring collision.

Once Jasmine has zipped through me, I spin to watch her progress.

She nearly steps into the Atlantic Ocean before she stops the charge.

When she faces me again, her eyes blaze with fury and a new power.

The connection she establishes to piggy-back off my Gifts tells me she's accessing Laser Beams. So, naturally, I shut that one down.

My figurative power control bank is looking sad and abandoned. It is also messy because of my mislabeling efforts.

Next, Jasmine teleports behind me, latches on like a clingy child, and moves us into the Bridgeway protective bubble.

I catch onto the plan midway through the teleportation. Since I haven't taken the time to remove their weapons, at least two of the Bridgeway guys still hold the stun guns, and another three have their police truncheons.

The truncheon wielders probably won't have enough swinging speed, but a stun gun blast will hurt like heck, scramble my brains, and ruin my day.

I consider blasting a hole into the ground for a new holding pen, but ultimately, I choose a slightly less destructive method.

Levitating the entire fishbowl prison, I move us about three hundred feet into the air. The jarring upward momentum keeps me safe from the stun guns.

Screams, curses, and a few prayers fill the space.

Next, I open a me-sized hole in the bottom and hop through.

Predictably, Jasmine follows.

I don't bother plugging the hole.

With their gear on, it isn't big enough for the Bridgeway gents to use our exit. I imagine the height also discourages them.

Upon reaching the ground, I move my flying prison over the ocean and lower it to about twenty-five feet above the water. This is a safety precaution because the shield will collapse if I stop willing it into place.

I still want the Bridgeway people to stay out of my business, but I'm not eager to see the aftermath of gravity vs. the human body.

With all the humanitarian concerns filling my mind, I lose track of Jasmine.

Terrifying two seconds, I can assure you.

Don't have to look for her long though since she appears behind me again and puts me in a chokehold.

Girl has a great grip.

I have ten to twenty seconds until unconsciousness and death ensue.

Panic makes me stiffen and fight for two of those seconds before self-preservation kicks in.

Our close contact of the violent kind gives me full access to Jasmine.

Using Absorb Experience, I pull every martial arts lesson she's ever been given.

Enhanced Intelligence lets me sort the lessons until I isolate all the breaking free tidbits.

Eight seconds into my allotted safety zone of nine, I discard all the lessons since Jazz will be ready for them.

Instead, I use High Jump and a good old-fashioned front flip to first deprive Jasmine of the advantage and then bust free. Traditional chokeholds rely on leverage and keeping the opponent off balance. When there's no ground, the leverage advantage disappears.

The timers for Dad and Doug flash somewhere in my mind, telling me I can't afford to keep entertaining Jazz's murderous intentions.

Fortunately, anger makes people impulsive and predictable.

I use my temporary freedom to fly to the ground.

Jasmine teleports in front of me this time.

Energy crackles between us as she accesses the thing I'd labeled Electrical Manipulation.

Jasmine reaches to grab my shoulders.

I catch her hands.

The Gift activates.

It is indeed a form of the power, just not the one she wants.

Every streetlight up and down the block surges, some even explode.

Meanwhile, I access the form of Electrical Manipulation Jasmine had been after.

I'd retitled it Nighty-Night Bedtime Tales.

50,000 volts of electricity flow from my fingertips into her palms.

She jerks her hands away.

Lunging forward, I catch her shoulders and zap her again.

While her body shudders under the tangible assault, I very carefully manipulate the level of oxygen reaching her brain.

It makes her sleepy, so she slumps in my arms.

I maintain the hold on the secret power until Jasmine is safely unconscious.

As I gently lower her body to the ground, several tears fall onto her face.

*I'm sorry, Jazz.*

Anger flare inside me.

I don't like having to hurt my sister. I also hate the invisible forces that have brought us to this. Reconciliation will be harder now.

Thanks, Evil Grandpa.

Though tempted to zero the emotional scales, I channel it toward determination.

Weariness and despair chip away at my morale.

That, I kick aside.

I don't have the time for a pity party.

Jasmine won't stay out of it for long, and both Dad and Doug need me immediately.

# Chapter 39

# Mission Report 2: Rescue Dad and Doug

**Objective:**

Rescue Dad and Doug.

**Location/Setting:**

Private dock and beach near New York City.

(I wondered how Bridgeway would keep my fight with Jasmine and my Bridgeway buddies hush hush, but then, I got curious and followed the money. The company owns all the beachfront property around here. The few people out and about are employees or the family of employees.

Middle of life-threatening situations usually isn't a great time for such investigations but being distracted during said life-threatening situations is far worse.)

**Quick recap of my craptastic day (a.k.a. background and notes):**

- Woke up to a blank whiteboard in my head, which was the first sign something had happened to Ellie.

- Found my family in three separate crises and went to investigate the nearest one.

- Found Mom talking with a woman who looked like Ellie.

- Met my long-lost twin, Jasmine, the homicidal Mimic.

- Stood by while Evil Grandpa had Mom poisoned.

- Found my brother Joe and his fiancée, Leslie, in a creepy cabin in upstate New York. Hauled their unconscious carcasses back to Bridgeway as ordered.

- Almost got my powers zapped by a nullifier.

- Had a mini-brawl with Jasmine.

- (Started searching for Ellie but haven't locked in a location yet.)

**Situation/Problem:**

Situation 1: Doug

My younger brother is in a shark cage being held at a depth of twenty feet. The boat suspending the cage is currently fifteen miles off the East Coast in international waters.

They knocked him out and gave him a twenty-minute air supply. That should be running out soon.

Bridgeway has two other divers down in cages armed with spearguns. They've also opened a cut along my brother's forearm, so there will likely be some finned company as well.

Situation 2: Dad

My father is in a piece of junk car about to be flattened by a car crusher.

Bridgeway has about fifteen guys on site around the junkyard to complicate my life and keep innocent idiots from blundering into the testing ground.

The problem:

Dad's Gift is Underwater Breathing. Doug's Gift is Super Strength.

Doug could have busted free of the restraints and escaped the car no problem. Dad would be fine in the shark cage for hours. He'd probably love the experience.

**Possible powers required (and why I think I'll need them):**

- Gift Transference – This is the only way to keep them alive until I can deal with the rest of their precarious situations.

- Time Manipulation – This has been in play thus far. It's the only way I had the time to get to Joe and Leslie, check in on Mom, and tangle with Jasmine.

- Teleportation – Even with my efforts to slow time, I've got two situations over fifteen miles apart.

- Super Strength – If either of them panic, I'll end up fighting them. Normal drowning people in full-panic mode are frightfully hard to rescue, let alone one used to having Super Strength.

- Shielding – This is always a good one to keep handy when anticipating a fight or a contested rescue.

**Live mission report:**

I completed the Gift Transference first, so Doug could breathe while he waited, and Dad could not be crushed while I ran through rescue scenarios.

**Rescue phase 1: Dad**

Dad would be mad I didn't go for Doug first, but honestly, my father was in greater danger.

- He had more Bridgeway goons watching over him.

- The car crusher had started doing its thing.

- He was still unconscious.

The unconscious thing cinched the deal. Doug's body should be able to figure out how to use Underwater Breath by sheer necessity, but Super Strength doesn't work like that. You need to be conscious to turn it on or off.

Since it wasn't that far, I used Flight to get to the junkyard, and Super Strength to yank the car containing Dad clear of the crusher.

By this time, the Bridgeway people started taking potshots at us, so I erected a shield around us.

After ripping off the door, I reached in to pull Dad clear. As I started to feel the rescue would go off without a hitch, I realized Dad's legs were trapped.

The seat had been jammed forward and locked in place.

I moved to push the seat back, but before I could exert any pressure, my hand felt hot as Danger Sense fired a warning through my hand.

Using X-ray Vision let me see the homemade bomb somebody had wedged behind the driver's seat.

Lacking time for finesse, I Transported that sucker to an empty patch of Antarctica, placed it in a shield, and let it explode. The only witnesses were some curious penguins.

Without the bomb, I got to move the seat mechanism enough to free my father.

I moved him back to the main Bridgeway building and set him in a cell next to Joe and Leslie.

Joe lay on a cot with Leslie sitting in a chair next to him, holding his hand.

The scene hit me with a sizable shot of guilt, but I brushed it off to teleport to Doug.

**Rescue phase 2: Doug**

I tried to teleport into the shark cage holding Doug, but instead, I bounced off the cage and into one of the excited sharks.

Mistaking me for a tasty fish morsel, another large shark tried to eat me. I phased my body enough to let the shark teeth pass through me.

When I had a second to look, I saw there was a shield surrounding Doug.

The confused shark took another pass at me.

Sensing the person holding the shield in place around my brother, I decided to deal with two of my problems at once.

Transported the shark that wanted to eat me onto the deck of the Bridgeway boat to play with the shielder.

The shield went away, leaving me free to teleport inside the cage with Doug and transport both of us to the deck.

The shark hadn't managed to eat anybody in the few seconds I'd left him unsupervised on the deck, but he did cause a glorious amount of panic and knock the shielder flat.

Two deckhands raced for spearguns, but they hesitated to use them.

Sensing my shark buddy had worn out his welcome, I put him back into the ocean along with the spearguns and every other weapon I could find.

A shield started forming around me, so I microjumped out of the pocket.

I considered using Induce Sleep on the man but didn't want to get arbitrarily penalized for not having it on my list of things to use during the mission.

So, my next microjump brought me next to the guy. I then used my newfound martial arts powers—the ones I'd absorbed from Jazz—to seize the guy's outstretched arm and flip him forward onto his back.

Finally satisfied, I jumped back to the spot where I'd dropped a sopping-wet Doug and moved us to the Bridgeway headquarters.

**Mission outcome:**

Successful, but not entirely smooth.

**Mission grade:** 74

Can't wait to see what stupid penalties they come up with this time.

- Overuse of Teleportation

- Misuse of Transportation – (I assume they mean moving the shark.)

- Needlessly endangering Bridgeway personnel – (Excuse me? You kidnapped my family.)

- Environmental endangerment – (No penguins were harmed in the removal of the bomb to a place without people. I might have chipped some ice though. I'll be sure to consider all the environmental ramifications next time I get three-quarters of a second to move a bomb. How about your office? No intelligent life there.)

**Private reflections:**

Haven't checked in with Dad and Doug yet, so I don't know how they're faring.

I'm being summoned to one of the practice arenas. I wouldn't go except it doesn't take much to sense that's where they took my mother.

# Chapter 40

# Superpower Review 20: Gift Transference

**Background and notes:**

Had to use this Gift recently to rescue Dad and Doug. Probably should knock this one out while it's fresh in my mind.

There is something therapeutic about composing these reviews that I don't have to run through separate experiments for.

(I'm stepping out of time to do it. That's different than Time Manipulation.

Ever see somebody space out? That's like a microversion of this.

Time Manipulation creates a slower—or faster—pocket within the current time.

Stepping out of time involves retreating to the 4$^{th}$ dimension. That's the one that allows for Transportation and a few other Gifts to work. Assuming I don't mess up, I should re-enter my timeline milliseconds after having left.)

Not sure I made it clear in my report, but after Dad and Doug were safely tucked in their holding cells at Bridgeway, I stopped using Gift Transference on them. Therefore, their Gifts reverted to the original owner.

**Explanation of the power:**

Gift Transference moves superpowers from one person to another.

Technically, it doesn't have to be a straight switch of powers. It can be one-way or multiple ways.

As mentioned while discussing Mimicry, this one tends to be confused for Gift Absorption and Mimicry.

Gift Absorption involves taking in knowledge of something. It doesn't necessarily have to be used on a superpower. That's how I benefitted from Jasmine's years of martial arts training.

Clarification on Gift Absorption. It can involve completely moving the power to the caster, but it usually involves a copy.

Transference involves a complete move of the Gift from one person to another person. That's a very distinct difference.

**Why use Gift Transference instead of Gift Absorption?**

- You can deprive someone of their power by moving it to another person.

- The effects are temporary. There's no need to actively move the Gift back. That will happen automatically once you stop actively engaging Transference.

- It's more thorough. Absorption is a quick copy that goes to the caster. Transference moves the Gift itself from one target to another.

The caster can be a target, but that's not typical. Also, it'd probably just be called Absorption at that point.

**Types of Gift Transference:**

- One-way – Moves a single power from one person to another.

- Direct two-way (Swap) – Moves two powers so that the targets essentially switch Gifts.

- Three-way (Triangle) – A's power goes to B. B's power goes to C. C's power goes to A. This pattern follows the triangle.

- Three-way (Target) – One person gets both powers from the other two. A's power goes to B. C's power goes to B.

- Multiple – There are other patterns. You can figure them out for yourself if you're so inclined. The skill-level of the caster will determine how many transfers can happen and how long they last.

Every Gift that's moved needs to be monitored because having a power and knowing how to use it are sometimes two different concepts.

**Demonstration:**

I swapped Dad's ability to breathe underwater with Doug's access to Super Strength.

This trade was uneven because the power types differed.

**What the heck am I talking about?**

Most of the powers involving breathing are auto-gifts. That means they activate automatically, without much fuss because of necessity.

Super Strength is a conscious gift. Those are activated by the user's will. It's a conscious decision.

Those might sound similar, but it's the difference between the need to think about breathing and the need to think about throwing a perfect baseball pitch. One you may think your life depends on it, and one your life actually depends on it.

**What happened:**

Dad was semi-conscious. I don't know if he used the Gift, but since his legs didn't look mangled, perhaps he used part of the power.

I used my Super Strength to rip the door off so I could get to Dad.

Doug used Underwater Breath for a few minutes while I got Dad out of the car crusher and played with sharks.

The shield that initially prevented me from getting to him didn't keep water out. He wasn't conscious during the rescue, which might have been a blessing.

The auto-gift of Underwater Breath took more babysitting than the conscious Gift of Super Strength.

**Expectations and reality:**

Expectation 1: Gift Transference is a set-it-and-forget-it power.

Reality 1: That depends on the Gifts being moved. At least some will must be exerted to keep the Gifts in place.

It can also be dependent upon the recipient's willingness to receive the Gift. I can't tell you how that's going to go because it depends on multiple factors including personality, consciousness, and the nature of the power.

Expectation 2: Transference is always successful.

Reality 2: Transfers can fail or be a terrible fit for multiple reasons, including the target's physical condition, mental capacity, and emotional stability. A suspicious mind might completely reject the possibility, which shuts down the person's access to a Gift.

It's not like belief is a power's automatic on-off switch but significant doubt can be crippling.

It's like fitting a round peg into a square hole. You might be able to accomplish it through brute force, but it's not going to be pretty.

**Complications and downsides:**

Complication: Gift rejection can get messy. It's like an allergic reaction.

The superpowers haven't been studied enough to dig deep into why some people don't take to certain Gifts well.

Downside 1: Most people consider the temporary nature of Transference to be a downside. The people whose Gifts are moved tend to be grateful for the temp part.

Downside 2: The target receiving the new-to-them Gift won't be as experienced with it as the original user. The Gifts come with a certain amount of inherent knowledge, but innate ability is a poor substitute for long hours of practice. Ideally, the two concepts—ability and practice—are combined to good effect.

**Combat potential:** medium to low

See downside 2 for the longer version.

I don't see much use for moving Gifts among allies.

There's some benefit to moving enemy powers to allies.

**Danger level:** medium

Having a negative reaction to a gift is unusual, but it's not unheard of.

One can never truly discount the possibility of people being destructively mean for a laugh.

**Usefulness:** medium

That honestly depends on the situations one finds themselves in. When helping Dad and Doug, I found it very useful, but that's not exactly a normal thing.

If someone with a specific Gift was indisposed, their power could be moved to someone else, but that would still require someone with Transference acting as a go-between. That's inefficient at best.

**Entertainment value:** low

Besides the prank value of moving someone's Gift away from them at an inopportune time, I don't see this being geared to entertainment value.

**Overall rating and conclusion:** 2.5 of 5 stars

I don't think this one was high up on the list to prep for the public, and I don't see it being a big seller.

# Chapter 41

# Journal Entry 19: Interesting Tidbits

Since I have already stepped out of the normal timeline, I decide to open a few of Mom's memories.

Afraid I might miss something, I had been pretty broad with which thoughts I snatched.

Throughout the time spent dealing with Jasmine and fetching Dad and Doug, I'd subconsciously been sorting memories.

I let the thoughts scroll past me and select the ones that are highlighted for one reason or another.

**Interesting tidbits I learn:**

- Mom had an older brother named Joe. Guess that's where my brother got his name.

- Uncle Joe died from a brain tumor when he was four. They didn't even know it was there.

- Mom was eighteen months old at that point, so she probably only saw her brother in pictures, videos, and digital scan archives.

- The incident kicked off Evil Grandpa's obsession with

superpower studies and Grandma's drinking problem.

- Grandma died a few years after her son. Technically, she died in an accident, but cars had pretty good anti-collision software even back then. She likely had to work very hard at overriding the safety system to drive off a cliff.

- After that, Mom practically grew up at Bridgeway. Guess that explains how she got her start here.

- Evil Grandpa wasn't abusive during Mom's formative years, just neglectful.

- Fortunately for Mom, Dr. Amy Leeta and Dr. Kyle Forchester let her hang out in their labs. That's where Mom's love of science was born.

- Evil Grandpa's name is Alexander Bridgeway. (Well, that explains some stuff.)

- Rolik was Grandma's maiden name.

- Mom adopted it when she went for her doctorate in Biological Engineering Science studies because she didn't want the pressure of dealing with the expectations and prejudices associated with her family name.

I know that is not a thing in your time, but it's exactly what it sounds like. It's the study of changing things in living organisms. I think it got a start through nanotechnology and branched into anything that enhances what's possible for humans.

- The Bridgeway name wasn't technically worth anything until Mom entered her teen years. That's when the government contract came along, and the small operation exploded into dozens of sites.

- Bridgeway does much more than superpower research.

That's the only part I knew about because it's the only part that concerned me thus far, but I'm starting to think otherwise. At least some of the technology has also deeply affected my life.

Ever heard of a Gift Predictor?

I hadn't until I open the memory called *Captured* and witness my mother tinkering with one.

The lab is mostly dark. The only light comes from emergency panels at sporadic points around the room.

From the furtive way Mom keeps glancing at the door while the machine does its thing, I guess she isn't supposed to be using it.

She has Baby Jasmine and Baby Me with her. With us bundled up to the neck I can't tell which is which, but Mom knows. I latch onto her knowledge and slap a label over us.

The nervous glances not aimed at the door go to one or the other of us.

The machine spits a microchip into a receiving tray.

Mom plucks it out and holds it between both of her hands. (That's outdated tech at this point, but this was twenty-plus years ago.)

The two-handed touch lets the microchip be absorbed into my mother's palms quicker, transferring whatever data they hold directly through her bloodstream.

"Ang, hurry. I think someone's coming." The male voice belongs to Dad.

"Someone's here," announces another male voice. "I'm supposed to be here. You are not. You've got three seconds to convince me not to light you up like a Christmas tree."

"It's okay, Ricky. It's just me," says Mom. "That's my husband, Winston."

"Dr. Rolik?" asks the guard. "I thought you'd quit."

"More like took an extended leave without permission," Mom murmurs. "Probably got terminated somewhere along the way." She picks up the two baby carriers and lugs us over to where our father stands.

"Why are you back?" The guard doesn't move from his spot in the doorway.

Mom answers the question with a question.

"Why are you asking?"

The guard's expression flickers from guilt to embarrassment to defiance before settling on righteous conviction.

"I didn't believe you'd be back." Ricky shakes his head in disbelief, then shrugs. "Ain't gonna question it though. I can always use the bonus money."

Mom stiffens at that statement.

"We just need to wait a little longer. My crew will be here shortly. Then, we can see where the boss wants you to spend the night."

Mom and Dad exchange some looks that convey a few questions and answers. Dad wants to know if they should try fighting. Mom wants to try reasoning, but she isn't very hopeful about either option.

"Ricky, please. You have a family. You know—" Mom doesn't get far with the pleading option.

"All I know is tonight's gonna pay for my kids' futures," says Ricky.

"At the expense of mine." Mom fires the verbal shot with quiet venom. "You know what he wants them for, right?"

Ricky shakes his head vigorously.

"Don't know. Don't care."

Dad uses the conversation distraction to punch the guard. The blow is fueled by panic and knocks the man out cold.

Next, Dad kneels by the nearest baby carrier—mine—and starts messing with straps.

"What are you doing?" Mom hisses the question, though she can clearly see what he's doing.

"You'll run faster without the carriers." Dad pulls me free and hands me over to Mom.

Baby Me starts fussing at being moved.

Mom cradles my head and makes a shushing noise.

"We don't even know what Superspeed will do to them." She backs up the statement with a solid glare aimed at Dad. "And I'm not leaving you to deal with my father."

"It's not about me," Dad snaps. "It's about getting them away from here. We shouldn't have come. Was it worth it?"

Mom nods, but she doesn't explain.

Ricky stirs.

Mom looks frustrated enough to kick the guard while he's down.

"Maybe we can hide." The half-hearted tone says she doesn't hold out high hopes for the plan.

Every light in the lab snaps on.

A new figure stands in the doorway.

"Welcome back. We have a lot to catch up on, but first, I'm sure you'll both want to see how family time has gone thus far."

Mom almost drops me.

One of the large wall screens light up and shows a security feed of the kid-version of my brother, Joe, playing with some toys.

# Chapter 42

# Journal Entry 20: Failing

Shaking off my mother's bad memory, I return to the present moment, check on a few things, and teleport to the room holding her.

I find Mom standing next to Evil Grandpa. She doesn't look pleased, but she also doesn't look like she's dying of a poison.

That relieves me and strikes every suspicious bone I own.

*Jasmine?*

My sister could pull off the mimicry event in terms of looks, but I don't think she can match the mark I'd placed on our mother.

**Right here.**

Jasmine appears next to me, looking none the worse for wear since our little altercation. She has changed from the imitation Bridgeway lackey outfit into jeans and a T-shirt.

"What's going on?" I don't hold high hopes somebody will explain things in a civilized fashion, but the question needs asking anyway.

Jasmine's emotional state feels suitably confused, but one can never truly trust such things with a Mimic. She could just be duplicating my own emotional state and reflecting it back to me.

I'd teleported near the main entrance, so we were within shouting distance of Mom and Evil Grandpa.

I don't see anybody with them until I switch my vision over to thermal view. That busts the simple illusion and reveals the presence of nine guards carrying nullifiers.

The setup shouts *trap*, but I can't pin down a rhyme or reason for the illusion pieces.

In hindsight, confusing me was probably the only point.

*Mission accomplished, Evil Grandpa.*

The mad scientist beckons us forward.

Jazz moves ahead a few steps, but I don't budge.

I am too busy flipping mental switches.

The best way to destroy an illusion is to re-map the room. That involves lots of the mind equivalent of echo location and math. Math's right up there with Physics on the not-my-favorite subject list.

Once I find the source of the illusion, I reach in and suppress the Gift.

The illusion collapses, so the projection of Mom disappears.

The room still holds the same number of people, but some of their positions have changed.

Evil Grandpa stands at the foot of an inclined hospital cot.

The bed holds my mother.

The nine Bridgeway guards toting nullifiers stand in a semicircle surrounding the bed.

The open side of said semicircle faces me.

Not sure I have it in me to walk normally, I use Superspeed to get to the bedside.

The nullifiers shift my way.

I put measures into place to deal with them, but most of my attention stays with my mother.

This version does not look okay.

A machine sitting on the bed's far side beeps slowly.

I tap Enhanced Intelligence and peek into Evil Grandpa's surface thoughts to get a handle on the readings. Even without that, I can tell the super shallow, barely-breathing status does not herald good things.

I reach to take my mother's hand.

"You may heal her now but note the wrist restraints she wears," says Evil Grandpa. "They're designed to prevent teleportation."

A molecular structure check tells me they've used silver chains, the ones Past Me had indicated I couldn't break free from by phasing. Guess they took that to mean I couldn't break them by other means too.

Stupid assumption on their part, but go Past Me.

Just in case I need to keep that illusion going, I tweak the chains to be platinum. The shade of silver color changes slightly, but one not watching for a change will never notice.

I also destabilize the chain structures enough that one hard knock will turn them to dust.

"Even after the healing, her life will still rest in your hands," Evil Grandpa continues.

I pick up Mom's right hand, then look at Evil Grandpa curiously.

"I don't understand. Why are you hurting your daughter?"

"Because she failed," he answers.

Though I want to question him about that, I need to concentrate on the healing efforts for a moment.

It takes more work than anticipated.

Essentially, I work my way through every cell in Mom's body, making a call about whether that cell is helping or hurting her, and destroy or remove the poison molecules.

The effort leaves me lightheaded, but at least I get instant feedback.

Mom squeezes my hand.

When the healing reaches the point it can proceed without me, I pick up the conversation again.

"How did she fail?" I wonder.

"Me." Jasmine's one-word, flat contribution somehow manages to combine resentment, disappointment, and hurt.

"You were supposed to have all the Gifts," says Evil Grandpa. "Now, it's going to be much harder to combine them."

I frown at Evil Grandpa, then at Jasmine, trying to wrap my head around their twisted logic.

"Let me get this straight. I was supposed to have every superpower, but instead, you got two baby girls with only most of the Gifts. And this is a tragic failing worth killing somebody over?"

"If I have other Gifts, I can't access them," Jasmine explains. "That's the failing I need to correct, and you're going to help me do it, one way or the other."

"Setting aside the horrific abuse of the word *failing*, can we back up to the leap in logic that brings us from failing to worth a death sentence?" I don't truly expect an answer, but I am irrationally disappointed at not receiving one anyway. A new thought pops into my mind. "And how exactly am I helping with your problem."

Mom squeezes my hand and answers.

"Steal ... yours."

"Not exactly," counters Evil Grandpa.

The guards change their aim slightly to stop targeting me. Instead, their sights fix on Jasmine.

Releasing a strangled, rage-filled beastly noise, Jazz lunges at Evil Grandpa. Three taser prongs spring out of the guard cluster.

Microjumping through Jasmine, I yank her clear with a spectacular tackle.

She thanks me with an elbow to the face.

We really must work on her gratefulness.

The move allows the Bridgeway goons to catch us both in the nullifiers' collective zone of influence.

# Chapter 43

# Superpower Review 21: Sense Danger (Heightened Danger Intuition or Precognitive Warnings)

**Background and notes:**

**Note:** I've had this review in an unpolished state for a while now. It never got finished because I had a few unexpected top-priority reviews surface and kick it to a perpetual back burner in my head.

I would categorize Sense Danger as a pseudo power because a form of it comes as a side Gift with many others, such as Flight and Superspeed.

However, because it's been officially recognized by the Superpower Control Council, people can also attempt to pass a SRT (Superpower Recognition Test) for it.

It's categorized as a Very Rare Gift.

Three people in known history have scored well enough to pass the SRT for this particular power. (Thank you, Google, for that little gem of information.)

**Fun and irrelevant fact:** A clerical error during the initial Council meetings about the power led to it being considered three times under different names.

That's why some of the textbooks and articles will go into nauseating detail about Heightened Danger Intuition, others will wax long about Sense Danger, and still others blither on and on about Precognitive Warnings.

I learned it as Sense Danger, so congratulations, that's what I'm going to use to refer to it. If you're dead set on having a different term, threaten somebody else's family or have Bess work her editing magic and find/replace each of the references.

**Explanation of the power:**

The type of Sense Danger recognized as its own Gift refers to the ability to see a few seconds to a few minutes into the future when something specific and dangerous is about to happen.

Depending on how much power manifests with the Gift, the range can vary a lot: a few meters to a few miles to a few thousand miles. (Yes, Bess, I just mixed the English and metric systems. I don't like yards. Get over it.)

There can be differences in range or depth.

**Random points about range:**

- Range can refer to physical distance or time into the future.

- Temporal—referring to time not spiritual state—range of a few minutes is typical. But I suspect the range is a few seconds up to a few hours.

- People with a physical range of a few meters may not even know they have the Gift, especially if they have no family history of superpower manifestations. (Sorry for making it sound like a disease.)

- The sweet spot for physical range is probably a few miles.

- Physical range of a few thousand miles has the same problems as a few miles if the Super's used to working solo.

**Random points about depth:**

The Gift could be calibrated to give warnings about every kind of danger or only a narrow range of dangers.

- Tripping, falling, and scraping a knee can hurt, but it's usually not life-threatening.

- Many types of avoidable accidents range in severity. Take car accidents for example. They range from scuff-the-paint incidents to break-into-the-car-before-the-fire-spreads incidents.

**Experiments:**

Not applicable.

This is one of the few powers where there are no experiments somebody could run. All Sensing Gifts fall into this category, but a few come as part of a package deal like Sense Emotional Distress, which is part of the Manipulate Emotions power.

I demonstrated by essentially acting like a supernatural dispatcher. In the few seconds I had the power on, I predicted twelve car accidents, two people tripping, eighteen people dying, and forty-seven near misses.

Grid cameras confirmed most of the predictions and eye-witness accounts backed up some of the remaining ones. Fourteen predictions went unconfirmed.

**How Sense Danger ability works:**

It's a bit like having a panicky, pessimistic radio blaring non-stop in your head. This is why I believe many people possess the Gift but simply never use it.

**Aside:** Unless they're crazy good at spinning tall tales, these people aren't even going to make it as fortune tellers. Nobody wants to hear constant doom and gloom that may or may not be changeable.

### Expectations and reality:

Expectation 1: Sense Danger is a Very Rare Gift.

Reality 1 (my personal educated guess): I don't think it's a VRG (Very Rare Gift). It's one of the few Gifts that if you make a mistake you die, which would certainly skew the data.

If you don't understand what it is or can't cope with the knowledge, those around you might just think you're not a complete deck up top.

Reality 1.5: A lot more people have this power but aren't even going to take a SRT because they have it switched completely off.

Expectation 2: Sense Danger automatically means you can do something about the event that comes with a warning.

Reality 2: Unless the Super is well-connected, the power isn't going to do much good since most people—besides Nobodies—get one Gift.

If that one Gift is a stellar warning system of something bad about to happen, but you can't get there in time to stop said bad thing, it's kind of useless.

Expectation 3: It's a very frustrating Gift.

Reality 3: That's accurate, but like anything, if one receives the proper support and training, the Gift can be successfully combined with others to good effect.

Expectation 4: The dangers sensed are all life-threatening.

Reality 4: Danger is danger. I suspect the life-threatening ones are the most exciting ones to talk about. (There's not much boasting mileage in having saved someone from a stubbed toe.)

Expectation 5: It's easy to use.

Reality 5: It's difficult to master. Essentially, if you have control over the Gift—some do, some don't—you would want to filter it just right so you can sense the dangers in whatever range you can reasonably intervene.

**Complications and downsides:**

Complication 1: Limited range.

Complication 2: Having to convey the danger in a way that doesn't make you sound stark raving mad.

Complication 3: Not personally having the ability to intervene in most cases can get frustrating. (Even my brief demonstration was emotionally rough. It's difficult to know somebody's headed for unavoidable pain. This leads into downside 1.)

Downside 1: You can't save everybody. Some people don't want to be saved. Some people can't be saved.

Downside 2: Knowing a danger and knowing how to help somebody avoid it are two very different things.

Downside 3: There's a stigma attached to using this Gift. Until very recently, a lot of work has gone into suppressing widespread knowledge of the existence of superpowers.

Bridgeway is working hard to prepare for an integrated, unified future, but the philosophy of making the whole world better by sharing our knowledge with the Normies is brand spanking new.

**Combat potential:** low

Those purposefully headed into danger would just get a constant *on* feeling. It's like setting an alarm and letting it blare for the next indeterminable time.

**Danger level:** medium to low

There's a very high risk of not being believed. Likewise, there's a high risk for soaring frustration levels, but the odds of direct danger if something goes awry is low.

**Usefulness:** 4 of 5 stars

If used properly, it can be a helpful Gift.

**Entertainment value:** 2 of 5 stars

Some people thrive off the adrenaline high that comes with solving crises.

**Overall rating and conclusion:** 3 of 5 stars

It's useful to have, but I don't recommend releasing this Gift to the general public.

Limited use for those already in public service roles sounds reasonable, but whether the Gift is a boon or a burden comes down to how well the Super is trained.

# Chapter 44

---

# Product Review 2-ish: Nullifiers

**Background and notes:**

I errantly labeled the clothing line evaluations as a superpower review instead of a product review, so this is technically the second time I'm sharing about a thing instead of a power.

Bess could totally fix it in about two hundredths of a second, but she said that would ruin the continuity already established.

**Translation:** She'd have to renumber all the power reviews. While I think that's an excuse for her being lazy, she has a point. It might confuse those who've already been keeping track to this point.

Anyway, I guess Superpower Review #9 gets to pull double duty as the first product review and my ninth official review.

As promised, here are my thoughts on nullifiers.

**Short version:** They're great if you're not the one staring down half a dozen of them.

If you are staring down six or seven and felt another three before the blasted things turned on, you're probably not going to be pleased with them.

Overkill much?

I'm not sure if I should be flattered or annoyed to warrant this much attention. (I'm going to go with annoyed.)

**Why am I doing this review now?**

Well, experience is one heck of a solid teacher. (I'm currently staring down seven serious nullifiers and there are three more backups hidden in the walls behind this cell.)

I can tell you more about how the actual capture thing went down later, but I'd been meaning to write this review for some time anyway. Might as well make good use of my timeout.

**Explanation of the product:**

Nullifiers do their level best to negate superpowers.

Nullifiers come in several shapes and sizes. I'm used to the bulky and obvious specimens like the ones I tangled with before my Dad and Doug rescues. They resemble skinny microwaves or overgrown ancient VHS video recorders. I saw one of those recorders in a museum once.

The sneakier versions are hand-held and roughly the size of a traditional set of playing cards.

**How do they work?**

I think the various versions have different targets.

- The large, cumbersome ones send out subtle signals at many frequencies. **Why that works:** The human brain still relies on sending and receiving signals. So, adding a few million contradictory ones trips the failsafe on most superpowers.

**Note:** A small subset of people suffer from nullifier errant activation or overload. (It means the signal causes their power to misfire or kills them.)

- The hand-held smaller ones are more directly vicious. They release a stream of picomachines to put the Super's entire brain in timeout. **Why that works:** It's a different kind of signal interference.

**Note:** The ones out in front are the first kind, and the three loaded into the cell itself are the latter kind.

- Medium ones use some combination of both methods. I think there are variants that do the signal disruption thing via electrical means instead of chemical or known electromagnetic radiation types.

**Note:** Bess is yelling at me for the multiple *I thinks*. They don't currently have one of the medium style nullifiers pointed at me, so I'm drawing my knowledge from archives that already exist in my head.

(**Internal note:** There are ways to beat nullifiers, but aside from the few hints I've already given, I will not be covering that part. A girl's got to keep some life-saving tips to herself.)

**Experiments:**

I suppose from a certain point of view, my entire life is an experiment right now.

My new digs are the Bridgeway equivalent of max-security lockdown.

The mysterious captors—new-to-me execs—haven't said so explicitly, but I gather I'm supposed to attempt escaping.

The seven nullifiers in front are cycling frequencies to provide wide coverage of neurological disruptions.

**How the experiment is going:**

- I have a headache, but oddly, most of my mental Gifts are intact. My guess about what's going on is that some mental Gifts come with self-defense mechanisms that send out counter signals. (It's like sending out the mental equivalent of chaff to intercept a missile.)

- I have a fever. My body temperature is 105°F. That would be really bad for most people, but it's only slightly uncomfortable for me. My body has a lot going on in preparation for using a Gift, so

101°F is my usual.

- I have sixty-seven partial plans for getting out of here, but which plan gets enacted depends on things outside my control. Since I have the thinking time, I'll probably generate another forty contingency plans just in case.

**Expectations and reality:**

Expectation 1: Nullifiers are all you need to control a Super.

Reality 1: False. If that was true, Evil Grandpa and company wouldn't have gone after my family to play twisted games.

Even if you only consider the physical aspect of control, one nullifier isn't enough.

Expectation 2: Nullifiers can nix any Gift.

Reality 2: False again. I wouldn't be able to work on this evaluation if they completely blocked my mental abilities. (I do find it ironic that certain mental abilities are the only ones intact right now.)

Expectation 3: Nullifiers are harmless to non-Supers.

Reality 3: False yet again. The definition of a non-Super is anybody who fails the Superpower Recognition Test, but life's never as simple as a one-size-fits-all evaluation. Therefore, it's possible for a nullifier to interfere with a partial or budding Gift.

**Complications:**

(Complication 0: With tremendous power, comes one heck of a battery drain. Nullifier batteries are notoriously short-lived. Probably at least one reason why there are multiple units in play here.)

Complication 1: Nullifiers interfere with stuff besides superpowers. That's why the door to this cell is physical rather than electronic.

Complication 2: The nullifiers that concentrate on brainwave signals are surprisingly difficult to aim accurately.

**Combat potential:** medium to low

If you want to control a Super, it will likely do the job. However, since the Gifted community has largely been hidden to date, most of the armies are still composed of bots, drones, and normal human beings.

**Danger level:** medium

They're finnicky machines at best.

**Usefulness:** medium

For their intended purpose, they work very well in the right conditions. Bridgeway did a lot of research to make sure this cell is up to the job.

**Entertainment value:** low

I'm going to assume we're not marketing this to run-of-the-mill psychopaths keeping Supers in their basements.

**Overall rating and conclusion:** 1 or 4 of 5 Stars

Once again, this comes down to your perspective.

Need to control a Super? Awesome, get thee a nullifier or three.

Being controlled by evil corporations through a nullifier? Sorry. Sucks to be you.

# Chapter 45

# Journal Entry 21: Lousy Family Reunion

You may ask how I came by those very detailed notes on nullifiers, and I will unfortunately answer: first-hand experience.

Baby Sister and Evil Grandpa sort of teamed up to capture me, but then, Evil Grandpa pulled a second betrayal and had the Bridgeway Goon Squad subdue Jasmine as well.

She occupies the cell to my right.

I should be pleased that we get to be jail neighbors, but the Older Sister in me is ticked off that people keep messing with Jasmine.

I always thought I had the perfect family. You know, loving parents, tolerable brothers.

Instead, I find out my twin sister has been raised to hate me and fed a steady diet of theoretical nonsense. In short, Jasmine believes that killing me might get my Gifts to transfer to her.

Evil Grandpa believes the exact opposite. He thinks he can correct my few flaws by forcing me to absorb Jazz's powers.

First off, that's crazy.

For the record, I do have Power Absorption as a Gift, but that lets me temporarily borrow a Gift, nothing more. A permanent version of that has yet to be invented or manifested.

Imbue Power exists in theory, but if anybody has it, they haven't exactly been shouting it from rooftops.

Second, I'm not going to try.

Third, I need to get out of this cell before they present me with some very uncomfortable moral decisions.

This is the lousiest family reunion ever.

Mom's doing okay. She's in a cell with Dad, one up and two to the left from me, directly across from the holding tank for Joe and Leslie.

Dad is crammed onto the cot with Mom, clutching her hand like it's the last time he's ever going to see her.

As far as I can tell, their cell looks like it lacks the modifications meant to prevent the use of superpowers.

Joe's up and stalking around his cell.

Leslie is napping on their single cot.

Doug is sleeping off some drugs in the isolation chamber across from Jasmine. He's got three nullifiers staring him down.

Jazz is curled in the far corner looking like a study in misery. She has four nullifiers facing her.

I really want to talk to her, but not with the entire family and a few random guards bearing witness.

Joe is the first one to meet my eyes.

"Fix this," he orders.

I want to protest since he seems to be giving me way too much credit here, but I barely muster the energy for a single nod.

*Don't you think I'm trying?*

The urge to scream that message burns through my head, but I can't let on that I have any contingency plans.

It's the equivalent of a shot in the dark with a Revolutionary War musket, but at least it's something.

Have I mentioned I hate waiting?

I'm not used to feeling helpless.

It's a terrible feeling. Highly not recommended.

As I prepare to think of the many ways I hate waiting, something happens.

One of the guards—a short guy with a forgettable face—presses a button on a flat disc.

The thing sparks.

By looks, it is very anticlimactic, but I feel the change as the nullifiers kicks off.

The two other guards turn toward the short guy.

One pulls out a taser.

The short guy executes an impressive roundhouse kick that catches Taser Guy in the chin.

The lady guard goes for a radio before remembering that Short Guy's opening move was an EMP disc. She then opts for the nightstick.

Short Guy plucks the weapon away before pulling another series of martial arts whammies on the guard lady.

I'm sure the moves have very formal, lovely names. When I copied the moves from Jasmine, I didn't exactly study up on their nomenclature.

To me, it looks like shuffle-shuffle-punch followed by jab-jab-lights out.

Everybody conscious, including me, rushes to the cell bars.

Short Guy stares down at his handiwork with a mixture of horror and pride.

Mom and Dad gawk.

Joe glares.

Short Guy slaps something onto my cell door and stands back.

Smoke curls up from the lock as the metal sparks.

A second later, a miniature explosion destroys the entire section holding the lock.

The plan goes perfectly until it doesn't.

The explosion is too hot.

It ends up fusing the metal that once made up the lock into a better lock.

Short Guy shoots me a panicked look.

I think as fast as my non-enhanced brain can think.

And come up with horrifying blankness.

"Try waking Doug," Dad suggests.

Hope relights the dying fires in Short Guy's eyes.

Racing over to Doug's cell, the helpful guard slaps another microbomb onto the bar next to the locking mechanism.

This time, it does the job flawlessly, providing just enough bang to rip the lock to shreds and drop those shreds to the ground.

My heart climbs into my throat and sets down deep, painful roots as I wait.

Short Guy tries light slapping and wrist chaffing, but neither method of waking someone can overcome whatever drugs they've given Doug.

*That's one more score we need to settle, Evil Grandpa.*

A soft curse and a longer groan emanate from Doug's cell.

Fear and despair make me twitchy, but they also force me to think.

Something my mother said earlier returns to me.

*Both of you.*

I look to Jasmine who leans back against the wall, facing me.

I practically fly across the cell to the bars separating me from Jasmine.

She eyes me with disinterest.

"Jazz, I know we have a few decades to sort someday, but I need you to trust me. I'm not him, and I didn't help you before because I didn't know you existed. You can scream all you want about that later, but right now, we need you."

Jasmine continues staring for so long, I fear her mental state has blocked my entire speech, but finally, she speaks.

"What's the point?"

A burning sensation starts at the base of my back and quickly intensifies, following the path of my spine. It feels like hot lava moving against gravity.

This must be the backup nullifiers kicking in.

Normally, the picomachines would travel the bloodstream from wherever they entered. My body fights back, confining the invaders to the area around my spine, but that only gives me a short extension on consciousness.

The pain changes flavors slightly, telling me multiple nullifiers have been activated.

That means they know of the escape attempt.

No doubt more guards will arrive shortly.

Sinking to my knees, I rest my fevered head against the cool bars.

I need to convince my sister to help but the part that controls speech fails.

Even thinking gets harder.

*Pick a side, Jazz.*

# Chapter 46

# Journal Entry 22: Secret Weapons

Remember that favor I mentioned oh so long ago? Might be calling that in soon.

But first, I just have to say I love Ellie.

Everybody needs a friend who will pick up their fights when they're being attacked by a few hundred million picomachines. (Not that I wish that fate on anybody.)

Fortunately, my epic struggle does not kill my ability to hear.

Several crashes sound as Ellie stalks out of Doug's cell and shoves nullifiers out of her way.

Too bad she didn't pack more microbombs, but they don't exactly leave those in convenient locations with Steal-Me signs on them.

My peripheral vision shows me Ellie has dropped the Short Guy look in favor of her own features. Okay, so this is the avenging-angel version of her with flushed cheeks and fire in her eyes, but close enough.

Gripping the bars in front of Jasmine's cell hard, Ellie presses her face into them with enough force to leave marks.

"Help her!" Ellie's voice skirts the line between rousing and desperate.

"Why should I?" Jasmine challenges.

"She's your sister!" A guttural growling noise escapes Ellie.

"She's the Perfect One." Bitterness soaks each of Jasmine's words. "No doubt she'll conquer the nullifiers and share a brilliant scheme shortly."

If my back didn't feel like my spine had been replaced with a lit torch, I would laugh.

"You can be jealous later," Ellie argues, "but right now, we have maybe thirty seconds before more guards show up." A sob turns into a cough, stalling her speech for a while. "If that happens, they'll find some other way to control her. Then, we're all dead."

"I don't care." The words sound even, but something subtle shifts.

I silently pray it will be enough.

Ellie lapses into silence, but her conversation with Jasmine starts to bear fruit.

Turns out, the Faruchi suit comes with some lovely self-defense mechanisms.

I even find a reason for the annoying cape.

It's incredibly creepy that the clothes heard my sister's advice, but I'll take creepy over back-on-fire any day.

I'd read about the voice commands but did not previously have any fun orders to give the clothes.

I also didn't yammer on about what made up each outfit either. Even Jabrie and Team Science Geeks didn't want to hear that stuff. Hence, me not mentioning that the patented color-weave-47 is 98% picomachines.

Anyway, Jasmine's suggestion activates the self-defense features, setting several things in motion.

Some of the itty-bitty wonders enter my body and start fighting the machines injected by the nullifiers. The rest spread out in three directions to cut off the source of evil picomachines.

It must look like the cape and clothes are melting off my body.

It's embarrassing—and probably too much information, but I'm glad I chose to wear normal, non-Faruchi underwear today.

Thank goodness because nobody thinks to order the machines to stop, so it's all-hands-on-deck for them.

End result: the entire outfit busies itself elsewhere, leaving me in my sports bra and underwear. At least I had the foresight to choose a fun color instead of tight and white.

Let me clarify that it isn't an instant cure, but once my Gifts starts coming out of nullifier lockdown, I shove all my energy into a massive cleansing effort.

Though not pretty, it effectively drives the picomachines out of my body. I don't have time to distinguish good and evil machines. This is an everything-must-go situation.

Even with the machines being individually invisible, the millions of them being evicted simultaneously creates visible hairlike strands.

Every exit from the body—sweat pores, front end, back end, ears, eyes, nose, and such—participate, but I don't have time to wallow in shame.

I set the entire prison wing into slow motion, teleport to my room, raid my snack stash for six power bars, and stuff my face while I dig out another Faruchi getup.

The yellow and green one had been sacrificed to the cause, leaving me with purple and blue or red and black.

Since I distinctly remember the purple being a tad too flammable for my liking, I choose the red and black one.

I pause for a mirror check and fix my scary hair, opting for the short look again. If a fistfight is in my future, I want nothing that invites pulling.

Upon my triumphant return to the cellblock, I finish what the good picomachines and Ellie had started by destroying every nullifier I can find.

Clearly, these people cannot be trusted with such machines.

Finally, I give Ellie a brief hug and thank her for being my secret weapon.

She probably doesn't hear me, but I like to think the thought counts for something.

I think about how easy it would be to whisk my family away from the chaos.

Super Strength would let me conquer the cell bars. One massive Transportation effort would let me take them anywhere. Preferably somewhere warm and far away from anything Bridgeway has its tentacles in.

With the slow time thing in effect, everybody looks frozen.

Mom, Dad, Ellie, Joe, Leslie, and Doug can start over elsewhere.

I don't enact the plan for one reason: Jasmine.

She will never forgive me if I sweep in and save the day. She needs to be a part of this.

Besides, Evil Grandpa and Bridgeway need somebody to teach them morality.

Like it or not, I've been elected to do so.

*All right, Jazz. You're going to help me with Backup Plan 33.*

Teleporting into my sister's cell and creating a new time bubble within the bubble are easy.

Not getting punched when Jasmine effectively comes out of stasis takes additional effort.

I eventually discard the idea of a fair fight, change the molecules in my sister's shoes so they stick to the floor, put her in a headlock, and activate the part of her brain that produces endorphins.

That's the body's natural happy drugs.

"I'm going to let you go in a second but stop fighting me." Following up the words with actions, I release my hold on my sister and let her shoes return to normal.

Jasmine whips around and saves me the trouble of shuffling to a better position to hold a conversation. For a moment, it looks like she'll renew the fight.

I raise both hands in the universal surrender gesture.

"I have a plan, but I need your help with it." I let a second pass to give her time to react violently if she is so inclined. "If you screw up while trying, the plan fails. If you refuse, it still fails. In both cases, nobody's getting out of this. What do you say? Want to be a superhero?"

# Chapter 47

# Superpower Review 22: Molecule Manipulation

**Background and notes:**

Set more stuff in motion and gave myself some downtime. Might as well make good use of it.

I've talked about this one a lot, so I should just make it official.

As previously mentioned, my older brother has this Gift. We found out about it because he got mad at me for stealing his toy dragon and drooling on it. (**Defense of actions:** I was two.)

Joe stole his toy back and fused my diaper to the ground. That got messy real quick because the diaper happened to be in business at the time, and I had recently mastered the art of shimmying out of pull-ups.

It would have been fine if Joe knew how to control the power to undo the change, but he panicked and tried to make the poop go away. Unfortunately, he ended up changing some of the clean diaper particles into the thing he was trying to get rid of.

Mom arrived on the scene in time to calm both screaming children. Joe's wails had more to do with his frustration. Mine were filled with delight.

I'd never experienced such freedom. (That kicked off a six-month stint of frequent diaper removal. Needless to say, my parents made potty training a priority after that.)

(Doesn't parenting Gifted children sound exciting?)

**Explanation of the power:**

There are two forms of the Gift, but people usually don't distinguish.

Basic Molecule Manipulation involves changing the chemical makeup of something. Essentially, the caster takes one form of matter and makes another.

Some of it happens by instinct, but to use it with a purpose—and not endanger yourself and others along the way—a deep understanding of chemistry helps.

It's like nuclear fission and fusion, only without the blow-up-everything part. You could also see some forms of it as controlled nuclear decay.

**Quick definitions for the execs who don't remember chem class:**

Fission – Is essentially messy molecular divorce. One thing becomes two and it gets explosively violent.

Fusion – Two smaller molecules join together to become one thing. The normal version comes with a side of crazy amounts of energy.

Nuclear decay – An unstable molecule burps up part and feels better.

**Side note:** Chemistry is not as evil as physics, though the high level, theoretical junk gets very blurry between the two subjects.

**Mini-chem lesson continued:**

Chemical identity is wrapped up in the number of protons. So, molecule manipulations usually deal with messing with proton numbers. One proton, you have hydrogen. Two protons, you have Helium. And so forth. These are the elements, the building blocks of all matter (stuff).

It gets rapidly more confusing from there because most stuff isn't made of pure elements. It's made of compounds, which are chemical unions between elements.

**Two types:**

- Change the molecules and atoms

- Change the combination of molecules and atoms

**Demonstrations:**

Since I'm still technically in a Bridgeway cell, these demonstrations had to be done virtually. I opened a space in my mind, recorded the changes, and wrote up notes about which chemicals were present at the start and finish.

- Demo 1: I changed water into hydrogen peroxide ($H_2O_2$) by isolating individual molecules of $H_2O$ and tacking on an extra O.

- Demo 2: Made wine into water.

- Demo 3: Turned lead into gold. (Yes, the advent of superpowers has made alchemy possible. But flooding the market with gold will only devalue it.)

- Demo 4: Changed moldy bread into fresh, new-ish bread. (I didn't just scrape off the mold, though I suppose that's one way to handle the situation.)

**What happened:**

- Demos 1 and 3 were easy. Lead and gold are neighbors on the periodic table. Lead has 82 protons and gold has 79, so I took each of the lead atoms and swiped three protons. When I had enough, I formed new gold atoms.

- Demos 2 and 4 were harder. Water to wine is the more popular direction of change, but I wanted to prove that more complicated things could be simplified.

**Expectations and reality:**

Expectation 1: No energy is lost or gained during Molecule Manipulation.

Reality 1: False, but the Gift comes with the ability to dissipate the energy into the 4th dimension. I suppose if you wanted the energy, you could harness it, but I don't recommend it as an alternative energy source.

**Why?**

Because in order to make usable energy in large enough quantities, the Super would need to devote their entire life to that cause.

Expectation 2: It's a Very Rare Gift.

Reality 2: My guess is it's not used very often. Thus far, more energy has been spent on suppressing Gifts instead of guiding them. A few parlor-trick type events might impress your friends, but that also attracts the Superpower Control Council's attention. Never a good thing.

Expectation 3: Whatever is made can be easily returned to its original form.

Reality 3: That depends on the caster's skill level. Atoms and molecules are very tiny. Changing a few drops of water into hydrogen peroxide might involve a few million molecules. Now scale that up to the amount you'd need to fill a glass.

Expectation 4: The change is perfect every time.

Reality 4: There's always the small chance of making a mistake. When that's scaled to many billions, even a very small fraction of errors can add up quickly.

Expectation 5: You can create something from nothing.

Reality 5: That's a different Gift called Conjuring.

**Complications and limitations:**

Complication 1: Giving the reverse instruction might be easy, but atoms and molecules don't always behave themselves.

Complication 2: Something can look perfect and have serious flaws.

Limitation 1: You're at the mercy of what's around you.

Molecule Manipulation isn't Conjuring. If I want to take lead and make it gold, it's a relatively easy thing to tweak. However, if all I have is hydrogen atoms, I'm going to end up with much less gold because I need to repurpose the proton from 79 of those hydrogen suckers.

Limitation 2: Range is highly limited. Though it varies some with skill level, few can manage to change things across a room let alone beyond.

**Combat potential:** 4 of 5 stars

Want to change table salt into chlorine gas? This is the power for you.

**Disclaimer:** Not recommended. Remember the range note? The caster would need to be within a few meters at the most, more likely less than a meter from the salt and the target. **Spoiler:** That's the breathe-it-in-and-die zone.

**Danger level:** 5 of 5 stars

See the above disclaimer for an example.

In short, the caster would be as likely to harm themselves as the person they seek to murder. (I've resigned myself to the fact that murder's just going to be a part of our discussions. Creepy government agendas.)

**Usefulness:** 4 of 5 stars

When used responsibly, this can be a neat and helpful power.

**Short list of uses:**

- Escape

- Breaking in

- Cleaning/ renewing

- Impressing people

**Entertainment value:** 3 of 5 stars

Unless your sole life goal is to become an escape artist or thief, you probably won't get much entertainment value out of this power.

**Overall rating and conclusion:** 3.75 of 5 stars

I hate to be the pessimist, but given the state of humanity, I recommend this not be distributed publicly.

Until society can safely dispense with instructions like *open box before eating pizza*, just no.

# Chapter 48

# Superpower Review 23: Eye Lasers (Laser Vision)

**Background and notes:**

Still trying to distract myself. Waiting to see if my plans succeeded or failed is awful.

I don't know why people want this Gift.

- It's destructive.

- It's hard to control.

- It takes a ton of energy.

- It makes your eyes terribly dry.

Once again, there's a discrepancy between the naming systems. I'm going to go with the broader term of Eye Lasers, though that does include Laser Vision.

There are a few other terms, but they're similar enough in intent, I don't feel the need to name them. (Optical anything sounds pretentious.)

**Explanation of the power:**

This Gift involves the creation of laser beams and the emission of said beams from one's eyes.

**Side effect:** glowy eyes

**What can you do with the Gift to control Eye Lasers?**

- Cut stuff (and drill holes)

- Heat stuff

- Kill stuff

- Move stuff

- Set stuff on fire

**Intent and intensity notes:**

To understand this section, you probably need to understand the nature of the laser beams created. People lump beams together as one thing, but light can be pure waves or particles.

**Warning:** More icky science coming. I shall try to be brief.

Lasers are most often portrayed in their snazzy form of monochromatic—it means one color—forms of light. But they can be any form of electromagnetic radiation and a few kinds of particles current scientists have slapped a figurative this-is-magic-and-we-don't-get-it sign on.

**Fun fact:** You can change the color of your eye glow by changing the nature of the beam. This isn't directly related to intensity. It has more to do with the Super's whims and will. By choosing a color, you are limiting the frequency and energy of your creation.

The Gift involves a particle even smaller than an electron, and those suckers are very tiny. (I would share the name of the new particle because it's kind of cool, but then Bess would just redact it and yell at me. And if she missed it, I'd get another visit from Security Panel agents, and they'd yell at me.)

Point is the lovely new particle can behave exactly as normal light or show off its unique properties. In other words, it can be harmless or destructive depending on how many there are and how fast they're traveling.

Because things you can't see usually weirds people out, think of it like a tennis ball. Thrown gently, it can be a fun toy. Fired from a machine at a few hundred miles per hour, it can be a weapon.

Same goes for the things making up laser beams. If a stream of a few million flows in gentle patterns, you get pretty light. If several quadrillion get fired at one spot for a few seconds, the thing they hit will likely give way.

The intensity of the beam determines if something will be warmed, cooked, deep fried, or burnt beyond recognition.

The surface area of the target zone usually matters when it comes to whether something gets knocked back or cut apart.

**Demonstrations:**

After doing some of the experiments, I might be approaching an understanding of the Gift's appeal.

- Demo 1: Cut an apple in half.

- Demo 2: Cut through a wooden door.

- Demo 3: Blasted marshmallows shot from a catapult.

- Demo 4: Cooked a frozen dinner.

- Demo 5: Moved a soccer ball.

- Demo 6: Lit a campfire.

It should go without saying that I didn't attempt killing someone, but sometimes, it helps to state the obvious.

**What happened:**

- Demo 1: I made a mess of the apple.

- Demo 2: The beams made short work of the door and the floor beyond.

- Demo 3: I blasted marshmallows like somebody skeet shooting, and now marshmallow launcher is officially on my Christmas wish list.

- Demo 4: The dinner was edible, sort of. I think the power can work for cooking, but I would need to practice more to not burn the heck out of half and leave the rest a block of ice.

- Demo 5: I might have gone through a few dozen soccer balls before I got the beams wide enough to move the ball without busting a hole in it.

- Demo 6: Still needed kindling and something to spark.

**Expectations and reality:**

Expectation 1: The caster might have trouble turning the ability off.

Reality 1: Only if they're very young, incompetent, or both.

Expectation 2: You can blow stuff up with the Gift.

Reality 2: Combustion—as in causing something to explode—is a different power. However, if something can go boom on its own and you heat it to unreasonable temperatures, it's likely to explode.

Expectation 3: Long, sustained laser beams require more energy than short laser beams.

Reality 3: It comes down to how intensely you're blasting something and how long you intend to blast this item. There's an initial startup cost to any laser beam formation. While sustaining a beam already in progress requires some energy, the cost is less than multiple start-stop incidents.

Expectation 4: Laser beams have the same intensity.

Reality 4: The intensity of each beam depends on the caster's intent. Want to point something out with a cute little pair of laser dots? You want to keep the intensity low. Want to cut through a six-inch steel slab? You will need a stronger beam.

**Complications, limitations, downsides:**

Complication 1: Controlling laser intensity takes time, patience, and practice. (None of which the general populous excels at when it comes to learning a new toy.)

Complication 2: Doesn't come with an undo button (unless you're me, of course, but if I'm fixing something, it's probably through a different power.)

Limitation 1: High energy cost. The user's energy level will factor in heavily to calculations about how long the person can keep up the power.

Limitation 2: Doesn't come with fuel, just the ability to start a fire. Sustaining is another matter.

Downside 1: Makes your eyes dry and itchy if you overuse it.

Downside 2: Cutting lasers don't stop with the thing you're cutting, so there could be potential collateral damage.

**Combat potential:** 4 of 5 stars

There are way easier—arguably less cool—ways to destroy stuff.

If we really want to have this tedious discussion about assassinations again, it's a lot easier to whip out a gun, vial of poison, or knife than ingest something that would induce laser beams to use.

**Danger level:** 5 of 5 stars

**Quick reminder:** A high score in this category is bad.

Would you hand out blow torches on street corners? Probably not, though they are admittedly relatively easy to buy. If you spend $50 at the right site, a friendly neighborhood delivery drone will have a nice, mid-range blow torch in your hands in 24 hours.

Okay, now pretend we're buying a pill that can turn anybody into a human blow torch, precision cutter, and high-powered flashlight combo. Some functions are harmless. All functions in their right context are helpful. Most are harmful if you misuse them.

**Usefulness:** 4 of 5 stars

I can see this having many applications: spelunking (exploring caves), construction, medical fields, waste processing, and so on.

I'd highly recommend using machine lasers instead of a Super's lasers for surgeries, but if you just want to burn some biohazardous waste, go for it.

**Entertainment value:** 4 of 5 stars

I'll admit I had fun. There is a certain joy to mild destructive acts. It's why people like taking a sledgehammer to drywall when they're frustrated.

**Overall rating and conclusion:** 4 of 5 stars

People aren't good at coloring inside moral lines. I think the uses if you find responsible buyers outweigh the dangers, but the Bridgeway legal team better be over and through and under the safety contracts before that product hits the shelves.

# Chapter 49

# Journal Entry 23: Backup Plan 33

What I'm doing now hasn't been tried before. It's risky and crazy, but it's also one of the slim chances we have at winning this twisted contest with Evil Grandpa.

I'm going to call it Soul Splitting, and it's part of my Backup Plan 33.

The name's a bit dramatic, but Mind Splitting sounded like a terrible headache.

Body Surfing and Head Hopping don't work for me either.

**Who are you talking to? And why am I walking up to a random house?**

*I'll explain soon. Knock and try not to scowl. You'll scare our Great-great-great—*

**Do you ever shut up?**

*The more you interrupt, the longer this will take, Jazz.*

Allow me to explain.

I'm here but not here.

The woman you'll see before you once you answer the door is my twin sister, Jasmine.

I have to leave most of me behind in my normal time at the Bridgeway headquarters to keep up appearances and monitor the situation.

The part I can spare grabs hold of the Time Travel ability and moves into my sister.

*Like a loud parasite.*

She doesn't mean that.

This wouldn't work if it went against Jasmine's will.

*I decided I don't want to die. Doesn't mean I'm happy about this.*

*Point taken. Let me finish my explanation so I can get out of your head and get you back to our timeline.*

Enclosed you'll find a laundry list of things to do.

They may not all make sense to you. They might seem stupid or trivial, but please, follow the instructions carefully.

Our lives depend on your efforts. (Not being melodramatic.)

**The laundry list:**

- Find the shiniest handful of coins you have and put them in a box. If you don't have coins on hand because they're already going out of style, get some from the bank.

- Buy small quantities of these stocks, bonds, securities, and interest-bearing accounts. (Jazz will provide you with a hand-written list because I'm not trusting mental communications across our current distances with sensitive information.)

**Note:** We can't pay you directly, but at least two of the stocks listed will see dramatic increases within the next few years as long as nobody—like us—mucks it up. That should compensate you well enough for running our errands.

- Check eBay for the following Lego sets. (See separate list.) They'll hold their value well, even opened as long as they have all the right pieces.

- Find a package of Twinkies.

That should do it.

After you gather the items, head over to the bank.

We'll be right there with you, but we have some other errands to run while you're in hunting-gathering mode.

I'll continue sharing our progress, so we'll know when to pop back to this timeline.

We're going to create one doozy of a profitable time capsule.

The trip back to our time goes smoothly, even if it does involve a half-dozen other stops. We need a clear line of succession for our fictional heir.

Jasmine plays each part of mourning child brilliantly. She doesn't need to bother with disguises.

I'd remembered to pack Manipulate Mind in my portable bag of tricks.

Since our current present is after business hours, Jasmine has to travel back one day to find a time when the bank will be open.

**Don't I need an ID or something?**

*Normally, yes, but we don't have time to get one made.*

**This from the Time Walker. Admit it. You just don't want to.**

*Jazz, we've broken about sixteen time laws today. More if our friend can find everything. What's one more abuse of Manipulate Mind?*

Technically, the stuff in the box belongs to us fair and square, but it still feels like stealing.

We get in and out as quickly as possible.

Jasmine ducks back into her former cell with me to let me transfer the normal version of Teleportation as I'd not originally thought to bring it.

Then, she moves us to an abandoned warehouse.

Though she is close enough to tap into some established neuronetwork hubs, Jasmine needs a link to make the connection. Since her ID and mine will likely send giant red flags through to Bridgeway, we believe it best to get an anonymous one.

She can't use any of my debit cards, but Dad and I are packrats.

I direct Jasmine to our collective stash of Buy-All gift cards. Nana—Dad's mom—never knew what to give us for birthdays and Christmas and whatnot, so we got gift cards. Joe always spent his, but Doug let me buy them for use of my credit and debit cards, since those were linked to game accounts—some of which he didn't want the parent units to know about.

After successfully raiding the stash, Jasmine purchases a generic link to access the neuronetwork and spends a few hours hawking our time capsule goodies.

This requires a few more backward jumps to set up the right accounts to meet the correct buyers, but it works out.

When we get the notice that you have what we need, we jump right back to do our first meet-and-greet with banking peoples and turn over the time capsule for the first time.

I can't help myself; I want to know what a Twinkie tastes like.

Since it isn't my body, I have to live vicariously through Jasmine. However, our connection lets me experience everything she tastes.

***That is the last time I let you choose the food. Ever. It was like eating a vanilla sponge.***

*It's not my favorite food, but it wasn't that bad.*

The unopened package of Twinkies sold for $63,000. (That's what happens when you have one of the last five known packages of something that went extinct over a hundred years ago. Don't worry, the buyer will never open the package. That would devalue it. Besides, I think nutritionally, those cakes are indestructible.)

Each coin sold well too. I won't go through all the numbers, but suffice to say, we make a pretty penny off the pretty pennies (and nickels, dimes, quarters, half-dollars, and weird, fake gold coin things).

Jasmine groans at that.

**Could you be any lamer?**

*Maybe. I'll keep you posted. You still have work to do.*

I don't envy Jasmine the remaining legwork. It involves lawyers and meetings and such to keep everything legal and binding.

As much money as we make on selling physical stuff, like the giant plastic containers filled with rare Lego sets, we make many times that by claiming the stocks, bonds, bank accounts, and other ancient pieces of paper.

Once every detail is quadruple checked, Jasmine returns to the cell block.

I very carefully untangle our souls and vacate the space I'd sort of hijacked in my sister's mind.

Next, I return to my cell and stop manipulating time.

Ellie shakes her head like someone who almost fell asleep and gives me a *what-did-you-do* stare.

# Chapter 50

# Journal Entry 24: Don't Mess with My Family

I don't have long to wait.

Pretty sure the Bridgeway reinforcements are just cooling their heels behind the sliding doors to this prison section. They burst in wearing riot gear, armed with police smack-down sticks and stun guns.

Two help the few Ellie had subdued.

Three move in on Ellie. She'd spent all her tricks in previous moves, so she wears her normal face.

They sweep my friend off to the side and bind her wrists with plastic flex cuffs.

I feel like a whole army of ants is hosting gymnastic competitions in my gut.

I'd created a clone to stand in for me while I impersonated Jasmine so she could run all the Time Walking errands.

She's back but invisible a foot to my left.

Before I can shut her out, Jasmine borrows a few Gifts, slips through the bars separating our cells, and modifies her looks to match the clone. I don't like where this is going but having her play me will go over better than the clone.

Clones make great body doubles, but they can't match a Mimic's skill at copying attitudes, demeanor, and actions.

When Jazz gives the signal, I flip the clone to invisible at the same time my sister makes herself visible.

Anybody paying very close attention will notice, but to the casual observer, the switch will register like them blinking. Their mind might note the difference and make an automatic adjustment to refocus, but that's about it.

Evil Grandpa's voice floats down through a speaker in the ceiling's center.

"You can drop the games, Jessica. Meet me in my penthouse office to discuss your next assignment."

**Do we tell them yet?**

*We can try.*

I had to mentally gag myself to keep from responding to Evil Grandpa, but Jasmine does a nice job channeling me.

"The only person who gets to call me Jessica is Mom, and that's only if she's got a good reason to pull the full name card."

"Are you even the real Jessica?" asks Evil Grandpa.

"What kind of a stupid question is that?" Jasmine fires the question with appropriate indignation.

"Inconclusive, sir." The guard who pipes up holds a scanner of some sort. He aims it first at Jazz and then at me. "Their vitals and brainwaves are identical. That shouldn't be possible."

*Oh, hello, Bob. This seems like a step down for you.*

I send an electronic pulse to mess with the man's machine and wrap his mind in the mental equivalent of mufflers.

While I'm at it, I molecularly destabilize the cell bars and inform all relevant parties of the changes.

Bob frowns down at the machine and tucks it away. He steps back from the bars like they will up and bite him if he gets too close.

"Why do you care?" I try to match Jasmine's level of disdain, but I think my efforts fall short.

"Because I need to discuss something with Jessica." Evil Grandpa sounds like he is spending his last ounce of patience.

"So, speak." The order comes from both Jazz and me.

It's weird using her voice and hearing my voice from her.

***Do you want to go see what he wants or should I?***

*Not eager to blunder into another trap. Just wait.*

"It's sensitive, and I'm not at liberty to speak openly about it. You either comply or lose your friend."

The Bridgeway goon squad brings Ellie to a position with a clear line of sight to both cells. They force her to kneel and make sure we get a good look at the nightsticks and stun guns.

Without better weapons, the best they can do is hurt Ellie, but I am not eager to see what their twisted minds will conjure next.

***Escalating kind of quickly here, Jess. Make a call.***

*Tell them. I'm spreading the word elsewhere, but it will take a while to trickle down.*

***We don't have a while!***

Jasmine clears her throat and speaks as evenly as she can.

"Everybody back off. It doesn't matter who's who. We own this company. That means, you work for us."

Nobody moves or responds.

I cringe internally. That is about the worst possible outcome, and it means we still have major problems.

"They don't work for Bridgeway," says Evil Grandpa. "They're my private security force. I took measures a few weeks ago when the lawyers started buzzing about a secret buyer approaching the major shareholders."

I'll have to add *paranoid* to Evil Grandpa's list of attributes.

His first statement offers me hope, but I will have to stall like a champ.

*Get them to safety. I'll go see what he wants.*

**Be careful. It's still probably a trap.**

*Then, you'll get to play superhero twice today.*

I modify my features back to the current look.

Jasmine does the same.

"Are you coming?" demands Evil Grandpa.

"Yes, but I can't work to my fullest under these conditions," I say calmly.

My statement signals my family to act.

Joe uses his Gifts on the guys threatening Ellie.

Their weapons turned to dust, and their boots stick to the floor as parts change into glue.

To keep Ellie from choking on the dust, I conjure a large fishbowl around her head and give her Dad's Gift for breathing underwater.

The oddity distracts the non-Bridgeway goons long enough for Doug to bust out of his cell and land a few solid punches.

Mom emerges from her cell and uses Superspeed to sweep Ellie aside out of the brawl zone.

One of the guys Ellie had tangled with earlier tries to re-enter the fray, but Leslie trips him. Next, Dad kicks the man before he can get up.

Mom free Ellie's hands.

Dad goes to help Doug, but he doesn't need much help because the encumbered state of the security guys leaves them at a distinct disadvantage.

Moral of the story. Don't mess with my family.

I drop the fishbowl from Ellie's head, let Dad's power return to him, and Transport everybody I care about into Jasmine's cell.

It's a tight squeeze, but they don't have to stay there long.

Jasmine nods good luck and farewell and grab Joe's left hand and Doug's right arm.

Everybody holds onto each other.

They disappear.

A stifling silence settles quickly.

I try not to think about the possibility of Jasmine double crossing me, but she doesn't exactly have the best track record on that score.

"All right, I'm alone. Let's talk," I announce.

I feel a presence appear next to me.

*No, you're not. It's my turn to hitch a ride.*

*What about Ellie and the family?*

*They insisted I come back.*

I welcome Jasmine back and open a space in my mind for her to occupy.

"Excellent. We'll be waiting."

The use of *we'll* does not bode well, but I am more than ready to get some answers.

# Chapter 51

# Superpower Review 24: Electrical Manipulation (Control Electricity)

**Background and notes:**

I've probably talked your ear off about the issues surrounding power naming.

Often, I'll title the reviews with the officially recognized term, as determined by the Superpower Control Council, then also list the non-stuffy version too. That's the version that pops up in conversation if you ask a Normie what kind of superpower they'd like to have.

Most people will say they'd like to control electricity.

Very few people will say, "I would like the power of Electrical Manipulation." (Yes, I said that with my nose suitably in the air. I'd wager some of you did too.)

This power came up earlier when I had that violent disagreement with my sister. She'd wanted the zappy form of controlling electricity, and I gave her the mess-with-lights-and-electrical-outlets version.

**Explanation of the power:**

Like Lightning Manipulation, this power encompasses whatever it takes to make, stop, or control electricity.

**Clarification:** Lightning is a form of electricity. So, I guess you could say that everything involving Lightning Manipulation is just a subset of Electrical Manipulation.

**What is electricity?**

It's one of the most useful forms of energy.

**Where does electricity come from?**

Under normal circumstances, you can get it by harnessing other kinds of energy such as coal, nuclear power, and so on.

If you're a Super who happens to have this Gift, then you can generate it. I suppose you could also claim this is a form of Molecule Manipulation, but it's an important enough application to warrant separate consideration.

**Electrical Manipulation usually involves one of the following:**

- Making electricity

- Directing electricity

- Dampening or stopping the flow of electricity

**Main applications:**

- Mess with existing electrical applications – the Super becomes a royal nuisance; i.e., turn lights on or off, blow out appliances

- Generate electricity – the Super becomes a miniature electricity-making machine (I say little because people don't compare to nuclear power plants.)

- Store electrical energy – the Super becomes a big human battery

- Unload a lot of electricity at once – the Super becomes a big stun gun

**Demonstrations:**

Teleported to a few different locations to show off various applications.

- Demo 1: First stop was at a remote campsite in North Dakota. Recharged all the electronic devices for a family. (Used a different Gift to repair the busted generator that was cramping their camping style.)

- Demo 2: Went to the lousiest grid I could find and overloaded it.

- Demo 3: After breaking the existing system, I increased my electrical flow so service wouldn't be interrupted for too long.

- Demo 4: I tapped into the memory of my physical altercation with Jasmine and registered it as my 4$^{th}$ demonstration.

**What happened:**

- Demo 1: I passed myself off as someone good with machines. Part of the difficulty of charging certain devices is not burning their components to useless slabs.

**Drinking water analogy:** There's such a thing as too much of a good thing. Think of electricity like drinking from a garden hose. Semi-useless fact of the day: water pressure varies by the length and diameter of your hose.

You could drink from a firehose, but it's highly not recommended.

Because me spouting (lousy pun unintended) waterflow rates in pounds per square inch would mean exactly nothing, I'm going to stick with generalizations.

- Garden hose – nice and gentle.

- Fire hose – usually fast enough to knock you over.

- Demo 2: I supervised the necessary repairs the system should have had about forty years ago. (The city council kept putting it off in favor of more *important* projects, like updating the nameplates for their office doors.)

- Demo 3: As with any project, this got much bigger very quickly. During repairs, I kept up the energy flow myself. I needed several powers to make it work without inadvertently burning out.

**More details:** I cloned myself a few hundred times and had half eating power bars and the other half working. (The bean counters at Bridgeway are going to get some hefty power bar bills shortly, but hey, now we know you can run a city for a few hours using this Gift and 472 power bars.)

- Demo 4: For the record, I don't recommend using Electrical Manipulation to zap people into unconsciousness.

**Expectations and reality:**

Expectation 1: It's the safest way to replace nuclear power.

Reality 1: Maybe true, but it's not practical because not enough Supers have the Gift.

Expectation 2: There's just an on/off setting.

Reality 2: The Gift usually handles the necessary physics calculations to make sure you're using the right amount of energy for the application. However, these can be overridden. So, it's a lot more complicated than on and off.

Expectation 3: It's a destructive Gift.

Reality 3: There are good applications. Power is the heart of this Gift. It's often easier to focus on the stopping power because that's the more visible aspect. Maintaining something that is already in place isn't exactly something people want to advertise.

Expectation 4: Every manifestation of the Gift is the same.

Reality 4: Some Supers love to create electricity and show off. Others concentrate on the destructive applications.

**Complications, limitations, downsides:**

Complication 1: It's not exactly a fun Gift to employ. It's a lot of work (literally, figuratively, metaphorically, philosophically).

Complication 2: I meant the end of the previous statement facetiously, but there's some truth to it. Forcing Supers to replace nuclear power is doable if and only if you're willing to cross about a thousand moral lines.

Limitation 1: Supers can generate energy, but they're still going to be limited by personal energy levels. Nearly any form of energy is going to involve taking it from one source and repurposing it.

Limitation 2: Physical distance is still going to be a factor. A Super can generate electricity, but it would still need a means to travel from wherever that person happened to be located to wherever you'd like the electricity to show up.

Downside 1: As with many Gifts, it's a one-way trip. You can't undo what you did. (I can, but I'm using other Gifts in those cases.)

Downside 2: Unless the Super has a lot of practice, they're going to be guessing at the amounts needed for each task.

**Combat potential:** 4 of 5 stars

Darkness can be psychologically difficult to deal with. Humanity has advanced far, but we're still dangerously dependent on creature comforts, including dozens of things that use electricity.

Soldiers tend to be a heartier lot than others but depriving people of light for an extended period of time can weigh upon them.

Bess tells me I need to be clearer.

The Gift has combat potential because you can scare people, leave them in the dark, or directly kill them by overloading their systems with too much energy.

**Danger level:**

To others: super high

I downplayed the destructive potential inherent to expectation 3, but that doesn't change the fact that it's still there.

To the user: medium to low

**Usefulness:** 4.5 of 5 stars

Responsible use of the Gift is possible.

The power comes with a deep understanding of how electricity works, so the person wielding such an ability would make an excellent consultant for power companies.

**Entertainment value:** 2 of 5 Stars

Overloading things can be exciting, but the power as a whole is pretty far down on the flashy fun Gifts list.

**Overall rating and conclusion:** 4-ish of 5 stars (don't try to make the math work)

This could go either way. It shouldn't be marketed as a fun Gift, but if you want to take some pressure off the existing grids, you could try to dole it out responsibly.

It would help if individuals could answer the power needs of their own homes. (I mean more than solar panels or something.)

I can also see it being included in emergency kits.

Cautious use recommended.

# Chapter 52

# Superpower Review 25: Illusions

**Background and notes:**

Illusions fall under Telepathic Gifts, but like Lightning Manipulation being under Electrical Manipulation, Illusions is important enough to warrant its own discussion.

There's a fine balance between attention to detail and artistic license when it comes to illusions.

It's a handy power to have around for many reasons.

The best illusions weave several powers together to create a specific impression within the target, including Manipulate Emotions.

**Explanation of the power:**

On the surface, Illusions are visual lies. That may sound harsh because the word *lies* comes packed with some serious negative connotations.

**Lies aside:** Even that definition can get tricky. It can be as concrete as true or false or as complicated as partial truths, lies of omission, and kind lies.

If you dive deeper, illusions involve the creation of images and impressions within the mind of another. That's why it's a subset of Gifts given to a Minder or a Telepathist. (I prefer to call them Head Talkers, but that is purely a personal preference.)

The list of applications could stretch on a very long time, even if you focus on generalizations.

**Sample applications:**

- Impersonate people – Mimicry is better for this, but if you only need a quick glimpse, it should be fine.

- Recreate crime scenes – This one isn't widespread yet because there aren't many police forces who specialize in crimes dealing with superpowers. The SCC (Superpower Control Council) has done a decent job keeping things quiet.

- Recreate beautiful locations – Companies already do a fine job of providing stellar visual tours. Some have even mastered the correct chemicals to release for certain smells, but a Gifted Head Talker can still create a more realistic illusion.

**Legal note:** The Superpower Control Council has determined that illusions are temporary enough—and hard enough to regulate—to fall outside the realms of copyrights.

If you want to get completely stuffy about it, illusions fall under a 5-level system. That's why you might hear someone referred to as an L1 – I. It stands for Level 1 Illusionist.

- Level 1 – visual only; this is most common; everybody with the Gift can handle Level 1 work

- Level 2 – visual and audio only; also very common

- Level 3 – visual, audio, olfactory; less common

- Level 4 – visual, audio, olfactory, tactile; rare

- Level 5 – all five senses plus internal bonuses

**Note:** I don't think taste is a popular illusion request, but emotions are hugely popular. It's one thing to experience something and react naturally and another to have the emotions amplified.

The level system gets complicated because there's a hierarchy of skills here too: novice, competent, expert, and master. Beyond that, you can add adjectives in front of these.

**Second note:** You don't have to tap all senses for an illusion.

**How does the Gift work?**

**Short answer:** It taps into various parts of the brain to recreate images, sounds, sensations, and feelings without the external part. (**Translation:** You can see an apple without there being an apple.)

**Long-winded answer:** I'm going to get science-y for a moment. Think of the brain like a musical instrument.

Different parts of the brain handle distinct tasks.

Some parts control stuff that should always be happening like breathing and pumping blood and such.

Illusions cover any Gift that will create an impression that's not real.

We could get into a deep debate over illusions being *real*. The emotional reactions are often real, so that argument has some valid points, but I don't have time to further dissect the point.

The person controlling the illusion needs to find the right controls then paint a picture within the target's mind.

**Demonstrations (and what they involved):**

Without other living beings, this Gift is kind of useless. Early in my time here at Bridgeway, I'd taken half a day to explore. I needed to map the facility in case things got dangerous anyway. The memories are still fresh enough to provide accurate recordings.

- Demo 1: A scientist was thinking about her recently deceased husband. I used some of her memories to recreate him for a brief

time. I kept this one to audio and visual only. She had enough
emotions to deal with.

- Demo 2: A kid was trying to comprehend some disgusting
  geometry concepts. We visited a few famous places around the
  world to study their geometry and how it applies to their
  structural function. Got sight and sound, but I steered clear of
  taste and smell. We went to some dirty places.

- Demo 3: A child wanted to go on a space adventure, so I made
  it happen. Sight, sound, and a muted feeling of cold or hot as
  required.

- Demo 4: A security guard was bored, so I gave him some
  phantoms to chase.

**Expectations and reality:**

Expectation 1: An illusion can be visual only.

Reality 1: A skilled Telepath can tap into all senses.

Expectation 2: Illusions always have a visual element.

Reality 2: Visual illusions are the poster child for the Gift, but there are
less popular applications involving only the other senses.

Expectation 3: All brains are the same to work with.

Reality 3: The stuff might be located in the same place, but every brain
feels unique. Think of it like cars, even luxury hovering cars have stuff
located about the same, but the interiors can still feel very different.

Same for house designs. Whether a hundred square feet or a hundred
thousand square feet, a house tends to have one or more entrances and an
appropriate number of windows. Style and size varies greatly.

**Complication, limitations, downside:**

Complication: Not every brain is equal. You can only work with what
you're given.

For the record, that's not me being mean. I'm stating facts.

Some people have very vivid imaginations. Those tend to be more fun to create illusions for because their imagination takes your suggestions and runs in its own direction.

There are people who have difficulty visualizing anything within their mind. That makes it easier for the illusionist to get away with some sketchy details, but it also makes it more difficult to know if your ideas are matching theirs because there's less in the memory banks to compare to.

Limitation 1: The normal version of illusions does not fool electronics. There is nothing to see since the power affects minds.

Limitation 2: You guessed it. High energy cost.

Downside: You can't always control how people are going to react to an illusion. One person might laugh at a ghastly specter, and another's going to have a heart attack.

**Combat potential:** 4 of 5 stars

The energy cost limitation will kick in and keep this from being the perfect combat Gift.

Level 1 things like decoy targets for the enemy would cost much less than direct attacks against enemy soldiers, but a few hundred well-directed bullets would be just as effective and a whole heap cheaper.

**Danger level:** 5 of 5 stars

The immediate example is creating an illusion to cause an accident, but misuse potential goes much deeper.

To use the Gift, you need to access people's brains. If you had a strong enough dose of the Gift plus zero scruples, you could potentially walk around suppressing people's will to breathe.

**Usefulness:** 3.5 of 5 stars

These are the uses I can see:

- Comfort – even this can go wrong because the illusion eventually ends; while that would be good from a business standpoint, we don't want a bunch of addicts getting ahold of it.

- Deception

- Entertainment

Use is in the eye of the beholder. If somebody wants to mess with another person's head, this would be highly useful.

**Entertainment value:** 3.5 of 5 stars

There's great business potential for a skilled illusionist. However, the cost to manufacture something that would give the user Level 3 illusion skills or above would likely make it unprofitable.

A brew aimed at Level 1 detailed picture illusions could hold its own with sales.

**Overall rating and conclusion:** 3.75ish of 5 stars

Mass producing Level 1 versions of this would likely invite lots of trouble.

Some people can't handle alcohol responsibly. Call me cynical, but I don't think teaching people to muck with others' minds sounds advisable.

# Chapter 53

# Journal Entry 25: A Lot of Uncles

I teleport directly to the center of Evil Grandpa's penthouse office. It looks like a traditional office in that it has a large desk, imposing chair, and two guest chairs.

That's where the similarities end.

Next to the desk sits a fancy hospital bed surrounded by three machines.

A figure lies on the bed, but I can't see the face from my current angle. Besides, two men in white lab coats stand at the foot of the bed, blocking most of the view. Not sure if they are busy or just trying to look busy.

To my left springs a sizable room that looks like a children's daycare center. It's a riot of loud primary colors and toys that look like they want to teach you something in an obnoxious, singsong voice.

I don't see or hear any children, but certain sections have been cordoned off with movable screens.

To my right is a room about the same size as the daycare center, but instead of bright colors, the room boasts a lot of grays and whites and gives off strong mad science vibes.

The floor-to-ceiling window behind the hospital bed turns opaque and holds the image of a young version of Evil Grandpa. If I had to guess, I would place his age at mid-thirties.

"There's a contract on my desk. Sign it."

I expect the words to come from the figure on the wall, but instead, the voice comes from the form on the bed. More specifically, the command comes from surround sound speakers built into the walls and ceiling. The quality tells me his strength won't last much longer.

*Nice to see you too.*

The figures standing at the end of the bed shift, one moving left and the other moving right. This gives me a clear view of Evil Grandpa, presumably in the fading flesh. This version looks three decades older than the one I'd seen inside Mom's mind.

I'm not the greatest at math, but even I can tell the wear and tear on the man's body goes further than normal aging.

Activating some Healing Gifts, I scan for problems. The initial report is grim. He has several inoperable brain tumors.

The Gift continues to search for ways to shrink the tumors to a point they can be safely removed.

"Stop her!"

One of the men taps something into a handheld device.

A mental shield slams into place, breaking my connection.

The main entrance opens behind me, letting the security team enter. The twelve men divide themselves, five left, five right, and two behind me. Most bear the standard Bridgeway goon squad weapons: nightsticks and stun guns. The two behind me have dart guns.

I track them through their clomping footsteps and buzzing brain activity.

The thought of an audience annoys me, but I ignore the newcomers.

*Why doesn't Evil Grandpa want to be healed?*

To my surprise, Jasmine answers.

***Because he believes the tumors are helping him think. He's been working on mind transfer technology for several years, and he believes he is close to a breakthrough.***

My sister's calm explanation gives me a bad feeling.

*Is he nearing a breakthrough?*

***I don't know. Maybe.***

The middle window pane turns dark. Soon, the image of a picturesque lakeside cabin forms. A large, four-person couch holds Dad, Mom, Joe, and Leslie. Doug and Ellie sit on the floor in front of the couch.

It would be a lovely family moment except for the blood running down Dad's face.

Mom wears deluxe restraints.

Joe is unconscious, and Leslie has a puffy black eye.

Ellie's head rests on my younger brother's right shoulder. She stares miserably at the recording device. Doug wears a sensitive shock collar and about a dozen zip ties around his wrists.

My heart lurches.

*This again? Jazz, you need to be less predictable.*

***Don't pretend you knew.***

*I didn't know. I just prepared for the worst.*

***Liar.***

I don't respond to her.

Oblivious to my side conversation with Jasmine, Evil Grandpa presents his case.

"I'm not asking much of you, Jessica. I need samples for my experiments. My clones and progeny ... lack your powers." After an awkward pause, he continues, "Show her."

The two men at the end of the fancy hospital bed turn around.

*Young men.*

Their facial features and bodies say teenager.

***Children.***

Jazz throws in the correction.

A brief touch upon their minds confirms as much. They might look like serious sixteen-year-olds, but their minds have that bright-spot innocence inherent in children.

The left clone dashes around the room and back to his spot in the blink of an eye. The right clone goes over to the desk, lifts it up, and balances it on one hand.

Demonstration over, the young man returns to his post at the end of the bed.

A door opens and footsteps announce three new arrivals.

*Five.*

Brainwave activity confirms the number.

The guards shift to let three boys approach. The older three bear enough features similar to Evil Grandpa to declare them clones.

The two smallest boys look slightly different.

An analysis of a few DNA strands shows me they aren't clones of Evil Grandpa.

I don't have my mother handy to do a DNA comparison, but I pull an image of her from the archives I'd raided during my earlier investigation. The youngest boys have enough similar facial features to her childhood form to confirm the connection.

*That's a lot of uncles ... and great uncles.*

Though not totally clear on the legalities of true clone status, I consider the teenage clones of Evil Grandpa to be his brothers. That makes them my mother's uncles. Hence, me assigning them great uncle status.

Circumstantial evidence says the two boys being carried are likely genetic brothers of my mother. That makes them my uncles.

My mind does these calculations in about two seconds.

*Weird.*

"You're going to help me fix this," says Evil Grandpa's portrait. This version of his voice is far stronger than the bedridden one.

I tense at his tone.

"There's nothing to fix." Lacking something better to do with my arms, I cross them. "They're fine."

I scan each child to make sure the statement holds truth.

It does.

Each child is perfectly healthy. One is a Shapeshifter, two can control elements, one has Telepathic Gifts, and the youngest will likely gain the ability to fly.

"They have multiple Gifts, but they can't access them. In addition to physical samples, you're going to help them unlock their true potential."

"If you asked nicely, I'd consider the training part, but this—" I stop speaking and rotate my pointer finger in a circle, indicating the dozen grim-faced guards. "Does not qualify as *asking nicely*."

Despite the defiance, the scientific problem intrigues me. I don't sense any other Gifts on my first pass of the Superspeed clone, but his body temperature is hotter than mine. The chemicals responsible for that have to do with enhancing growth.

*Stopping the growth treatments might help.*

**Thanks. I'll pass the suggestion along.**

*You do that.*

**You can't stall forever, Jess. Just make this easy on everybody and cooperate.**

"We can do the sample gathering with or without you being conscious, but I'd prefer not to taint the samples." Evil Grandpa's tone conveys how much of an inconvenience it would be to have to get samples from a drugged version of me.

Not eager to be drugged anyway, I scan people's surface thoughts for their least favorite creature.

Then, as Evil Grandpa loses patience and orders the two men with dart guns to fire on me, I do some quality illusion and shapeshifting work and charge.

# Chapter 54

# Journal Entry 26: Mirror Gift

I don't like being a squirrel. Just going to throw that out into the universe and hope I never have occasion to experience that again.

I choose squirrel as one of the forms because I need the mass to be around 650 grams, and they have better danger sense than chinchillas. On average, chinchillas are a hair heavier than squirrels.

That *better danger sense* is what makes squirrel form annoying. The heartrate in danger (about 415 beats per minute) is enough to leave one with a nervous tic.

Without going into exactly how much mass I need to distribute because nobody needs to know that information, I'll just say I form a few hundred spiders, a dozen cockroaches, four snakes, nineteen bats, and a squirrel.

I don't have time to customize a creature for each guard, so I go with generalizations. I need fast and agile or terrifying.

Some of the Bridgeway goons have weirdly specific fears anyway.

One guard fears sharks, so I create an illusion to cover that one. A) Because I don't have the mass to spare for the task. B) Because I don't want to deal with the logistics of keeping a shark version of me alive out of water.

The only ones I don't seek to terrify are the youngest two of the uncles crew. For them, I make a puppy illusion. They squirm enough to be set down and follow the puppy illusion to an empty corner of the lab to hide.

The middle three of the uncles get a normal, civilized instruction to back away. Two listen, one does not. The ungrateful little brat takes it upon himself to smash as many of my spider forms as possible.

I change a few of the dead spiders into wasps to bother the kid until he backs off.

My main goal is avoiding the knockout drugs coating the darts. The two I know about have already fired, but I disintegrate the triggers to prevent them from being a future threat in this encounter.

The discussion escalated from revelations to actionable threats crazy fast.

A couple of Spider-Me versions get squished in the chaos. The sensation is similar to something landing on my foot, only the feeling manifests wherever on my body those molecules originate.

The combined feeling is similar to being pummeled with pebbles. It stings but doesn't do any lasting damage.

As the spider forms die, I let the mass return but turn incorporeal.

I suppose I could have gone with Incorporeality as an opening move, but I had been feeling closed in anyway.

The creatures and the illusions bring me some breathing room.

As you can imagine, the noise level is significant. I might have added a few snake hisses and spider purrs to the mix. Yeah, spiders purr, that's new to me too. Fun fact, in most animal forms, you can do whatever that animal does.

It hardly matters.

I get drown out by cursing, shouting, and screaming men.

**Jess, stop.**

Jasmine's command comes paired with an emotional whammy that flattens me. I reform in my normal body and drop to my hands and knees. It's that or outright pull a proper faint, and I really want to stay conscious.

I'd not thought to remove Jasmine's access to Emotional Manipulation, and it wouldn't have mattered anyway. Her Mimic abilities would let her mirror the Gift if anybody near her had it.

In a building housing a few thousand people that wouldn't be too hard to find.

People tend to think of Emotional Manipulation in terms of what it can suppress, but you can dial feelings up as much as down.

In this case, Jazz takes everything in me that can channel a sense of tiredness and throws them into overdrive.

She stops pressing a second later, about the time my defenses kick her out of my head.

Jasmine must have found somebody nearby with Teleportation because she uses it to bring her body to Evil Grandpa's penthouse office.

That part makes sense as most of the intriguing stuff was happening here.

Bringing our mother with her does not make sense.

*You are really starting to tick me off.*

**Welcome to my world.**

*What'd I ever do to you?*

**You don't have to do anything. You are the problem.**

The statement hurts more than it should, and I don't think the gut reaction has anything to do with Emotional Manipulation.

This blind hatred thing is new territory for me.

My brother, Joe, might have hated me for a time, especially those middle school years when I took my annoying kid sister duties seriously.

And Doug probably resented me for having way more freedom due to the age difference.

Both are perfectly acceptable reasons for sibling rivalry.

We've traded the usual number of bruises and semi-vicious pranks over the years.

As a sibling, Jasmine has been in my life for a matter of hours, and it's like some inner demon drives her to make up for twenty-plus years of missing petty grievances with hefty interest.

Mom still wears the criminal restraints. Foot manacles attach her feet together with enough chain to let her stand and walk sort of normally, but they will keep her from running. Another chain runs up from the foot chain to wrist bindings that hold Mom's hands near her waist.

Instinctively, I give Mom Impervious Skin, so she will have better protection in case one of the slightly traumatized guards gets it in his head to shoot her.

That is my second major mistake.

Combined with the first mistake of trusting Jasmine after a couple of key betrayals, I'm sort of surprised I live long enough to share the tale.

Partly a perk of Evil Grandpa really wanting something from me, I guess.

The other part isn't luck.

A benefit of being betrayed multiple times is a healthy sense of paranoia.

Normally, I would give away my only copy of a Gift and get it back when it has served its purpose, but this time, I activate Impervious Skin as a Mirror Gift.

Ironically, it's something Mimics do.

They see a Gift they want, copy the power, and use it.

I go the other way.

I saw one of my Gifts I wanted to use, so I activated it, and then, bestowed a copy of the same power on another.

That's why the needle Jasmine stabs into my back breaks.

You'd think that would be the end of the horrible situation, but I keep forgetting that bad guys get to break moral rules of engagement.

The unwritten but should-be-binding rules say you don't harm puppies or children.

During those brief moments while I ensure that Mom and I will be safe, one of the Evil Grandpa clones snatches up one my two-year-old uncles and places a blade an inch from his neck.

Mom draws a sharp breath and whispers one word.

"Joe!"

# Chapter 55

# Superpower Review 26: Emotional Manipulation

**Background and notes:**

Can't say I've given much thought to Emotional Manipulation as anything more than a way to keep it together during stressful situations.

Having recently been on the wrong end of the Gift being used as a weapon, I guess I can attest to it being such. Can't say I'm comfortable with the thought of treating it as a weapon, but people do a lot of things they never considered when pressed.

**Explanation of the power (State the Obvious):**

Emotional Manipulation encompasses everything related to changing emotions as desired. The change can involve suppression or amplification.

Usually, only one emotion is controlled at a time, but it is possible to tug on related emotions.

**Common emotions to control:**

- Fear, worry, anxiety

- Horror, disgust

- Devotion, admiration, awe, love, lust

- Anger, rage

- Passion, will

- Surety, confusion, embarrassment

- Contentment, calm

- Joy, satisfaction, amusement

- Intrigue, interest

- Sadness

- Surprise

- Alertness

**How it works:**
- Suppression – dialing an emotion down; making the target feel less of something

- Amplification – dialing an emotion up; making the target get a stronger dose of the emotion, whatever it may be

Emotions can't be simultaneously moved in opposite directions. Think of the emotions being on the same sliding scale, such as joy being on one end and sadness on the other. If I enhance your joy, I'm simultaneously going to be suppressing your sense of sadness.

Trying to do both would have no effect or slight effect, depending on which was being amplified to a greater extent or suppressed to a lesser extent.

**Possible targets:**

Listed naturally in order of most likely to least likely.

- Self

- One other

- Two others

- More than two others

- A crowd

**Proximity:**

Tends to be important. The closer the target is to the caster, the stronger the effects.

Think of emotions like threads that can be tugged on. They're a jumbled mess inside most people. Identifying the emotional threads to pull is a natural part of the Gift.

**Duration:**

The effects last as long as there is energy behind the Gift. The caster can also willingly end the manipulation at any point.

**Demonstrations:**

- Demo 1: Jasmine threw most of my emotions that dealt with being alert and pulled them as far down as they'd go.

- Demo 2: I made a montage of several recent instances of using the Gift to level my emotions so I could think clearly.

- Demos 3-12: I systematically worked my way up from one target to ten. I targeted the same emotion, in this case joy.

- Demos 13-15: I went to a rock concert and tried calming batches of 50, 100, and 200 people.

**What happened:**

- Demo 1: I have better defense mechanisms than many people, but the move still stopped me in my tracks for a bit.

- Demo 2: Putting this together helped me learn a little about the Gift. I thought the panic zeroing thing was a one and done button, but it's more like pulling on a lever and holding it in place.

- Demos 3-12: Proceeded as expected.

- Demos 13-15: I managed to calm the chosen cohort, but the effects didn't last long. I wasn't going to waste my time getting a headache over trying to dampen their excitement. There wouldn't have been much point to that. I'd already proven to myself it could be done.

**Expectations and reality:**

Expectation 1: It's all or nothing.

Reality 1: While turning an emotion completely on or off is often what happens, it's not the only thing that can happen.

Expectation 2: The energy costs are always going to be the same.

**Aside:** This is true for many Gifts that only have an active or dormant state. Take Flight, for example. Unless you intend to do it under extreme conditions, the energy cost should be predictable based on your mass and altitude conditions.

Reality 2: The target's current emotion may deepen or offset the energy cost. Let's return to the sliding scale analogy.

If the marker running between sadness and joy is already on the side that favors joy, it should cost less to move it completely over to maxed out joy.

Conversely, it would cost me more to drag the marker down to deep sadness because I have to cover the ground between joy and neutral before making headway on my quest to make this person sad.

It helps to work with emotions already activated.

Expectation 3: It would be amazing therapy.

Reality 3: It might be all right for temporary relief, but the false feeling goes away whenever the Super stops activating the Gift. You'd have to deal with the issue's root to cure something.

**Complications and downsides:**

Complication 1: Subtle manipulations can be resisted.

Complication 2: The way the Gift works gets complicated because I suspect there are multiple ways or mechanisms for the power to be activated.

Being the curious soul that I am, I found a few people with the Gift and asked a bunch of nosy questions. Chief among these was: describe what it feels like to use your power.

I got every analogy from pushing buttons to sliding levers to twisting dials to opening vials of chemicals to singing songs that evoked the right emotion.

Complication 3: Atmosphere can interfere with the work. This is the crux of the difficulty I had calming the crowds at the rock concert.

Complication 4: Results can be unpredictable. People have some automatic self-defense mechanisms that kick in. How quickly, depends on the person.

Downside 1: It's easy to overuse. Unless one practices a lot, they won't have a great handle on how much they can safely use the Gift without hitting a burnout level.

Downside 2: Emotional Manipulation comes paired with strong empathy. The Super may be forced to actively block that aspect of their Gift to maintain their own peace of mind.

**Combat potential:** 4.5 of 5 stars

Warfare has largely moved away from many soldiers clashing on a chosen battlefield. In some cases avatars, robots, and enhanced humans have replaced normal recruits. However, humans are still the common factor.

If you can manipulate the emotions of soldiers at key points, you can make them reckless or ineffective.

**Danger level:** 4 of 5 stars

I suppose the danger to self depends on how recklessly the Super uses the Gift. It is sort of like a muscle in that it can be strengthened over time through frequent practice. That said, it's also possible to overuse the Gift. Burnout for this power most often shows up as a listless state.

Danger to others is very high. It's one of the easiest powers to abuse. Emotions often control actions or inaction.

If you suppress somebody's will to open their eyes and shut down their danger sense, you could potentially force them to walk into a busy street.

**Usefulness:** 4 of 5 stars

Testing this Gift has reminded me that even negative uses of something count.

It's probably easier to use this power for more evil-minded purposes than good ones.

**Entertainment value:** 2 of 5 stars

Unless someone genuinely enjoys messing with other people, I don't see it having high entertainment value.

I suppose you could view it like a recreational drug for personal use. It could act as an upper or a downer.

**Overall rating and conclusion:** 3 of 5 stars

My sister proved it could be handy to have in a fight, but I'm going to go out on a limb here and assume most people aren't looking to get into a fight.

The same lack of predictability that plagues those who come by the Gift naturally will likely hold true for those given a temporary version of the power.

If the Gift could be limited to only changing one's own emotions, it may have some value as a treatment for severe depression, but I'm not sure how far along the Bridgeway scientists are with unlocking an artificial version of this.

I don't recommend wide public distribution of Emotional Manipulation.

# Chapter 56

# Superpower Review 27: Gravity Manipulation

**Background and notes:**

Manipulation sounds like it only has to do with bending the thing to one's will, but as with Lightning Manipulation, the Gravity Manipulation Gift encompasses several subpowers.

I don't always mention every subpower that goes along with a Gift. For example, Superspeed comes paired with the ability to keep one's clothes on and intact despite traveling at speeds that should rip them off your body and tear them to shreds or leave them 900 miles behind you.

**How can this be?**

**Short answer:** Magic.

**Slightly longer answer:** Much like working your current clothes into your shapeshifted forms, it's just a part of the Gift.

Technically, Flight is a subset of Gravity Manipulation, but it's cool enough to have garnered its own fans.

My point is that sometimes what makes it into a discussion comes down to marketing. The word *gravity* conjures up a gut disgusted feeling from many people due it its association with physics.

**Explanation of the power:**

Gravity's definition considers any two objects in the universe, but I'm going to narrow that down to Earth, since that's really what we're interested in here.

**Overly simplified version:** Normal gravity is created by the attractive force that exists between two things with mass. Earth has mass. I have mass. Still not telling you how much mass but suffice to say it's way less than Earth. Therefore, I get pulled toward the center of the Earth.

The other factor that needs to be considered is distance. The closer the distance, the stronger the pull between the two objects.

Manipulating Gravity can be accomplished by tricking the Earth into disregarding one or the other of these two factors.

**Spoiler alert:** Most people with the Gift mess with the mass not the distance. It's a lot easier to fake the Mass Manipulation part by temporarily sticking some of the object into the 4$^{th}$ dimension than it is to actually change the object's mass. Different Gift. Different discussion.

**Note:** On the surface, this Gift can be mistaken for controlling people or objects because that's what it looks like.

**The subpowers:**

- Increase gravity's effects

- Decrease gravity's effects

- Alter gravity's effects

We usually think about how this Gift affects a complete body, but the subtle effects can be more devastating.

**Demonstrations:**

**Note:** No demonstrations were done on living beings. Many watermelons sacrificed themselves for the cause.

- Demo Set 1: I decreased gravity's effect on a watermelon.

- Demo Set 2: I increased gravity's effect on a watermelon.

- Demo Set 3: I altered gravity's effect on a watermelon such that it traveled through a makeshift maze.

**What happened:**

**Clarification:** I called them Demo Sets this time because I had a little too much fun playing with watermelons. They make fantastic splatting sounds. Yes, I cleaned up the old-fashioned way afterwards. (The other options would have involved Time Manipulation or Alter Reality.)

- Demo Set 1: I made a watermelon fly. The first eight experiments I must have done it too fast because they struck the ceiling like canon balls.

- Demo Set 2: I made a mess. Might have cracked the floor before the watermelon imploded and spilled its pink guts everywhere.

- Demo Set 3: Once I got the hang of it, I enjoyed leading a merry band of watermelons around the room. The watermelon probably had less fun because it took me a few tries to perfect the control. I changed gravity's effects to draw watermelon left, right, forward, or backward.

**Expectations and reality:**

Expectation 1: The Gift only has an on/off setting.

Reality 1: Like many Gifts, there are degrees to this one. I've got 134 bruised and busted watermelons that agree with that statement. Dropped the salvageable ones off in a remote village in Senegal.

Expectation 2: It takes a lot of energy.

Reality 2: Not from the caster. It's like playing with valves that control the flow of water. The Earth's still responsible for normal gravity. You're mostly messing with how it affects a target.

Expectation 3: Bigger objects are harder to move through gravity manipulation.

Reality 3: To a point, I'd argue that it's easier to move larger objects through this Gift. People often like dealing with things they know. If I know a car has a mass of 1800 kilograms, then I can calculate how much mass needs to be disregarded to lessen gravity's effect effectively.

**Complications, Limitations, Downsides:**

Complication 1: Using it effectively requires some experimentation. How much is too much has enough variation to warrant experimentation. What will lift one person and give them an exhilarating pseudo flight experience, will reduce another person to tears.

Complication 2: If the target is alive, there's a chance for the Gift to be resisted.

Limitation 1: It may not take a lot of energy, but it makes up for that by requiring extra concentration to use safely.

Limitation 2: It's a close-range Gift. For best effect, you should be in the same room—like within twenty-five feet—of the object you are trying to affect.

Downside 1: It's what I'd call a manual Gift. Once you stop messing with gravity, it will revert to normal. This can be very, very bad if you're not paying attention and are floating a few hundred feet off the ground.

Downside 2: There can be lingering aftereffects, such as dizziness, nausea, and vomiting. Basically, anything that could come with motion sickness.

Downside 3: The chance of accidentally killing someone is very high. In addition to the normal damage sustained from striking objects along the way, unbalancing the fluids in a person's head could cause brain damage, paralysis, or death.

**Combat potential:** 4 of 5 stars

If you can successfully get in range, it can be great for close quarters fighting if you don't care about the enemy's fate.

**Danger level:** very high

Did you read the list of downsides? Even if you're not out to kill somebody, you could accidentally off them. People are relatively fragile. They generally don't do well when all the fluids in their body decide to dance one way or another.

**Usefulness:** 3 of 5 stars

I can see it being helpful to lift heavy objects, but it takes a lot more practice to use well than something like Manipulate Mass.

If you're just looking to break stuff, then I guess it's very useful.

**Entertainment value:** 2 of 5 stars

Besides a malicious sense of wanting to make a mess, I don't see this being a fun Gift.

**Overall rating and conclusion:** 2.5 of 5 stars

The opportunities for destruction far outpace the chances of this one to be used for good.

Small batches to practice ways to combat it might be fine. Packing emergency kits with it to lift objects off unfortunate souls being crushed would also be fine, but this should not be made available to the public.

# Chapter 57

# Journal Entry 27: Soften You the Hard Way

Mom really means Brother Joe, not Son Joe.

It's confusing because she named her firstborn after an older brother who died while she was a toddler.

Guess she hadn't counted on Evil Grandpa cloning the tyke.

Movement in the penthouse office ceases.

The Evil Grandpa clone holding the younger Uncle Joe clone hostage stares at me stonily.

I'm not sure what kind of reaction he wants.

To be safe, I give the kid temporary Invulnerability.

If I wasn't already using Impervious Skin, that would have been my go-to option, but I had stretched that one far enough by making it a Mirror Gift. Extending it to cover a third person would cost me almost as much energy as Invulnerability.

Powers get harder to maintain if you have multiple instances of them running. It's not like you get a discount for stretching a power.

Invulnerability is one of the most draining Gifts in existence because it prepares for dozens of possibilities simultaneously.

Since my kneeling position doesn't allow for easy movement, I spend some energy watching Jasmine's emotions. If I am about to enter a delicate negotiation, the last thing I need is an unmonitored, stab-happy sister standing behind me. She's already broken one needle on me. I would not put it past her to try again.

Since my movement happens to be in the direction of the hostage situation, the aggressor stiffens. This brings the blade even closer to the toddler.

The Invulnerability will protect the kid, but I also tweak some of his emotions to keep him calm.

If this situation keeps up, I will have to drop Invulnerability and switch to a different plan.

Evil Grandpa's portrait figure breaks the awkward silence.

"Drop the protection powers, Jessica. That's the only way nobody gets hurt."

I don't bother telling him his logic is garbage or that it makes no sense for him to threaten one of the clones he'd presumably worked very hard to create.

"Conserve your strength. You'll need it soon," he continues.

"For what?" Frustration turns my tone petulant. I honestly don't expect to get an answer.

"The transfer." Jasmine tries to keep her voice steady, but I hear uncertainty anyway.

My strength drains at an alarming rate, mostly due to keeping Invulnerability active, but I manage to push myself to a kneeling position that doesn't involve my hands.

I even send Evil Grandpa's portrait a decent glare.

"I see you require more convincing," says Evil Grandpa.

Mom's emotions flop about as shock gives way to horror, anger, and disbelief before landing on desperation.

"Don't do this. It won't work." She shoots me a panicked look.

I'm not completely clear on what the *this* is that he wants to do, but I figure clarity will come soon enough.

My creature attack has broken the Bridgeway guys' neat lines.

Several of them disappear and reappear a few seconds later with a guest.

Doug, Ellie, and Leslie vanish from the cozy cabin scene and appear near my mother.

Leslie stands with her escort to Mom's right, and Doug and Ellie are guided to positions to her left.

In eerie unison, they kneel.

The Bridgeway guys step back and cover them with weapons that look like laser pointers but probably do a lot more damage.

Doug, Ellie, Leslie, and Mom have grim expressions. Someone has obviously explained the score to them, though I'm not sure when that could have happened, unless Evil Grandpa possesses telepathic powers.

**Very good, Jessica.**

*Nope. You do not get to share headspace with me.*

I shut down that line of communication, but not before noticing that his mental voice sounds like Bob.

*Great. He's already been in my head.*

When a buzzing headache starts at the base of my skull, I shut down the protection powers.

The great uncle clone sets the uncle clone down.

The boy scampers back to the corner currently holding his brother.

*I've been played by a toddler.*

I don't have the spare energy to work up decent indignation.

"Now, get up and wait for my men to bring the gurney," says Portrait Evil Grandpa.

I reluctantly follow the instruction.

Two Bridgeway guards dash into the lab section and disappear behind a divider.

One of the great uncle clones whispers something I miss.

"That's an excellent idea. Do we have one prepared for her?"

Portrait Evil Grandpa's enthusiasm kicks up some anxiety in my gut.

The clone nods and strides off with purposeful steps.

"Jess, get out of here," Mom orders.

I send her a questioning look.

The current setup implies very bad things will happen to her, Doug, Ellie, and Leslie if I take that advice.

Ellie catches my eye and sends a message.

"Hush, Angela, you don't mean that." Evil Grandpa's portrait speaks soothingly.

"I do mean it," Mom insists. "I won't let you do this to her!"

"Do what?" Part of me knows, but I want the confirmation anyway.

"Stop playing dumb," mutters Jasmine. "I already told you: the transfer. You get his body. He gets yours."

"Or I could just heal the body he has," I say slowly. "Why isn't that an option?"

"It's not a matter of health," chimes in Portrait Evil Grandpa. "It's about your Gifts."

Ignoring him, I address Jasmine.

"I thought you wanted to kill me to absorb the powers. Can't have it both ways."

The Bridgeway guards return from the lab section before Jazz can answer. They wheel in a tricked out medical gurney.

In addition to normal restraints, it has a few extra restraints and several leads connected to a large battery located underneath the main body of the gurney.

Soon thereafter, the clone that cheered Portrait Evil Grandpa returns from his errand too. He carries a heavy-looking straitjacket.

Silver strands have been woven throughout the material.

Once again, I silently thank Past Me for dropping that little tidbit into a report.

"Hold still and let them work," says Portrait Evil Grandpa. "Once they secure your arms, lie down on the gurney."

The Bridgeway goons fumble with stuffing my arms into the straitjacket.

I don't fight them, but I also don't help them.

I could mold into the form without them undoing the straps, but their struggle buys me an extra few seconds of thinking time.

I try thinking forward the next few minutes.

Most plans and pieces of plans hit the same snag. If I weasel out of a complete resolution, Evil Grandpa and company will haunt me and my family forever.

Also, my body will defend itself instinctively.

The only way to lower natural defenses is to knock somebody out or hinder the thinking process.

*That happens through drugs or pain.*

"If you help with the transfer, this will be much less painful."

Portrait Evil Grandpa's threat rolls off me.

**If you don't help, he'll soften you the hard way.**

*You almost sound concerned.*

If Jasmine answers, I miss it because every effort goes into finding a way to avoid the next few unpleasant minutes.

When I don't move quickly enough, four Bridgeway lackeys knock me over and lift me up onto the gurney.

It takes a lot of effort to hold still while they fix electrodes to both sides of my temple and at the base of my neck.

# Chapter 58

---

# Journal Entry 28: Essence Transfer

When I first heard Evil Grandpa wants to switch bodies, I picture messy Transportation jobs where his brain will move into my body and vice versa. I say messy because it will take some fancy healing to deal with the spacing differences and the many nerves and blood vessels that need to be reconciled.

What he has in mind—an Essence Transfer—is much less disruptive but no less disturbing.

If I let it happen, my brain will rewire itself to clear out some space for Evil Grandpa to fill with thoughts and memories.

It's called an Essence Transfer because it takes the important pieces of a person and relocates them to a new target.

I would be a prisoner in my own head.

Desperate to avoid that fate, I do something arguably crazier.

I transfer most of my Gifts to Ellie along with a crash course on how to use them.

Had to review several people's memories to piece together what happens next.

Was personally too busy being a diversion to pay much attention.

Why would I let 100,000 volts of electricity enter my body for several seconds?

Because it's really difficult to ignore somebody screaming their head off and twitching uncontrollably.

I also need Evil Grandpa, the Clone Crew, and the Bridgeway guys to lower their guards. I don't care what Evil Grandpa says about them being private security. They still wear the Bridgeway uniforms, so they still get that label.

There's a tiny fraction of a second where someone is vulnerable during a transfer.

The shocks are meant to lower my defenses to allow Evil Grandpa to hijack portions of my mind.

That part of the plan works swell, but I have Ellie mess up the next step.

As Evil Grandpa initiates the Essence Transfer, Ellie activates the power I'd labeled Redirect.

It surrounds me with the thought equivalent of glue traps.

When Evil Grandpa's essence makes its move on my brain, he runs headlong into Ellie's trap.

Next, I ask her to identify a safe target.

I don't get a chance to spell out what qualifies, so I shouldn't be surprised that Ellie chooses one of the few surviving spider forms skittering about the penthouse office.

Since the target was too small to accommodate Evil Grandpa's essence, she has to enlarge the spider form.

It's a good thing she does, or Evil Grandpa might escape the spider form.

Initiating another Essence Transfer might have been tricky, so I suggest Ellie tag the target and let the initial momentum do the rest.

About this time, Ellie returns my Gifts with a whiteboard note that says: *Being u is ...* and follows the words with an animated illustration of the exploding head emoji. *Please tell me u r my Jess.*

I dash off an acknowledging message.

Okay, so it's a check mark.

She catches the point.

The effort to move his essence proves too much for Evil Grandpa. Without me filling the empty shell, the body he left behind expires.

I can't exactly say he dies because he's been given a new body.

It just wasn't the one he'd planned on getting.

The transfer still counts as a success. The spider form was technically part of me until the me part got kicked out.

Figuring I can spare the mass, I conjure a cardboard box from one of the dumpsters outside the building and drop it around Spider Grandpa.

Shock keeps the Bridgeway guys and Clone Crew members stationary.

Mom cries.

Jasmine glares at me.

Doug breaks free of his bonds and watches the remaining Bridgeway guys carefully.

I hadn't counted them closely to begin with, but it appears we are light several Bridgeway guards.

Spider Grandpa jumps inside the cardboard box, making little thudding noises.

Leslie and Ellie stare up at me.

I fully return to my senses in time to realize I am floating in the room's center about two meters off the ground.

Thank goodness the penthouse office comes with a vaulted ceiling that would have made a cathedral jealous.

Still rocking the straitjacket, I must look like a giant moth chilling in its cocoon.

Instead of trying to figure out the mess of buckles, I turn incorporeal and slip out of the confining thing. With nothing to hold it up, the straitjacket plummets to the ground.

While restraints linger on my mind, I change the chemical structure of Mom's bonds. Ellie and Leslie hadn't been bound, and Doug doesn't need my help.

One of the older clones rushes for the desk which still holds that contract Evil Grandpa had wanted me to sign.

I use Transportation and bring the contract to hand. Since the paper version is forty-eight pages long, I need Speed Reading and Enhanced Intelligence to absorb the gist of the document.

After all that, I probably should have spent a solid 48 hours thinking it over and re-reading the fine print.

Below me, Jasmine folds her arms. Her glare softens to disappointment, weary acceptance, and curiosity.

I only recognize all that because I still channel broad spectrum Enhanced Intelligence, which includes emotional identification.

"Will you sign it?" asks Jasmine.

"You ... don't have to," says Mom.

I slowly descend because I don't think it's fair to maintain literal high ground in the conversation.

"What's the alternative?" I wonder.

"You die!" The hissed statement erupts from one of the middle grade clones.

He shoots me.

Six times.

I manage to don Impervious Skin in time, but it still feels like being repeatedly whacked with a sledgehammer. My body flips the kinetic force into heat and directs it to the ground under my feet, leaving scorch marks.

The flattened slugs bounce off me.

I clutch at the area on my side that caught the most bullets.

*That's gonna bruise.*

**You're a Healer, dummy.**

Jasmine might not be cheerleader material, but she has a point, not that I have time to acknowledge the thought.

Crazy Clone Great Uncle is already lining up more shots.

I don't have much energy left, but I try to telekinetically pull the gun from my wayward great uncle before he can blast somebody else.

It doesn't work, but it does force him to tighten his grip, which buys me a few seconds.

As the energy reserves descend to the *here-be-headaches* zone, Ellie catches me in a bear hug.

The whiteboard blazes with an all-caps message: DO IT.

Many years of friendship let me follow the order. She wants me to draw the energy difference from her.

We've talked about it in passing, but I've never considered trying it in a real situation before.

If the people around us join forces, we could still have one heck of a fight on our hands.

My headache grows worse as I heighten my awareness.

I do not want any more nasty surprises like homicidal great uncles.

Ellie offers me an easy energy fix.

Still, I hesitate.

If I miscalculate, I could kill my best friend.

# Chapter 59

# Superpower Review 28: Impervious Skin

**Background and notes:**

Might as well talk about some of the things I've used recently.

**Caution:** Do not leave this one active too long.

**Frequently asked questions:**

**Isn't this covered by Invulnerability?**

Yes. Impervious Skin can be one of the things activated by Invulnerability.

**Why have both?**

Think of the Invulnerability Gift as a multitool set and Impervious Skin as the regular knife part within that set.

The set may come with several knives, scissors, pliers, three kinds of screw drivers, bottle openers, and such, but sometimes, you just need the normal knife.

There's also an energy cost difference between the two Gifts. Just because you have an ability does not mean you use have it dialed on constantly.

Impervious Skin costs much less to use than Invulnerability.

**Energy cost aside:** It's hard to say how much less because individual energy costs differ when it comes to activating and maintaining superpowers.

**Explanation of the power:**

**Base definition:** Impervious Skin prevents things from passing through the skin.

**Original and most common intent:** To prevent bodily harm due to conventional weapons attempting to pierce, tear, rip, or otherwise breech the skin.

**Note:** This does not generally cover instances of crushing, blunt force, or large scale, high-speed impact. (It's not going to save you, if you get hit by a car.) See limitations for more details.

**Hidden effect:** Impervious anything goes both ways. Nothing in. Nothing out. This includes things like sweat. That's part of why I said not to leave it active too long.

I tend to use it like a very close personal shield.

**Side effects:** If left active for too long, Impervious Skin can cause—or make worse—several skin conditions, including acne.

**Experiments (Demonstration Proof):**

Perspective is an amazing thing. Had I been forced to do these demonstrations, they would have been much less enjoyable. Perhaps enjoyable is the wrong word.

Not a psychopath, promise, but I do have a dangerous curious streak.

**Disclaimer and reminder and plea:** Please don't try any of these experiments at home. I have a lot of Gifts—like Healing—that can keep my irresponsible self from accidentally permanently damaging something.

I also donned a sensor package and turned off my pain receptors during each test.

- Demos 1-8: Tested various things with piercing or stabbing potential, specifically various needles, knives, swords, and arrows.

- Demos 9-15: Tested various types of blunt force weapons, including types of bats, hammers, maces, sticks, and sticks with fancy names.

- Demos 16-20: Tested various types of guns and explosives.

- Demos 21-25: Did some chemical and biological agent picomachine simulations.

**Side note:** I did not try nuclear weapons. The expense did not warrant proving that point. Besides, the fallout from those is much greater than trying to break skin.

I also did not try stepping off the planet into outer space.

**What happened:**

- Demos 1-8: My skin held up with nary a scratch.

- Demos 9-15: Skin held. I got some nice bruises and broken bones though.

- Demos 16-20: Good to go with firearms. Would have died with explosives.

- Demos 21-25: Results varied based on where the weapon struck (or moved to). Acids on the skin was fine. Poison gas would have won. Creepity little breathable bioweapons snuck through.

**Expectations and reality:**

Expectation 1: It provides a little less protection than Invulnerability.

Reality 1: Define *a little*. It prevents the skin being perforated by small weapons and normal sharp objects.

**Quick look at the difference:**

- Impervious Skin will help against bullets, arrows shot by humans, and knives. Machine fired bolts could do some damage, not by piercing the skin but by slamming into it with considerable force.

- Impervious Skin will usually not do much good against blunt force things, explosions, and other types of harm that involve crushing or impact zones.

Expectation 2: It can be left on just in case.

Reality 2: Not recommended. Most people develop skin problems if Impervious Skin remains active for more than a few hours.

Expectation 3: It's all or nothing. Either all of your skin is covered by the Gift or nothing is covered.

Reality 3: If you have enough skill, you could selectively protect certain parts better than others. This too is not recommended because it's kind of difficult to predict where a threat will land.

**Complications, limitations, and downside:**

Complication 1: Doesn't protect against concussive force from explosions or the Gift (Concussive Force). You can still die if a bullet strikes the right spot.

For example, if you got shot in the hand, Impervious Skin would likely prevent much damage, but if you got shot in the head, you could still die from the concussive force.

Bullets can strike with hundreds or thousands of pounds of pressure. Even if the bullet can't enter your head, it can knock your brain about inside your skull. I shouldn't have to tell you that would be very bad.

Complication 2: The Gift does not always turn off pain receptors.

Limitation 1: Doesn't protect you against temperature fluctuations.

Potentially, you could walk through fire, but you'd still have problems with smoke inhalation.

Limitation 2: Without getting too graphic, humans come equipped with several orifices. In other words, there are multiple points of entry and exits for oxygen, food, and such to get in and out. This is normal.

Impervious Skin doesn't batten down those hatches unless absolutely necessary. (Also, a good thing. You'd die if you couldn't breathe whenever the Gift was activated.)

Downside: Can cause skin diseases and conditions.

**Combat potential:** 4 of 5 stars

The Gift would make useful temporary armor for soldiers.

- It's lightweight.

- It's relatively low energy cost for short-term use.

**Danger level:** medium to low

The answer depends on how you define danger.

- Mortal danger? Low.

- Danger of unpleasant side effects? Medium, though that can depend on how you use it.

**Usefulness:** 3 of 5 stars

Can be handy for emergency workers to keep around. I would recommend Hostage Rescue Teams have some.

Construction workers doing dangerous things may also want to keep some around.

The use isn't marked higher because it's a Gift geared to preventing damage in hostile situations only. It won't do much good in accident situations because those are unpredictable. Using it enough to always be prepared would likely trigger the adverse skin reactions.

You'd want this power active if you intended to enter a swordfight or a small arms firefight.

**Entertainment value:** 2 of 5 stars

Impervious Skin is more of a workhorse power than a recreational Gift.

**Overall rating and conclusion:** 4 of 5 stars

(Don't try to make the star average make sense. It got some bonus consideration due to really being nice to have in a fight.)

I'm slightly biased because it's helped me out of some tricky situations.

It should be safe enough to market to the public, but the stable of lawyers should go over the disclaimers and warnings thoroughly.

# Chapter 60

# Superpower Review 29: Invulnerability

**Background and notes:**

This is one of those powers people naturally assume every superhero gets. I blame the entertainment industry.

Invulnerability didn't come up earlier because it's not being considered for public release. Hence, it got buried on the priorities list.

While it's a highly useful Gift, I doubt it'll ever earn the distinction of being my favorite power simply because of association. If this one is activated, things have gone very, very wrong.

**Explanation of the power:**

**Short definition:** Conveys temporary immunity from any kind of physical harm.

Emphasis on the *physical harm* part, and nobody would want the Gift to extend itself to emotional harm anyway.

**Pre-emptive explanation because I know I'm going to get asked to elaborate:**

This is a classic case of be careful what you wish for.

If you extended the Gift to emotions, the universe may decide you can be harmed by words. If that happens, the easiest fix is to shut down various senses.

Can't be upset by audible message if you can't hear them. Likewise, you can't be harmed by nasty written things if you can't see them.

**End result:** The Gift would shut down your ability to see and hear. That would really ruin your day.

### Addressing the temporary part:

The most common limiting factor will be the Super's energy level.

Even if you started at full-energy, well-rested status, keeping Invulnerability active would wear you down in a matter of minutes.

### Why?

Because this is the closest most people will come to multiple powers.

**Side note:** I have multiple Gifts, but I don't walk around with every single one of them active at the same time. That would be crazy.

### Common Gifts included in Invulnerability:

I'd probably bore you if I listed out everything that could come with Invulnerability, but here are the usual suspects.

- Impervious Skin

- Immunity to harmful chemicals, bioweapons, etc.

- Immunity to crushing, tearing, pulling, etc.

- Disease Immunity

- Elemental Immunity – fire, cold, wind/air, water, etc.

- (Yes, it could handle nuclear damage and attempts at disintegration, but I did not get clearance to test these. Besides, no conventional recording device would survive long enough to tell the tale.)

**Side note:** Even though a lot of these list immunity, Invulnerability goes beyond immunity to destruction of whatever was causing the threat in the case of harmful chemicals and bioweapons.

### Dynamic Gift:

Invulnerability is a dynamic Gift. That means, it changes as the nature of the threat changes. It also has to decide what is a threat and what is not a threat.

For example, if it's supposed to be fighting a biological agent, the Gift needs to identify the invader, isolate the troublesome spot, and eradicate the problem. At the same time, it must avoid taking out good bacteria already in the body.

### Demonstrations (proofs):

I think the Bridgeway lackeys helping me with the demonstrations had far too much fun trying to hurt me.

- Demos 1-5: stabby things

- Demos 6-10: flat-edge pain causers

- Demos 11-15: bang-bang and boomy things

- Demos 16-20: creepy little invaders, both living and nonliving

### What happened:

*I spread the demo sets out so I could rest and recover in between. I'm decent with knowing my limits, but it would really stink to overestimate my energy levels midway through dealing with a biological agent trying to kill me.

- Demos 1-5: I survived without bruises or scratches.

- Demos 6-10: I think I broke some weapons with my face, but better an angry bean counter who has to buy another mace than a visit to the dentist.

- Demos 11-15: Apparently, 10,345 bullets approaches the limit of my personal Invulnerability level. The next one winged my left arm. Since another 3,000 were milliseconds away, I teleported behind the line of shooters and let the sandbags do their job.

- Demos 16-20: Creepy things, big or small, aren't my favorite. Big might get more press, but it's the small, deadly invaders you should really worry about.

That might sound alarmist, but nobody ever hired me for my good cheer.

**Expectations and reality:**

Expectation 1: This is the perfect Gift.

Reality 1: It's nice and very good at keeping you alive, but I'd only count it perfect if it didn't come with the threat of a violent headache.

Expectation 2: If you have Invulnerability active, nothing can harm you.

Reality 2: I suppose the answer depends on how philosophical you wish to get. Invulnerability protects you from physical dangers. Mental, emotional, and spiritual trials and tribulations are beyond the scope of this Gift.

Expectation 3: There's a steady, predictable energy cost.

Reality 3: There's a steady, predictable *initial* energy cost to run the diagnostics and deal with little issues. If actual violence breaks out, energy costs can quickly spike.

**Complications, limitations, and side effects:**

Complication 1: It's harder to turn off than most Gifts. Picture Invulnerability like an active control panel.

The quick but risky way to handle things is to turn everything off simultaneously. The safer but slower way is to shut the individual effects off in manageable batches.

Complication 2: Giving the Gift to somebody else is dangerous. It's like handing them a limitless credit card linked to your energy reserves.

Limitation 1: Energy. Unless you have a way to augment your energy, you run the risk of coming up short at an inopportune time.

Limitation 2: Prevents harm from physical threats only.

Limitation 3: It doesn't remove fear. If you have a healthy fear of being stabbed, shot, or blown up, you're still going to feel everything a normal person would feel in that situation. At best, Invulnerability will take the edge off enough to let you function, but that's about it.

Side effect 1: Tends to elevate one's body temperature.

Side effect 2 (healing hack): If you don't have the healing Gift, but can access Invulnerability, activate it briefly and whatever ails you should clear up.

**Combat potential:** very high in short, regulated doses

For best results, I'd recommend having one person dedicated to giving two to three others Invulnerability from the safety of a nearby bunker or hidden safehouse. That way, those fighting in the moment won't experience the energy crash.

Giving individual soldiers Immunity is also an option. It's a very expensive option and comes with some risks, but with proper training, it's doable.

**Danger level:** 3 of 5 stars

This is a purely defensive Gift.

The danger is mostly a very high risk of energy crashes.

**Usefulness:** 5 of 5 stars

I can't exactly knock the usefulness of something that prevents 99.99% of ways to die when it's active.

**Entertainment value:** 2.5 of 5 stars

I suppose there's a wee bit of satisfaction knowing bullets, knives, and other weapons can't touch you. However, like a video game set to god-mode, the novelty of being immune to every kind of physical attack, would quickly grow old.

**Overall rating and conclusion:** 4 of 5 stars (usefulness boost in play)

Bridgeway has some contracts to create limited batches of Invulnerability.

I highly suggest they're trackable and limited. Otherwise, we run the risk of creating a black market for the stuff.

I don't mind having this around for protection. I do not want to be having violent altercations with idiots who stole some instant Invulnerability. Besides, drug dealers don't have the best track record with not messing with the products they're selling, and the chemical formulas for anything out of Bridgeway Labs are very specific.

# Chapter 61

# Journal Entry 29: Energy Vampire

I freeze time and brace, trying to anticipate the points Ellie will make in our coming discussion.

**DO IT!**

Her second iteration of that whiteboard order is followed by a few dozen exclamation points, but I see no reason to be that authentic with my account.

Ellie wants me to draw energy from her.

**MAKE WAY.**

*You're mighty demanding for a guest in my head.*

Nevertheless, I clear some head space and create avatars so Ellie and I can have the oddest, most civil argument in our friendship history sort of face to face.

Seeing as my energy reserves hover just above the red danger zone, following her instruction would be the smart thing to do.

I perform a dozen calculations.

It should be a breeze to draw exactly what I need, but fear of failure rears its ugly head, bringing self-doubt with it.

"I could accidentally hurt you."

"But you won't." Ellie crosses her avatar's arms and gives me the make-your-next-dumb-point stare.

"Maybe I should draw it from the kid trying to shoot me." I'm not sold on that idea, just thinking aloud. From a tactical standpoint, that too makes sense.

"You'd regret it." Ellie quirks an eyebrow at me. "Next."

"Why do you think I'd regret it?"

"Because you couldn't shoot the Rabid Hell Hounds in *Apocalypse IV*."

I struggle to follow her logic. We haven't played that game for at least five years, and besides, those hounds were cute. I also wanted the extra experience points one could earn by redeeming the hounds instead of killing them.

Ellie grunts at my slowness in picking up her point.

"It'd make you feel like a bad guy."

"True, but how does that make drawing energy from you the better option?"

"I told you to do it."

I roll my eyes at her.

"Yeah, that'll be great comfort to your family at your funeral."

Ellie's bared teeth expression is more feral creature than sweet smile.

"So, don't screw up."

Past Me would have taken Ellie up on her challenge but Present Me is all about doing the unexpected.

I come back to my senses a hairsbreadth from the trouble I'd hit pause on.

Crazy Clone Great Uncle's finger rests snuggly against the gun's trigger, ready to try his luck again with the rest of the clip.

Ellie's warm embrace gives me an idea.

Since breaking Ellie's hold in my energy-drained state would have been a struggle, I draw some of the needed energy from her and some from every other person in the room.

I draw in heat energy first.

It's an easy energy form to draw even from afar, but it's not the simplest to use.

Direct contact would be the most efficient transfer method, but I don't need most efficient, I need quickest.

There's a difference.

That initial draw gives me the energy I need to cast a wider invisible net that sucks heat energy to me like a plant absorbing sunrays.

At best, I get scraps from each person, but since I happen to be in a very large building occupied by a few thousand people, those fragments add up.

I also draw direct electrical energy from the nearby wall sockets.

The lights flicker.

When I have enough energy, I direct some of the excess into the handgun staring me down.

Crazy Great Uncle screams and tosses the gun away like a hot potato.

It sails my way in slow motion.

I don't dodge because that would leave Ellie in the flight path.

Instead, I set my right hand on fire and snatch the superheated piece of metal out of the air. Using a fire ability gives me temporary immunity to the effects, but I drop the gun and extinguish the flame as quickly as possible.

As expected, the display captures everybody's attention. Fire has a way of doing that.

My left hand still clutches that darn contract.

For a second, I consider burning the contract to a crisp, but I have already decided to sign it and that would be counterproductive. Besides, my heightened awareness tells me there are two other viable copies of it in a wall safe in the room next to the day care center.

"So, how's it feel to be an Energy Vampire?" Ellie's teasing tone pulls me back to the moment.

"Siphon," I correct absently.

Ellie waves off the technical term.

"I like Energy Vampire better."

"Fine." I really have bigger fish to fry than what Ellie calls the power.

Jasmine, Portrait Grandpa, guards, former hostages, and Crazy Clones all watch me warily. Some are behind me, but I can feel the connection through the faint energy bond I'd forged between us.

Narrowing the energy bonds to the people in the room, I subtly go the other way and move small bits of my energy into them. This slips me past mental guards and puts me in touch with each target's feelings.

I also turn so I can face most of the action, but I keep a few senses trained on the Crazy Clone and set a Stasis Field on a six-inch invisible trigger. Essentially, if the kid moves, he'll be flash frozen in place for a few minutes.

That should keep me safe enough, but I don't like having the kid behind me. Paranoia makes me shift position so that the massive desk stays behind me. This leaves Crazy Kid to my left and the bulk of the others to my right.

Mom feels weary, Leslie relieved, and Doug suspicious.

Got nothing from Jazz because she is using her Mimic abilities to block me.

Crazy Clones vary from accepting to resentful.

Most Bridgeway guys feel confused, except for two who radiate mild satisfaction.

Mr. Odd Emotions One steps toward me, but Doug sticks his right arm out to create a barrier to block his way.

"It's okay, Doug. I know him."

*About as well as anybody can know Shapeshifter clones.*

"Are you sure about this?" The young Crazy Clone I'd just relieved of a gun looks between the two Bridgeway guys who felt off.

I am getting awfully tired of people not wearing their own faces.

This is not a hard concept. Wear your own face.

"Know him how?" Doug demands.

"That's Malcom North. Henry Rathbun's on your other side," I say. "They've been my ... watchers for months."

Doug shoots me a dubious look.

"Not doing a great job of convincing me they're not threats, Jess."

"Show your faces." Mom speaks the quiet instruction.

North and Rathbun dutifully shift features. Both resemble the Uncle Joe Clones.

"I don't like it much either," Jasmine admits, moving to stand behind Young Crazy Clone, "but she's the best we're going to get for a teacher."

I clamp down on a snarky thought about that ringing endorsement.

Before I lose my nerve, I fetch a pen from my room because it's easier than searching Spider Grandpa's desk.

Then, I sign the contract.

That's how I inherit a multi-billion-dollar company and a dozen pain-in-the-posterior apprentices.

# Chapter 62

# Journal Entry 30: Bounty Hunter

I really want to write: *They lived happily ever after*, but the story ain't over yet.

It might not be over for a while.

We got problems, and most of them have names.

But before I explain that mess, let me tell you a quaint story.

Once upon a time, there lived an ambitious young scientist named Alexander Bridgeway.

He had almost everything life can give a man: a modest research company, a beautiful family, and one of the rarest, most heavily coveted and controlled Gifts: Precognition.

But the Gift was stingy and uncooperative.

It showed him only the barest glimpses of possible futures. If he wanted to make any of them happen, he'd have to take matters into his own hands.

His work became his obsession and consumed him from the inside out.

Then, tragedy struck, and his son died.

And Alexander blamed himself.

Pain from the first tragedy drove him deeper into work.

He withdrew from his wife and young daughter and vowed to find a way to get other Gifts. If he could only get other Gifts, he could change things for his son or at least save others from his fate.

The new obsession made him miss every warning sign of his wife's downward spiral. When an accident took his wife's life, Alexander finally remembered he had a daughter.

He brought her to work, trusting his colleagues would keep her safe while he threw himself into more experiments.

The government got wind of his progress and sent some investigators. They watched his work for years.

When he showed the right amount of dedication and progress, the government envoys offered Alexander a very large contract.

He accepted it on a few conditions.

**The conditions:**

- First, he wanted assurances he and his people would never be prosecuted for the ambitious experiments prior to the contract.

- Second, he asked for a Time Pass to visit his son.

- Third, he sought permission to retrieve enough samples to clone his son.

- Fourth, he demanded a say in all research conducted by his company.

- Fifth, he asked for the freedom to exercise his Gift however he wanted.

- Sixth, he wanted permission to experiment freely on samples from his daughter.

He was granted all but the last demand.

The Superpower Control Council liaison said he wasn't comfortable condoning experiments he didn't understand, but he did give his blessing to drawing samples from a past version of the girl.

That disagreement almost halted the deal, but Evil Grandpa bargained for some legal mumbo jumbo that essentially meant he could experiment on persons born on Bridgeway properties. He also got immunity from prosecution for crimes against persons under climate emergency acts.

Basically, that translated to Evil Grandpa getting a stay-out-of-jail free card as long as his company stayed useful to the United States government.

They wouldn't approve his actions, but they also wouldn't stop him.

Suit deniability and all that.

Anyway, suffice to say, the mad scientist got a pass on past misdeeds and an immunity card to play in the future if anything he did crossed legal lines.

He did his experiments, waited patiently, did more experiments, and refined the batches of clones for himself and his deceased son. He considered cloning his daughter, but some colleagues convinced him not to do so while she lived.

Guess that was the other reason Evil Grandpa felt free to threaten Mom. He's got frozen spares around here somewhere.

Didn't expect the man to win Father-of-the-Year awards, but that is so twisted.

Upon learning his daughter married a test subject and tried to break away from the family business, Evil Grandpa's scheming kicked into overdrive.

He wasn't quick enough to bring the couple under control until after their son—my brother Joe—was born.

Undeterred, Evil Grandpa continued to manipulate pieces until his daughter—my mother—couldn't stop thinking about heritable diseases she might pass on to future children.

Her mistake lay in turning to Evil Grandpa for help during the screening process. By the time she realized the tests were yet another experiment, it was too late. He'd already exposed the children—Future Jazzy and me—to drugs that should increase their likelihood of unlocking Gifts.

**Must you call me that?**

*Must you lurk in my head?*

**You read the contract. I get to lurk as part—**

*Yup. Got it. Lurk quietly.*

**I don't know why you insist on flashing the family affairs in front of strangers, even if they are related.**

Long story short, the drugs worked, and the bouncing baby girls got multiple Gifts.

Then, came Mom's bargain due to philosophical differences in training methods.

Evil Grandpa got to train Jasmine in the lab-regimented, just-the-facts way, and Mom got to train me, all-natural style.

You heard most of the rest of the tale.

I had as normal a childhood as a Super can get.

We did regular check-ins at the Bridgeway HQ until I turned five or so.

High school and college were normal-ish experiences.

Finally, Evil Grandpa figured I'd had enough normal and should start earning my keep at the family business.

Being Evil Grandpa, the man couldn't bring himself to ask normally. Not-normal asking resulted in the last few months of my life: kidnapping, coercion, skyrocketing stress levels, threatened friends, threatened family, and so on.

**You wouldn't have listened to a normal invitation. His Gift told him so.**

*Doesn't mean one shouldn't have been offered.*

For the record, I didn't kill Evil Grandpa.

He's still rocking Spider form.

I'm going to get flack for selling out, but I signed that contract because the government's been desperate for years.

Much as I'd like to think the trials, tribulations, and trust issues are confined to my immediate family, Uncle Sam funded dozens of programs as ambitious as Evil Grandpa's quest for many Gifts.

Lest you think the folks raised a fool, I tweaked the contract before signing it.

**My non-negotiable demands:**

- My family members (and friends) get to choose to join the family business or get a fresh start somewhere far from Bridgeway's reach.

- Bridgeway goes through a comprehensive overhaul of recruiting practices.

- I get veto power on missions and experiments.

- I get to design the training regimes or experiments if I feel like it. (If I'm getting shot at, I would at least like the comfort of knowing I chose that path.)

- My contract expires in five-year terms. At the end, either party can walk away. (Thus far, I've been aging normally. I might be in my twenties now, but I do not want to be doing this forever.)

**My responsibilities:**

- Train the clones who want training in whatever Gifts they develop.

- Continue testing superpowers and reporting on their uses and downsides.

- Be available for intervention and de-escalation procedures if a crisis involving a Super arises.

End of negotiations.

Okay, I'll admit, point three terrifies me.

My watchers try to brush it off as a hypothetical, but North is tense enough to eat carbon dust and spit diamonds whenever he mentions it.

North and Rathbun might be clones but they're also card-carrying government lackeys.

Unfortunately, point three is something they wouldn't budge on. I manage to put a few limitation clauses in, but that's about it.

Like it or not, I may have a future as a Super Nutbar Retrieval Expert.

**Bounty Hunter.**

*That's what I said.*

**Bounty Hunter is cooler.**

I concede the point so I can move on. If you missed that part above, Jazz gets to ride shotgun in my head as part of the government oversight team.

**You're the one who wanted to bond.**

*They didn't give me much of a choice. It was Spider Grandpa or you in that saddle, and he's still ticked off I won't complete the Essence Transfer. You might have gone along with all that double-triple-quadruple-crossing, mess-with-my-head-to-test-my-true-superhero-worth junk, but at least you didn't come up with it.*

The Superpower Control Council isn't just a US thing.

They're an international organization.

The talking heads I pretty much sold my soul to have decided that Supers might be needed to help humanity reach the next step.

Whatever that means.

**You know exactly what that means.**

*Yeah, I get the gist.*

Bridgeway's Bottled Powers Project isn't going to be an isolated thing. Other companies will be selling similar things. And some won't have wise people telling them it's not a great idea to give Normies Laser Eyes for funsies.

The whole world gets to be part of a new evolutionary experiment.

Thus, I get to be a very well-paid first responder to crises created by the experiments gone wrong.

***That's surprisingly cold and pessimistic of you, Jess. I approve.***

*Thanks. I think.*

***Admit it. You can't wait to be a Superhero Bounty Hunter.***

*Well, I do look good in Faruchi duds. I might even start to like capes. I'm going to leave it at a solid maybe on actually liking the job.*

**The End of Season 1**

# Thank You for Reading

Dear Reader,

This story started on Kindle Vella. I had a blast writing it. (So much so that I continued in a second season, then a third.)

I asked my students what superpowers they wanted and got a lot of Flight and Teleportation requests. That got me thinking about the good, bad, and ugly parts of the powers. Then, Jess popped up outta nowhere and started telling me about them. The rest is history.

Did you know there's a bonus zone on the Vella? It starts with Episode 63. The first episode talks about the Spotify playlist, but the rest, so far, have been training modules and memory capsules.

If you want to continue Jess's normal story, check out Superhero Saga Season 2 (and 3) on Kindle Vella.

If you liked this but want to sample a slightly different flavor of fantasy, try Casual Gamers (litRPG fantasy) on Kindle Vella.

You can find out more about my other works at linktr.ee/juliecgilbert.

Sincerely,

Julie C. Gilbert